# IN HOT PURSUIT

3rd Age World Publishing. Vancouver and London.
www.3rdageworld.com

# IN HOT PURSUIT

Terry Oliver

# Dedication

To Wendy,
for her encouragement and support.

# CHAPTER 1

Barney Roper was in a good mood – hell, he was euphoric. He felt the wave of delight sweep over him like an orgasm. As he sat staring out the window watching the airline ground-crew loading baggage and meals aboard the Airbus 310, he caught sight of his reflection in the little rectangle of glass.

"Sixty-eight years old and grinning like a schoolboy," he grinned. He pored over the details as people roved in and out of view purposefully carrying out all the endless checklist of last minute preparations. He had seen them go through this routine many times before but today everything took on a heightened significance. "This must be what an ex-con feels like – let out after serving a twenty year life sentence – seeing everything again like new," he thought. Only he had done thirty years with no parole and now he was staging a breakout – at sixty-eight! He grinned again - "Barney the Kid."

A pair of workers standing in one place under the wing caught his eye as they stood motionless staring upwards while everyone swirled around them. A moment or two later another man had joined them – Barney scrunched down in his seat to try to see under the wing but he could only make out the lower half of their bodies. One of those strange-shaped airport vehicles with no top half pulled up and two more men clustered around the others under the wing. A woman brushed past his seat and he looked up with a start.

"Alice?" She turned and glanced at him - one of the cabin crew members, an older woman, checking luggage and seatbelts – she must be the chief flight attendant, Barney reckoned, judging from her age.

"Get a grip," he told himself. From the back, she had reminded him of Alice, his wife, and he felt a sudden pang for that soft curving back he loved to mold himself to in bed – each night telling himself he could never give that up – never prise himself loose from that comforting embrace as he fought off drowsiness to prolong his delight.

And now here he was, deliberately distancing himself from her – not that he had enjoyed that warm curling back for a while – it was only a pale memory, since they hadn't slept together for – how long? – It seemed to him an age since he had been exiled to the narrow bed in the spare room while Alice luxuriated in their king-size bed across the hall.

"Excuse me, but I think this is my seat."

Barney turned to see a woman standing in the aisle looking pointedly at him.

"Sorry." He hurriedly gathered up his jacket, cabin bag and Guardian newspaper, which he had dumped on the seat beside him and pulled them all on to his lap. The woman continued to stand there.

"Actually, mine is the window seat."

"Oh, sorry." He struggled to stand with all his belongings but fell back down into the seat in the cramped space. "Sorry," he said again.

The woman smiled briefly. "Never mind, I'll sit here."

"No, please –" Barney attempted to stand again but she was already sliding into the aisle seat.

"Actually, I prefer an aisle seat. I can stretch my legs out and walk up and down whenever I like – I don't know why I always ask for a window seat – habit, I guess."

"Me, too," he nodded. "All that clambering over other people every time you need to go to the loo – and now that we're supposed to march up and down every hour so we don't get DVT – Are you sure you wouldn't like to sit here?"

The woman laughed and shook her head. "No chance." Her dark auburn hair was streaked with grey at the temples and looked an inch or two longer than most women her age would have worn it, Barney reckoned, but it somehow suited her. She was wearing a longish skirt and a tailored jacket and looked faintly over-dressed amongst all the casual jeans and comfortable tops favoured by most long-haul passengers nowadays.

He remembered when a flight abroad was an occasion to wear brand new smart clothes and matching luggage – it had all seemed quite important in the fifties and sixties – must have been damned uncomfortable, too, judging by the rumpled state of most people by the end of those marathon flights in the old turbo-prop Super Constellations – 'Superconnies', as they used to call them. His first flight from Toronto to Prestwick

Scotland on Icelandic Airways had taken over twelve hours with a refueling stop at the RCAF airbase in Gander, Newfoundland. He grinned at the thought of it.

"What's so funny?"

"Pardon? – Oh, I just had a déjà vu about my very first flight."

"Was that to Canada, too?"

"No, the other direction. I come from Canada originally," Barney said.

"You don't sound very Canadian – more English."

"Ah, well. Thirty years is a long time."

"And now, you're going home." It was a statement more than a question.

"I suppose I am, in a way."

"Actually, so am I," said the woman. "I haven't been away thirty years though– only two but it seems a lot longer."

"Here in England?" asked Barney.

"No, China."

"China – wow! Whereabouts?"

"Guangzhou– in the south, - near Hong Kong but on the mainland."

"And you were traveling in China for two years – on your own?"

"No, no. I was studying. Chinese medicine – at the university."

"Oh, a doctor."

"A nurse, actually- you can't become a doctor in two years – not even in China."

"Sounds fascinating," said Barney.

"Exhausting is a better description," said the woman. "I'm glad it's over and I'm going home."

"You didn't like it?"

"I didn't say that – just that it was very tiring. You never seem to get any time to yourself. You're either studying or continually socializing with the Chinese – they never leave you alone – always wanting to practise their English – sometimes I just used to go to my bedroom and lock the door."

"Wasn't it difficult, being on your own? Did you get harassed by men much?"

"Mostly businessmen. They wanted to take me along on their business trips –"

"To translate?" asked Barney.

"I don't think translating was primarily what they had in mind," she said. "But I don't know – I never took them up on their offers. - More of an acquisition, I would guess, to impress their business colleagues." The woman looked around. "I wonder why they're taking so long to get going? I'm gasping for a drink. – Miss!" She hailed a passing attendant. "Has the flight been delayed or something?"

"No, not really," said the girl. "The captain should be making an announcement shortly."

Barney glanced out the window. The cluster of men under the wing was dispersing and the baggage handlers had gone. A few moments later the pilot made his usual bluff speech of welcome and apologized for the delay – technical hitch with the hydraulics – ready to go – forecast was for sunny weather in Vancouver.

"Ha!" said the woman, "that'll be likely."

The plane lumbered out to the end of the runway. Barney said nothing; he was staring out the window at the wing. He clenched his hands in his lap as the plane surged forward, recited his favourite Buddhist chant under his breath and concentrated his whole body into helping the pilot lift the plane into the air. When he had succeeded in getting the huge ungainly structure level and no longer tipping either forward or to either side he slowly exhaled and un-hunching his shoulders, slumped back into his seat.

"Do you always do that?"

Barney turned to see the woman smiling at him. "Huh? – Oh, yeah, I guess I do. Little ritual I've got into over the years – back seat driver."

"Good trick," she said, "– you got us up here."

"Yep, never fails – at least, not yet."

"But can you get us back down?"

"Piece of cake," said Barney. "Getting down is easy – you don't need engines for that. We can just glide down if we have to- but getting up is another story."

"So do you think it's safe enough to take off my shoes, yet?"

"Absolutely." He grinned as he watched her bend down to ease her shoes off and push them under her seat. Her hair fell forward, partly hiding her face and giving her briefly the appearance of a young woman although Barney reckoned she was probably in her late fifties. She sat back, wiggling her stockinged toes and sighed.

"Now, if I could just have a drink."

The plane's passengers were settling themselves, sorting and shifting and re-storing coats and duty-free purchases as the flight attendants were threading their way through them passing out headsets for the film. Barney could see that it would be awhile before they got around to passing out the drinks.

"It just so happens," he said, fishing out his shoulder pack from under the seat where he had stuffed it earlier, "-I have a drink here in my bag." He produced a pack of six miniatures of Scotch and a can of ginger ale. "Emergency supplies," he said. "Never fly without them. Only one snag – no glasses. I usually just open the can, drink a bit and discreetly pour one of these in."

The woman leaned over conspiratorially." How about if I go get a couple of paper cups from the washroom?"

She slid out of her seat and Barney watched her as she stood waiting to get into the aisle past a large Indian woman in a sari who was stuffing packages into the overhead luggage bins. She seemed tiny compared to the Indian woman and her tailored jacket accented her trim waist. Barney revised his estimate downwards – early fifties, he decided as she squeezed past the other woman and disappeared down the aisle.

He opened the Guardian and tried to read but his attention drifted off and he gazed idly round the cabin. The flight attendant he had earlier mistaken for his wife came down the aisle and handed a baby bottle to the large Indian woman holding a child on her lap. As she turned to go, she smiled briefly at Barney. She was not remotely like Alice, he realised.

His mind returned unbidden to his recent separation, picking at the scab, refusing to let it heal over. It was as though they had been moving in slow motion like those TV documentaries he had watched of plants gradually unfolding and then flowering, fading and wilting and sinking back into the ground. Was that what had happened to them, he wondered? How often had she turned away from his urgent longing on some pretext or other until finally pride had stopped him pressing her and he turned away too, so that then they slept back to back, badly. Alice tossing, turning, and poking him with her elbow to stop snoring.

In the end, it had seemed easier to give in and go to the other room in order to get some sleep. After that, it was as though the irritability with each other in bed had seeped into their waking hours and they had picked and prodded at each other over the smallest thing. Soon, a word, a look, a gesture could cause a flare-up which only subsided into a smouldering ember of annoyance, ready to break out again at any hint of a possible slight.

They had made half-hearted attempts to talk about it, but this invariably degenerated into point scoring – a habit they had foresworn years ago. They drifted along in limbo – tip-toeing around each other in elaborate rituals of politeness or sitting staring miserably at the television.

"This is ridiculous," Alice said and Barney agreed.

They thrashed out a plan, born of desperation, to take a page from their children's book and have a gap year apart. Barney would go on his own to Canada. Alice would stay and resume her career. They would keep in touch and in a year's time review the situation to see if there was anything to salvage or to go their separate ways.

It was the best they could come up with and they had parted stiffly - the awkwardness and the painful feelings would catch Barney in unguarded moments so that he had to stop and look about to get his bearings – he hoped Alice was making a better fist of it than him – did everyone their age go through this pain of adjustment when their kids were gone for good?

He knew there was even a term for it now – 'empty nesters' – a flimsy sort of expression for what they had been going through, Barney thought. He tried to recapture his euphoric mood and looked out the window at the bright sunlight bouncing off the wing – he looked further down but there was nothing except a solid bank of cloud spread out like some endless white duvet covering the land.

"At last. You wouldn't believe that one airplane could hold so many weak bladders – I nearly gave up." The woman handed Barney two paper cups and he pried one of the miniatures free from the six-pack.

"Whole or half?" he asked her.

"Half is plenty," she said. "And fill it up with dry ginger please – I need a long drink after that wait." She took the proffered cup and raised it to him. "Cheers." She took a big swallow. "My name's Trish – Patricia, actually."

"Cheers. My name's Barney – Bernard actually." He smiled and they leaned back sipping their drinks. Trish took another long swallow and Barney asked, "Okay? – Not too weak?"

"Oh, this one won't even touch the sides," she said. "You know, I hardly drank at all before I went to China – but all the young doctors and nurses at the hospital drank whiskey like water – Chinese scotch, too – real paint remover – I've probably done  more irreparable damage to my liver in two years than I did in the past thirty."

Barney fished in his bag for another miniature. "– No problem, there's more where that came from."

"I think I'd better start pacing myself now that I'm going back home or people will start getting the wrong idea." She took a small sip from her cup. "– Not that anyone's expecting me."

"You didn't tell anyone you were coming home?"

"Oh yes, I just didn't say when exactly. I told them I'd be dropping off in England to visit my sisters for a few days. They live in Birmingham."

"Ah. Well, somebody has to live there, I guess," said Barney.

"Yes, I know what you mean. Still, it's nice to go back home, even to Birmingham."

"Is that where you're from, then? You don't sound very Brummie."

"Actually, I've lived in Vancouver since I was a teenager – went to Kitsilano High School for my last two years. I soon learned to drop my Brummie accent."

"-But your sisters?"

"They were older. They stayed for a year and then came back to live with Dad. My parents split up and my mother had moved us all out to Canada because her brother was there and he offered to help her get set up in Vancouver."

"I thought Kitsilano was a posh part of town," said Barney. "With the beaches and UBC and all."

"Depends where you are," Trish said. "– We were a long way back from the beach and the university, in a basement apartment. Not a patch on our house in Birmingham – we had lots of Chinese neighbours."

"In Birmingham?"

"No, Kits. That's where I first learned to speak Chinese."

"You speak Chinese? I'm impressed –"

"It's not that hard, actually. It's the writing and reading that's the difficult bit. I never really mastered that – only Pinyin."

"Pinyin? What's that?"

"It's a kind of westernized phonetic version of Chinese – uses our alphabet."

"Say something in Chinese for me," said Barney.

"*Hao. Wo yao hu shi White. Quing he ye yao putaojiu ma? Ni ne?*"

"Sounded like you said 'white something'."

"I did. I said, 'Okay, my name is Nurse White. Please may I have another drink – what about you?'"

"Is that what they called you – Nurse White?"

"In polite conversation or at work, yes. That's the convention – title plus last name." She held out her empty paper cup .Barney unscrewed the top off the miniature and poured her another.

"In two years you must have got pretty good at it."

"Not really. – The lectures were all in English- for the foreigners - and everyone always wanted to practise their English on me – also I used to go to Hong Kong a lot and there's a big expat English community there – it was a kind of haven from the unrelenting demands to practise English in Guangzhou. - Cheers," she raised her cup.

"Cheers," said Barney, topping up his cup. "I've always wanted to go to China – ever since I finished school."

"Why didn't you?"

"I toyed with the idea – but the language seemed so impenetrable, somehow –"

"Like I said, it's only the reading and writing – the speaking is easy."

"Hardly easy," said Barney.

"Relatively easy, then. Once you've mastered the tones – and there's only four of those in Mandarin – and hardly any grammar. You should try it – there's lots of classes in Vancouver – you'll be speaking like a native in no time."

"Mmm," said Barney, doubtfully. "– Tempting, though."

"Only please don't ask to practise on me. I need a break for awhile," Trish smiled.

He laughed, "I think you're probably safe for the time being. I'll be too busy getting my act together to think about studying Chinese any time soon. – Unngghhh!"

His drink flew across Trish's knees as the plane lurched suddenly sideways. A moment later, the ping of the 'Fasten Seatbelts' sign came on above their heads. Trish clutched her drink firmly as the plane shuddered and bucked again.

"Better get this down my neck – feels like rough weather ahead." She gulped the last of her scotch as a flight attendant hurried past towards the rear and people all around quickly sat down and fumbled with their seat belts.

More shuddering followed a sickening lurch to the right. The plane levelled out again only to make another lunge right – Barney glanced out as the wing rose up to block his view – he sat bolt upright, his empty cup crushed in his hand gripping the arm rest – Oh god, he mouthed softly as the wing dipped back level. The plane cabin had gone silent and the normal background murmur of conversation stilled – all heads facing forward as if waiting for a signal.

The shuddering continued as if they were driving over some bumpy road, each time followed by the rightward lurch before the plane slowly levelled out. Trish gripped Barney's arm tighter with each tilt of the cabin, saying nothing. He remained rigidly still throughout every gyration, mouthing 'no, - no', over and over.

A sudden sinking forward and a sharp steep veer to the right brought an involuntary moan from the passengers. Trish looked at Barney whose face had drained of colour.

"Are you alright?" she asked but he said nothing and stared straight ahead, his hands clamped on the seat rest, the spilled whiskey making a widening dark stain on his pale blue shirt.

No announcement had come from the pilot – obviously, they had their hands full and the flight attendants had vanished from sight – presumably buckled into their little jump seats at the back of the cabin. The stomach-churning lunges, always to the right, increased in intensity, the passengers whimpering quietly in anticipation of each turn and groaning more loudly with every lurch.

"Oh god," breathed Barney.

The plane's shuddering and bucking and rightward lurches stopped almost as suddenly as they had begun and it seemed to settle into its bumpy road mode. The intercom pinged and the pilot's voice came on, slightly terser and less bluff.

"This is Captain Wilson. Sorry about not speaking to you earlier, folks, but we've been kind of busy up here. It seems our little technical hitch didn't get ironed out after all. When we ran into that turbulence, it re-occurred and – well, you saw the result. We've been advised to divert to Reykjavik, Iceland and barring any more turbulence, should be there in about twenty minutes. Meantime, please remain seated and keep your seatbelts fastened. Thank you."

A buzz of excited voices spread through the cabin as the passengers digested this bit of information. Trish released her iron grip on Barney's arm and straightened up slightly from her crouching position in her seat.

"Oh thank God, we're going to be okay, Barney."

He remained rigidly upright, still gripping the armrests.

"Barney – Barney? – You alright?" He seemed not to hear her and Trish prized his hand from the armrest and began stroking it. – "It's okay," she soothed, "it's okay – you heard the captain – we'll be landing soon."

Slowly he slumped down from his erect position until his head and arm rested on his lap like some deflatable doll. He began to shake and long juddering sighs rolled down his body. Trish continued stroking his hand, obviously glad of the chance to let her training occupy her mind. She made no attempt to stop him shaking, only making soothing noises. Slowly his shaking subsided and he fumbled for a handkerchief. She quickly pressed some tissues into his hand and he blew his nose.

"Oh god," he sighed, breathing deeply "– oh god –" He looked up slowly and saw the large Indian woman across the aisle. She smiled warmly at him and he managed a weak smile.

"Sorry," he said to Trish. "Sorry. I –" But she only shushed him and patted his arm.

"Are you okay?" he asked.

"I think so," said Trish. "I'll tell you for sure when we're on the ground."

Fifteen minutes later the plane began its descent into Reykjavik airport and landed – rather shakily, but without further incident and the passengers erupted out of their seats, cheering and congratulating each other and hugging the cabin staff who abandoned any attempt to maintain their professional demeanour and hugged them back.

"Its my turn to buy you a drink," announced Trish and she took Barney's arm and steered him towards the long bar in the huge glass cavern of Reykjavik terminal where extra staff were being rapidly pressed into service to deal with the revellers as they poured off the wounded aeroplane. A large cheer went up as the uniformed flight crew passed through on their way to debriefing and they grinned and waved in acknowledgement.

"Two Johnnie Walkers, please," said Trish. "– Doubles." She turned to Barney. "You want anything else – a snack?" He shook his head. They took their drinks and headed for an empty table facing out onto the featureless moonscape of Reykjavik airport.

"God, I love this place," said Barney fiercely. "I don't ever want to leave."

"Here's to Reykjavik," said Trish. "– Cheers." They both drank deeply and gazed blankly out at the dusk settling rapidly beyond the wall of glass. Finally Barney spoke.

"Look, about that – thing. I mean the way I behaved – I just want to apologise –"

"There's no need," Trish interrupted. "I understand, really–"

"No," Barney said, "I don't think you do – I'd like to explain –"

"It's not necessary, honestly –"

"It's just that I felt about seven years old and I got completely swamped by a wave of fear – it sort of paralyzed me, the same as when I was a kid in the dark – afraid to make the slightest movement – even to breathe – it's completely irrational." He took another big mouthful of whiskey and shuddered slightly. "Phew! – That's strong – I'm not used to doubles."

"Do you good," said Trish, working on her own glass. "– Look, we were all afraid. Everyone. It's normal – natural. That was very scary. I'm still trembling – in fact –" she rose," Excuse me a minute –." Clasping her handbag, she walked unsteadily in the direction of the washrooms.

Barney resumed staring out at his own reflection in the plate glass. He wondered idly if he could make her understand what had happened to him or even if he should try. He hadn't told his wife about it until a couple of years ago – how do you explain to someone that you're still afraid of the dark when you're sixty-six years old?

He had never told her before because he was afraid she would no longer respect him. But after the kids had all left, he thought he should risk it. So he told Alice in a light-hearted manner, she had taken his cue and they had treated it in a joking kind of way. She would ask him, if she was going to be away for the weekend in London, if he was sure he was going to be okay on his own. And Barney would say yeah, he'd be fine as long as he had the dog with him.

And they had left it at that – he never told her about how that fear had come to govern his life – how it had sort of linked up with his physical fear of fights with other boys; of how he avoided any situation which might become threatening, until he became so convinced of his own cowardice that he decided he could never get married and have a family – how would he ever protect them? – And even when he did finally start in his late thirties, he hid his fear with elaborate ploys and when it cropped up as it eventually did, he relived his shame alone and silently.

When he was going through the breakup with Glenys, his first partner, he had gone to a therapist and told him how he had pissed his pants once when another boy threatened to punch him at a club – he could still burn with shame at the thought of other people seeing him so afraid – what had the therapist said? – he must have made some comment but Barney couldn't remember – probably he was too wrapped up in his own embarrassment in telling the incident – he had never told Alice about that – he was sure it would erode her feelings for him – there were some things you couldn't tell even to those you loved and Barney hadn't risked it.

There was no sign of Trish so he wandered around the few duty-free shops idly fingering cigar lighters and ludicrously expensive decanters of perfume. Seated apart from the other passengers was the large Indian woman and her family, quietly eating from an assortment of plastic containers, which she kept extracting from her multi-coloured hold-all. She seemed very serene, calmly feeding her husband and children as if nothing untoward had happened at all. Barney continued his tour of the enormous terminal.

Theirs was obviously the only flight in and they were nearly swallowed up in the acres of glass and open space. He drifted back to his seat by the window and took another sip from his drink. Trish's glass was missing and he saw her standing over at the bar chatting to the bartender. She turned round, saw him and waved her hands to ask if he wanted another drink but Barney shook his head and she came back and sat down.

"The barman says they're sending out another plane for us from Manchester."

"How does he know? I didn't hear anything."

"He took a tray of drinks to the crew lounge and they told him. Looks like we'll be here for awhile," said Trish, swirling the ice in her glass.

He leaned back in the leather armchair. "I feel exhausted. Think I'll try to snooze for an hour – do you mind?"

"You go ahead, I'm going to read my book – I can't sleep in these places – it's like being on a park bench."

Barney closed his eyes and began silently chanting his favourite Tibetan mantra. "*Om mani padma sidi hum, om mani padma sidi hum*" – up and down it went in his brain, smoothing and soothing and ironing away the creases and jagged edges of his mind – it was more like humming, really, he mused. "*-Om mani padma sidi hum,*" he hummed to himself, smiling behind his closed eyelids. He would say nothing to Trish about his fear – after all, he barely knew her. She might think he was some kind of weirdo. And she seemed to like him – despite what had happened.

He felt quite fond of her already – maybe we could go out together in Vancouver – nothing heavy, just meet up for a walk on the seawall and a coffee, or perhaps a concert at the Orpheum and a meal. Or a film maybe and then I could drive her home afterwards "*– Om mani padme sidi hum,*" he hummed– the odd trip over to Salt Spring, stay at some off-season bed and breakfast – we could alternate – one weekend at her place and the next at his – but no living together, he admonished himself. It's taken me too long to get my freedom – don't surrender it immediately.

A line from Martin Luther King's famous speech swam into his head –'Free at last, free at last, thank God in Heaven we are free at last' - he could hear the soaring cadence of that powerful voice, charged with emotion – "free at last," he hummed silently, *"-om mani padma sidi hum."* He drifted off, his arm curled protectively around Trish's warm naked body and his hand cupping her breast – a smile spread over his face and his breathing deepened into a gentle snore.

A muffled voice saying something he couldn't make out brought Barney swimming back up to consciousness. The voice seemed to be in English but he couldn't understand what it said. He opened his eyes and looked at his watch –the dial showed seven-thirty – in the morning or evening? The muffled voice echoed again in incoherent English – 'gate five' was all he could make out. He looked about for Trish and saw her sitting at the bar again, still swirling her drink and reading her book. He rose stiffly and crossed to the bar. She looked up, smiling.

"– Good sleep? You looked like you were out for the count."

"Yes, I feel better."

"Mmm, you were looking a bit unravelled – want a drink?"

Barney made a face, "Coffee, maybe – my mouth tastes foul."

"You were snoring – with your mouth open, that's why."

"Charming. Why didn't you wake me?"

"What for? We weren't going anywhere."

"I'm starving," Barney said. "– Let's get something to eat."

"No time," Trish said. "Didn't you hear the announcement?"

"I heard it –but I don't know what they said."

"We're boarding at Gate Five in ten minutes. You've got time for a coffee, though."

"Okay," said Barney. He beckoned the barman. "– You want one, Trish?" She shook her head and indicated her glass. "I'll just finish this." Barney went back to their chairs and collected their hand luggage. He returned to the bar with it and drank his coffee. "– Should have had orange juice – it cuts the fur," he said.

"Not as well as this," Trish said, draining her glass. "– We'd better go–" She stood up, unsteadily and picked up her things. Barney noticed she had a new duty-free bag.

"Doing some shopping?"

"Insurance." She held up the bag obviously holding a bottle. "–Don't want to be caught out again. Look – the barman even gave me some paper cups – no more queues this time. Let's go," she leaned heavily on his arm and they made their way to the boarding gates.

As the replacement aeroplane made its way across the Atlantic, Barney watched the TV screen where the little plane symbol inched across the map, following its Great Circle route. There was something comforting about seeing their progress every half hour or so – he much preferred it to watching the in-flight movies, which were usually inane comedies aimed at ten-year olds.

Trish had been making headway, too, working steadily through her bottle of duty-free scotch, stopping only to switch to wine with their meal when it arrived. She'd had a second glass of wine but declined the tea and coffee, reverting instead to another cup of scotch. Barney had long since ceased to keep pace with her and now as he sipped his tea, he watched Trish out of the corner of his eye.

She was in the middle of telling him about some lavish Chinese banquet she had been invited to in Guangzhou at which they had apparently served all sorts of delicacies like snakes and locusts and monkey brains and puppies – none of which she could bring herself to even taste, let alone eat. So she just drank instead – round after round of toasts and counter-toasts until she nearly passed out and they had politely put her in a taxi and paid the driver to take her back to her hotel.

"I was so embarrassed - I mean I was sort of the honoured guest –the only westerner - and a woman, and I had messed up big-style. Not only had I refused every delicacy I was offered, I had got helplessly drunk as well – and they were so polite! God, I still blush when I think of it –" she took another big swallow of her scotch "– talk about losing face – I reckon I single-handedly set the West and womankind back ten years in one evening."

"You're exaggerating," said Barney. "It couldn't have been that bad."

"It was. It was awful – terrible – one of the worst evenings in my life – and believe me I've had some disastrous ones."

"How long ago did it happen?"

"Last week. The night before I left China – it was my leaving party – all my colleagues from the teaching hospital where I studied." Trish shook her head mournfully. "– Some of the senior professors had been invited, too…."

"Ah well, you survived," Barney said. "Probably a few months from now you'll be dining out on that story –"

"Never," said Trish, vehemently shaking her head "– What a way to end things - they had planned to see me off at the airport but I couldn't face them – I sneaked off early in a taxi – bloody hell." She finished off her drink. "– Story of my life – one big cock-up." She began to pour more scotch into her cup.

"I'm sorry," said Barney. "It does sound god-awful." Trish turned to him and smiled ruefully and he grinned back. They both started to giggle.

"Oh don't," she said. "It's not funny." She took a sip of her scotch and snorted in the middle of it, the whiskey spraying out her nose. Barney hand her a paper napkin and sniggered, setting her off again and the two of them giggled convulsively. Trish wiped her nose and her eyes.

"You see?" he said, "I told you you'd be dining off this in no time."

"Who with?" said Trish. "– The way I'm going I soon won't have any friends left."

"Oh come on," said Barney, "- It can't be that bad." He began mopping up the spilled whiskey with a paper napkin.

"You don't know the half of it, brother," Trish said. "That's just so typical of me."

"You mean there's worse?" asked Barney, smiling.

"Much worse."

"Tell me."

"You don't want to hear, believe me-"

"Try me" – but she shook her head. They sat silently staring at their hands, Trish working away at her drink. Several minutes elapsed.

"My husband left me because of that –" she announced suddenly. "– Said he couldn't take one more scene like that –"

"-You've done this before, then?" Barney said.

"God, yes – dozens of times. My husband said every time we went to a party I'd make a scene. That's not true of course – it wasn't every time…. A lot, though," Trish conceded.

"– I didn't mean to – never intended to – I always started out vowing this time it would be different – but somehow –" her voice trailed off.

"What happened? I mean each time –" asked Barney, curious now.

"Oh nothing much," said Trish. "– I didn't dance on the tables or do a strip or anything. It's just I would start out in a good mood, having a few drinks and then I'd start to feel bad so I'd have more drinks and then more, until finally I'd pass out and my husband would have to take me home. Only now he doesn't have to anymore because he left-"

"Is that why you started drinking – because he was leaving you?"

"No – long before that – when I knew we weren't going to have any children."

"Oh, I'm sorry."

"Do you have any children, Barney?"

"Yes, - three," he said apologetically.

"Well I never had any," said Trish, looking down into her empty glass. "None. My husband didn't want any. Anthony said there were already too many children in this world without us making things worse. Only he didn't tell me this until after we were married – after he told me he was having a vasectomy so we didn't need to worry. I guess it was around then I started to drink whenever I wanted to forget about all my babies that never had a chance to be born. That's when I really got to know Johnnie Walker – I just poured him into that big empty hole inside me – let him fill me right up – only he never could quite succeed because I always let him down – couldn't last the course." She stood up abruptly. "– Excuse me, must go to the loo." She drifted into the aisle and

23

headed towards the rear of the cabin, still clutching the bottle of Johnnie Walker.

Barney decided he'd better go to the washroom as well. He could freshen up at the same time, wash and brush his teeth before the main rush – they must be getting near – the little aeroplane symbol on the map was edging its way down over northern British Columbia. The passengers lay about in crumpled heaps on their seats in a vain attempt to find a comfortable position.

He locked himself into the toilet and consulted his image in the mirror. For the thousandth time he asked himself who was that old guy staring back at him. He stuck out his tongue and examined it, then began methodically brushing his teeth.

By the time he was finished his ablutions a small queue had formed outside the door and the passengers were beginning to bestir themselves. A young mother in the seat ahead with twin girls was combing their hair into ponytails. The large Indian woman was packing and repacking her plastic containers while her husband sat passively with his hands folded and one leg tucked under him.

Trish was still in the loo so Barney used the space to sort out his things and reshuffle all his belongings into his carry-on backpack. He prided himself on travelling light and one day vowed he would have no luggage to check in – only his carry-on bag. But that day had not yet arrived and he told himself that he had an excuse because this time he was moving and not simply travelling. He resumed his seat and gazed out at the snow-topped crests of the mountains below, stretching into the distance in the bright sunshine.

"Excuse me sir." A flight attendant leaned over the empty seat. "Is your wife feeling unwell? She's been in the lavatory a long time and the other passengers –"

"Oh, she's not my wife," said Barney. "What's wrong?"

"Is she a relative, sir?"

"No, we've only just met – do you want me to go with you?" – He started to rise from his seat. The flight attendant seemed uncertain.

"You say she's not travelling with you?"

"That's right," Barney nodded, "But I talked to her quite a lot – I could come and speak to her –"

"Do you know her name, sir?"

"Trish – Patricia. – Sorry I can't remember her last name – I know she mentioned it, but …."

The flight attendant turned to go, checking the seat number above Barney's head. "We'll find it on the passenger list."

Barney rose and followed her down the aisle to the rear cabin where a small knot of people stood by the toilets. She squeezed past and Barney followed in her wake. She rapped on the door.

"Patricia – are you alright?" She looked at Barney and nodded towards the door.

"Trish – Trish, it's Barney - can you hear me?" He knocked tentatively at first, then more firmly. "– Trish? Trish! Please open the door." – He pressed his ear to the door – "Trish?" – Nothing. He leaned over to the flight attendant and whispered, "She's had an awful lot to drink. – I think maybe she may have fallen asleep." – He banged on the door again. "Trish! – Trish?" Still nothing.

The flight attendant nodded to another one hovering nearby. The woman approached and inserted a hexagonal metal handle into a small hole at the top of the door and turned it. She pushed the middle of the folding door, which opened inwards a few inches. Trish sat slumped on the closed toilet seat her head leaning against the wall. The attendant tried to push the door open but it appeared stuck. The other woman squatted down and reached in behind the door feeling for the obstruction. She pulled out the empty bottle of Johnnie Walker and gave the first attendant a meaningful look.

"-Trish," said Barney, over her shoulder "– Are you okay?" But already the two women were taking over, obviously familiar with this situation.

"We'll look after her sir. Thank you for your assistance. Could you please return to your seat?"

"Don't you want me to help you get her back to her seat?" asked Barney, but the attendant only shook her head.

"She'll be better back here with us – there's a spare seat right here she can have." She turned back to the toilet and squeezed in beside her colleague who was leaning over Trish and shaking her shoulder. Trish's head lolled forward. A strong whiff of whiskey caught Barney's nose as they lifted her awkwardly between them and hauled her out of the toilet.

"Please sir – just return to your seat – we'll look after her now."

Barney nodded and backed away as they half-carried, half-dragged Trish into the crew kitchen space and propped her on a jump seat. The curtain swished closed behind them and the small group of onlookers shook their heads as they resumed queuing for the toilet and Barney walked back to his seat.

He sat staring at the little plane on the TV map and saw that it seemed to be hovering over the word Vancouver. As if to confirm it, the intercom pinged and the pilot announced they would be beginning their descent and should be on the ground in approximately fifteen minutes. Barney looked out the oval window at the sun starting to set over the mountains. In the top corner of the window, he could just see the sunlight glinting on a strip of water.

"The Pacific Ocean," thought Barney, "- I made it."

As soon as the plane had bumped down on the runway, Barney pressed his light button to summon a flight attendant but no one came. He craned his neck around to see if he could catch someone's eye but there was no sign of anyone. Not until the plane came to a standstill and the jets sighed in relief as they shut down, did the attendant approach him.

"How is she?" he asked. The young woman shook her head.

"We're not sure – we still haven't managed to rouse her – we've called ahead for a doctor and he'll be coming on board as soon as they open the cabin doors."

"I'd like to wait for her," said Barney. "See that she's okay." The attendant was checking under the seat. She held up a handbag.

"Is this hers, do you know?"

"Yes," said Barney, "I'm pretty sure. And that other one is too. The coloured material one." The attendant fished it out and rose.

"You could let all the other passengers leave first and then wait to see what the doctor says, I guess. You say she was just a fellow passenger?"

"But I feel I know her quite well," said Barney. "We talked a lot. I couldn't just leave."

The attendant nodded. She began threading her way back through the milling throng of passengers filling the aisle. Barney gathered his coat and bag on to his lap and waited. After an age, the crowd thinned out and he was able to look back over the seats to the rear but the curtain was still closed. He watched the baggage handlers piling up the chain of wagons and snaking their way into the terminal. Still he waited. Two uniformed cleaners worked their way down the aisles stuffing rubbish into black plastic bin liners. Finally, the young flight attendant approached.

"Hasn't the doctor arrived yet?" asked Barney.

She nodded. "Oh yes. He's gone. They've taken her to the airport infirmary. He thinks she's only passed out but they want to keep her in overnight to make sure. It's Mr. Roper, isn't it?"

"Yes, Barney Roper. – Look, couldn't I go and see her?" The attendant shook her head.

"Sorry, sir – but you're not a relative."

"But I don't even have her address or phone number – how will I find out how she is?" A thought struck him. "Did you look in her handbag? – she must have her phone number there."

"Yes, we found it – but we're not allowed to give out that sort of personal information." She looked at him for a minute. "You could phone the infirmary in the morning – I can give you that number, if you like."

"Yes, please," said Barney, and he stood waiting in the aisle as she went back to the crew area. A moment later, she handed him a slip of paper. "Thanks," he said. "Thanks very much, miss –" He tried to read her lapel tag.

"Becky," she said.

He nodded, "Becky. Thanks Becky." She smiled at him, then turned back down the aisle and Barney hefted his shoulder bag and headed for the exit.

In the bendy-bus driving into the city, he watched the other people all sitting silently with that condemned expression common to bus passengers everywhere. He got off at the Burrard Street station and consulted his notebook with the directions to his address. He knew the city fairly well from previous holiday trips but the darkened streets with their splashes of bright neon lighting disoriented him at first and he headed off in the wrong direction. He had walked two blocks before he decided he must be going the wrong way and asked someone, which was the way to Bayshore. The man pointed back in the direction he had come from and Barney turned and trudged back past Burrard and on down Georgia.

Eventually he found the building – a tall high rise, all glass, balconies and bright lights. He opened an envelope, took out the set of keys to let himself in. It took him awhile to work out the security fob that operated the front door and the elevators but he finally arrived on the twelfth floor and walked down to number 1203.

He knocked first, just in case, then opened the door and dropped his bags in the hallway, found the light switch and began exploring the apartment, turning all the lights on as he went. He slid open the balcony door and stepped outside. He still had his coat on and the September night felt cool on his face.

He watched the lights of the harbour reflecting off the forest of sailboat masts for a few minutes then stepped back inside and went into the gleaming kitchen and opened the fridge. He took out a carton of orange juice and started looking for a glass in the cupboards. His foot kicked something and he looked down at a plastic bowl half full of water that had splashed out onto his shoe.

Taking the glass of orange juice, he wandered into the bedroom and eased himself down onto the bed, still wearing his coat. He kicked off his shoes and stretched out full length, sipping cautiously at the juice, before setting it down. He stared up at the ceiling and closed his eyes. As he drifted off, he realized his euphoric mood had completely evaporated.

# CHAPTER 2

When Barney left for Canada, Alice Roper smiled secretly to herself. She had been working towards this day for a long time and she intended to savour it to the full. Crossing to her old roll top desk, she unlocked a small drawer and took out an official-looking envelope – it had arrived three days before Barney had left but she hadn't allowed herself to open it. She knew exactly what it contained but still she had waited – just to be sure. She carried the letter into the living room, sat in her favourite wingback armchair and picked up a glass of whiskey that she had just prepared. The old longcase wall clock only stood at eleven a.m. but she raised her glass, took a good deep swallow and gently eased open the envelope.

She began to read –"*...pleased to inform ...officially accepted ...master's degree program...archaeology department ...St*

*Swithens College, Oxford ... thesis topic... Roman household rituals... tutor Professor Hector Bradley...."* Her eyes scanned the letter absorbing the comforting phrases and the slightly formal language. They stopped on the last paragraph and reread it. It was an invitation to attend a graduate students' informal get-together with department teaching staff for drinks at six-thirty pm on October the first – exactly one month from today.

Alice folded the letter carefully and put it back in the envelope. She leaned back in her armchair smiling contentedly. God knows she needed a break, she thought. Her caseload at work had become more and more impossible and when the new girl they brought in to share the work left after only five months to have a baby, all her cases defaulted to Alice.

She struggled on, feeling frustrated and unhappy knowing she was not doing justice to all the families entrusted to her care. Her sixtieth birthday was looming and she agonized over her decision to leave and pursue a totally different career at this age. Not that she wasn't familiar with it. After all, archaeology had been her first choice and she had never really given it up, even after her parents had persuaded her to switch to social work so she could at least earn a living when she graduated and support her baby daughter Netta.

Alice was still living at home with them in the big old mansion flat in North London on the edge of Hampstead Heath. She was determined not to live off them any longer than she had to and that had clinched her decision to switch careers. Her father had pointed out that she could continue her interest in archaeology as a hobby and this she had done ever since – going on digs for a day here or a weekend there and keeping up with developments in the academic journals.

They were right, of course. There were no jobs in archaeology when she graduated but social workers were in huge demand. She had never stopped working throughout her married life, except to have her second daughter, Cassie, and then only for six months. So when Barney had first mooted the idea that he might return to Canada to pursue what he called his Third Age Explorations now that the kids had all flown the nest, Alice too had begun hatching her own backup plan.

She drained the last of her whiskey and went to sit at her desk. Choosing a clean sheet of her letterhead paper and her favourite fountain pen with the wide gold nib, she started to compose her letter of resignation, effective exactly one month from today. She handed it in the next morning before she began working out her notice.

All through the turmoil that followed, Alice remained serenely unperturbed and happy, dealing with all the crises in a calm, efficient manner, smiling and nodding and listening to the stream of problems that flowed over her desk and in and out of her office. Her boss had gone from incredulity, to anger, to despair and then finally resignation when he realised that Alice was not to be dissuaded. Her colleagues and friends too, had come to accept her decision and secretly envied her new-found confidence, wishing that they had the nerve to pack it all in and go off – where? – To do what? They reluctantly went back to their overflowing desks and insistently ringing telephones thinking some people have all the luck. Alice just smiled at them and the piles of case-notes on her desk grew daily smaller while the clamour for attention from her clients diminished as she quietly but firmly transferred them to her bewildered replacement – another new graduate whom Alice was relieved to find had no current boyfriend likely to derail her with an unexpected pregnancy. Alice was one of those people who believed that you made your own luck and she was enjoying making hers.

At her leaving party on the last day of the month, her women colleagues and friends had first taken her for a raucous meal at their regular Friday night bistro and then for a last night of ten-pin bowling. It was something they had started doing rather sheepishly at first after they were all sent on a stress-management course by a department head worried about increasing absenteeism.

There was a bar at the bowling alley and a team of regulars from a machine tool factory on a nearby industrial estate – young men bored with the routine of their work who came to let off steam. The women flirted with them, emboldened by drink and numbers and soon what had started out as a duty became a social engagement they looked forward to as each hectic week took its toll on their stress levels.

Tonight was no exception and they had started with a round of drinks at the bar and a surprise gift from the machinists. Tony, their spokesman, usually so vocal in his teasing of the women was almost tongue-tied as he made the presentation. "To Alice, from all the lads – hope this helps you find your buried treasure." The barman passed over a long awkwardly shaped bundle from behind the bar. Alice unwrapped a stainless steel spade, which the men had retooled so that the blade was much smaller and narrower – she hefted it experimentally.

"It's beautiful," she said "– and so light. Thank you." And she hugged each of them in turn.

Al, one of the older men, shook his head. "If I gave my wife a present like that she'd probably hit me over the head with it."

"Come on," said Alice, picking up her glass and carrying her spade. "I feel lucky tonight," and she headed for the bowling lanes.

They started with a mixed team of the men and women and Alice was allowed to go first. She had never been much good but enjoyed the chance to unwind with all her women friends. Tonight her first ball wobbled a bit, then smoothed out and gaining momentum, took out all ten pins cleanly – a strike. A loud cheer went up from both teams and Alice bowed and took her seat. She had never mastered the scoring and left it to the others to do the complicated calculations, which they did with increasing arguments as the game progressed. On her next two turns, she bowled spares and then another strike.

"Go for it, Alice," the women called encouragingly. "You're on a roll!" She finished the game with the second highest score, beaten only by Tony, the men's best player. More drinks followed and the teasing, flirting and innuendo grew in volume.

After an hour or more, Alice bowed out for a game and she and her oldest friend, Stevie retreated to the bar to cool off. They ordered mineral water and Stevie pressed the chilled bottle against her forehead. She was a big-boned woman, used to physical work in her large garden but she was still perspiring freely.

"You know, it's not too late to change your mind, Alice."

"Don't be absurd, Stevie – it's way too late for regrets now – anyway I've burned all my bridges - and boats –"

"But what about me, Alice – what's going to happen to me?"

"You'll be fine – you've got your house and your beautiful walled garden – and Charles."

Stevie snorted. "Charles! – What good is Charles? – Who am I going to talk to, that's what I want to know –"

"Stevie, you know everyone in the whole county, practically."

"Yes, but I can't talk to them, Alice – not like you."

"You'll just have to come and visit me, then. It's only Oxford, Stevie – I'm not going to China."

"It won't be the same, though – you'll be meeting all these clever new people – sophisticated –witty – charming –"

"Are you trying to frighten me, Stevie? – 'coz it's no use - I don't care how clever or charming they are, I'm going – they can charm the pants off me –" Alice grinned, "I hope they do." She set her bottle of mineral water down on the bar and headed for the loo.

Their final game over, amid much good-natured joking, the rest of the team came out to join them at the bar and ordered coffee. On her return from the washroom, Alice noticed Stevie was missing. She was about to enquire, when she spotted her talking near the exit door with the barman. He nodded and left and Stevie walked back over to join the group.

"Just before you all leave," she announced, "I have been asked to say an official goodbye to Alice from all her friends and workmates. She will be sorely missed and so we decided to have the usual whip-round and get her a leaving present. We had thought of buying her a new Mini – but there wasn't quite enough money. And anyway everyone knows the parking in

Oxford is hopeless – so, as more befitting her new role as a poor student, we settled for this instead…."

Stevie gestured towards the exit door and on cue, the barman opened it and wheeled in a gleaming new bicycle, complete with wicker front basket and 'sit up and beg' handlebars. Everyone applauded and cheered as Alice hugged Stevie and took the bike from the barman.

"No excuse to be late for school now, Alice," said Al.

"It's perfect," exclaimed Alice. "My favourite colour – British Racing Green – now I feel like a proper student at last." She wheeled it up and down between the tables holding it with one hand and hugging everyone in turn with her free arm.

"Let's see you ride it, Alice," called Tony, holding the door open. They all grabbed their coats and followed him outside.

"Someone hold my spade," she said, brandishing it like a sword. Stevie took it from her and she pushed the bike out between the two lines of friends forming a guard of honour. In the car park, everyone cheered as Alice gamely mounted the bike and wobbled off between the cars. She circled round and headed back towards them.

"I don't know how to stop it," she shouted, as they all scattered from her path. "Squeeze the handles," called Tony, running beside her. "Here," he pointed. The bike halted abruptly and two of the other men who had joined the chase, caught Alice.

"I think you'd better practice in the morning, Alice," said Stevie. "We can put it in the back of my car."

"No, I want to ride it home," insisted Alice. "Does it have a light?"

"Right here," said Al, switching it on.

They all gathered round, calling their goodbyes and shouting encouragement as Alice rode off again, looping through the car park and then sailing past them, all cheering and waving as she headed off down the street, her red tail-light winking in the dark

# CHAPTER 3

Aloud insistent buzzing brought Barney struggling back up to consciousness. He lay for a moment listening to the sound. The buzzing had stopped but then started again and he opened his eyes to the unfamiliar surroundings and looked down at his fully clothed body. Another buzz brought him sitting upright and he realized it must be the door intercom and not the telephone. Padding down the hall in his sock feet, he found the receiver and spoke into it. "Hello?"

"Mr. Roper? Is that you?" said a woman's voice. "It's Rozalin LeClair."

"Oh, yes, sorry. How do I let you in?" said Barney.

"It's alright, I have my own keys – I just wanted to make sure you were awake. May I come up now?"

"Yes, of course - please," said Barney and replaced the receiver on the wall. Looking in the hall mirror, he saw his dishevelled appearance and his rumpled clothes. He pawed at his face and hair ineffectually and tried to brush the wrinkles out of his clothes. His bags lay on the hall floor where he had dropped them last night and he picked them up and carted them into the bedroom. He was debating having a quick wash when a knock came at the door. He walked back down the hall, still in his sock feet and opened it. A tall, dark-haired woman in her late fifties stood smiling at him. She held out her hand.

"I'm Rozalin Le Clair." She glanced at his clothes and smiled again. "It looks like I did come too early, but I haven't much time. May I come in, Mr. Roper?"

He shook her hand. "Please, yes." He stood aside and let her lead the way into the apartment.

"I hope you found your way around alright," she said over her shoulder. "It's not very large, but it's quite comfortable." She crossed to the balcony doors. "Did you like the view?"

Barney came and stood beside her to look out at the harbour and the mountains beyond.

"Yes, it's stunning," he said "Afraid I've only seen it at night – my flight was delayed several hours and I guess I just sort of conked out when I got here – what time is it, anyway?" He fumbled for his pocket watch.

"Eleven o'clock," said Rozalin. "I expect you're still jet-lagged."

"Yeah, I guess I am." nodded Barney. "Uh, would you like some coffee? – Is there any coffee?" He headed into the kitchen area and looked for some familiar hint.

Rozalin followed him. "Why don't I make the coffee and you can have a wash and freshen up," she said, opening the freezer door of the fridge and removing a packet.

"You keep the coffee in the freezer?" asked Barney. "Good thing I didn't try to make any last night – that's the last place I would have looked."

"My mother always said it kept fresher," said Rozalin. "I don't know – just habit. – Would you like a croissant? I picked some up on the way."

"A croissant would be nice," he said, standing in the doorway.

"Okay." Taking some chunky dark green cups from a cupboard, she noticed him still standing there. "It's alright, I'll manage –" and she made shooing motions with her hand at him. "Sorry to rush you, but Eugene will be here soon with Ralf."

Barney stared at her, uncomprehending. "Ralph?"

"Ralf's my little dog. Remember? – You did agree you'd look after him."

"Oh, Ralf – sure. Yes, of course. I'll just have a quick wash," said Barney walking back down the hall and opening the first door he came to. He stared blankly at the washing machine and dryer, which blocked the entrance.

"Other side," called Rozalin from the kitchen. "Towels are under the counter." He collected his toilet bag from his rucksack and entered the bathroom. He debated having a shave but the socket didn't match his electric razor so he settled for brushing his teeth and splashing hot water on his face. He found his comb and smoothed his thinning white hair.

Going back to the bedroom, he removed his rumpled jacket and pulled on a sweater from his bag. When he emerged from the bedroom, Rozalin had set a cafetière of coffee and the croissants on a little table on the balcony.

"I thought you might like some fresh air," she said. "It's still fairly warm for September and I can enjoy the view for the last time." She poured coffee into the heavy cups.

"Those croissants smell good."

"I warmed them in the microwave," she said, handing him one on a plate. She leaned back in her chair and gazed out over the harbour. "Every year, I tell myself to go in the spring instead so I can stay here for the fall colour - but then I'd miss the whole summer here - and Europe is crammed with tourists in the summertime, so it's hard for me to work undisturbed."

"You mentioned in your email that you'd be travelling in Europe but you didn't say where," said Barney, wiping flakes from the croissant off his pullover. "Are you a landscape painter?"

"Not really. Mainly houses, street scenes, markets, and harbours. Nostalgia stuff, mostly."

"Nostalgia?"

"Yes. Most of my clients are ex-pat Europeans. They like to see paintings that remind them of home, so that's what I give them – sort of," she said.

"How do you mean, sort of?"

"Well, they want to see things the way they remembered them, so I have to edit out the modern buildings and just paint the old stuff. That's why they like paintings more than photographs – everything looks too new in photographs – not how they like to think of it."

"I see," said Barney, intrigued. "- And you can give them what they want?"

"'He who pays the piper'," she said. "It's a niche market but it pays well. I stumbled on it by accident, really, through some of my mother's old friends. Women she played bridge with – all expat French women like her – widows mostly. She used to show them my paintings when I was at art college and one of them asked me if I could paint her a picture of her old house in France from a photograph she had.

It was in black and white and blurry, too but she told me everything about it – the colour of the paint, what kind of trees and shrubs in the garden – even the stained glass in the front door. She remembered every detail so vividly I was afraid she would be disappointed with my painting but she loved it – it was just how she recalled it, she said and she hung it over her mantelpiece in her living room.

Of course, all her friends saw it and they wanted one of their house or village, too. Some of them wanted their church or favourite café or street or chateau or bridge but they didn't have photos. I had finished Art College and was going to France for the summer, before I had to get a job. My mother had insisted on it and had saved enough to pay my fare.

She was the one who suggested I go to all these villages and towns, find the places the old ladies had lived, and paint what they wanted. So off I went with my sketchbook and paints and my Eurailpass. But of course, it all took a lot longer than I thought, so I ended up taking lots of pictures as well, to use to remind me when I got back home."

"Did you enjoy it?" asked Barney, thinking how much he would have loved a trip like that when he was young.

"Loved it," said Rozalin. "It was kind of like a treasure hunt - finding all those old buildings - and the old ladies had given me dozens of names and addresses of relatives and neighbours to look up if I needed help and a place to stay.

Of course, some of them had moved away or died but most of the time I found someone who remembered them and they insisted I stay with them while I sketched and painted and photographed. Sometimes I got passed around the village and fed huge French lunches and drank so much wine I'd fall asleep over my sketchbook in the afternoon."

"What a brilliant way to see a country," said Barney enviously. "And you never looked back, since then?"

Rozalin laughed, "Not quite. There weren't that many old French expats in Vancouver, so I had to widen my net a little. My mother took some of my paintings and sketches around the community centres and seniors' clubs and came back with some requests for pictures from several European countries."

"Your mother sounds like quite an entrepreneur," said Barney.

"Oh, she was - somebody told her she should go to Victoria because there were tons of expat English people on Vancouver Island - so we took the ferry over and did the rounds of all the clubs and seniors' centres we could find and came home with enough commissions to keep me busy for the next two summers."

"How long have you been doing this?" asked Barney.

"Ever since," Rozalin said. "But after a while I got fed up with just painting old houses and started doing other stuff as well - I used to ask around the villages for the most popular locations and views. They sold pretty well, too and I started getting requests for favourite views that people remembered - they said photographs were always disappointing and never really caught the scene. Nowadays I pretty much paint whatever I want – as long as it's someplace people know." She stood up. "Would you like to see some of them?"

"I'd love to," Barney said, following her back into the living room. She went to a hall cupboard and started pulling out canvases.

"These are some I'm still working on, but you get the idea" – she handed them to him and he saw at once the appeal they must hold for lonely old people far from their native country. Barney was sort of expecting some chocolate box thatched-cottage paintings but these were quite simple and unfussy, capturing the mood in an unsentimental way.

"Why, they're very good," he exclaimed.

"You sound surprised – I have been doing it for many years," said Rozalin.

"Sorry. I guess I was thinking they'd be like those idealized calendar paintings the card shops are full of back home," apologized Barney. He turned over a few more canvases and then flipped back to one. With a shock, he realized that he recognized it. "This is Tintern Abbey." – It was a statement rather than a question. Rozalin looked over his shoulder at it.

"That's right," she nodded. "I was working my way down the Wye Valley when I did that –"

"I've been there dozens of times," said Barney, holding up the painting and walking over to the window. He examined it intently, looking for all the telltale details. "You left out that big ugly car park right beside it - there's no grass there," he said accusingly.

Rozalin laughed. "A bit of artistic licence – you sound like one of my clients."

"Definite improvement though," he grinned. "I can see why you're so popular. I wouldn't mind having this myself."

"It's not finished yet," she said. "And anyway you probably couldn't afford it. I charge quite a bit for these things now - you told me you were on a pretty tight budget when we negotiated the lease -" It was her turn to sound accusing.

"No, you're probably right," said Barney, handing her back the canvas.

She was packing the others away in the cupboard, "Tell you what. You can have it on loan while I'm away. Hang it in the hall if you want." Rozalin held out the painting to him.

"Well, thanks," said Barney. "– I'd like that – remind me of home."

Rozalin laughed again. "Just like my expats." She stood up and closed the cupboard door.

Barney tilted the canvas back and forth. "It's good," he said, "-very good."

"Thanks," she said. "But it's not really what I'm interested in – it's just a living now – bread and butter stuff." She glanced at her watch and he noticed her strong hands and ringless fingers. –"Eugene should be here by now." She went back out and looked over the balcony. "He usually comes back along the seawall." – She sat down again and poured Barney some more coffee. "I haven't really showed you around the apartment, yet, but it's all fairly obvious – I'm sure you'll be fine."

"I'll be fine," Barney assured her, drinking his coffee and leaning back in his seat. "– I don't plan on moving off this balcony for at least a week – I'll just sit here and soak up the sun and the view."

"Enjoy it while you can," said Rozalin. "This is Vancouver, remember."

"You say you're not really interested in your painting anymore?" probed Barney.

"I never was," she said. "– I just sort of got side-tracked. My real love is abstract painting, but it doesn't put bread on the table. I've got a basement full of unsold stuff." – She got up and leaned on the balcony railing, looking down at the seawall.

"I'd love to see it," offered Barney, but Rozalin shook her head.

"No time, I'm afraid. I'll have to leave as soon as Eugene arrives with Ralf – If you really wanted to see it, Eugene could show you sometime. He's my only admirer – and patron – except he has no money."

"Who is Eugene – a friend?"

"Yes, in a way. I hired him to walk Ralf every day. He's an art student at the Emily Carr Institute – he walks people's dogs to earn money. He takes Ralf out and I pay him with my abstract work – one a month. He must have quite a collection by now."

"Abstract painting," said Barney. "Pretty radical departure from this." He held the canvas out at arm's length trying to imagine how it might look through the eyes of a Braque or Picasso.

"I loved collage work when I was a student," said Rozalin. "And then when I travelled around the continent on my sketching trips, I used to go into all the little local galleries to see what the local painters were doing – pinching their favourite views. Lots of the places were showing modern stuff as well so I kept abreast of what was happening in the art world all over Europe and tried to incorporate all the new ideas in my own paintings. I've shown some of them to a few galleries here – but nobody seemed interested so I just hang them in my basement store."

Barney frowned, "I didn't notice anything like that inside."

"Oh, I don't keep them on view here. I don't think my regular clients would want to see them – ruin my street cred," she smiled ruefully. She looked over the railing and waved suddenly. – "There they are." She looked at her watch again. "My God, look at the time. My flight's in three hours." She turned to Barney. "I don't suppose I could persuade you to drive me out to the airport in my car," she asked him. "– It's quite close really. You can do it in half an hour at this time of day."

"Of course, I will," said Barney. "It's the least I can do, seeing as I'm having the use of it while you're away."

The intercom buzzer sounded and Rozalin hurried to answer it. "Come on in, Eugene. I'm waiting for you." She opened the hall closet door and began removing two battered leather pieces of luggage. "I'm all packed and ready to go," she said to Barney. "I'll just introduce you to Eugene – and Ralf, of course." She opened the apartment door and stood waiting in the doorway.

The sound of an elevator door opening was followed almost immediately by a small grey dog hurtling into the apartment hallway. It came to an abrupt halt when it saw Barney and cocked its head to one side inquiringly. Rozalin smiled, "Barney, this is Ralf. Say hello, Ralf."

"Ralf" barked Ralf. "Ralf, Ralf." He kept a discreet distance from Barney who had hunkered down to pat him. He held out the back of his hand for the little dog to sniff. Ralf sniffed briefly and then allowed the back of his neck to be stroked.

Rozalin beamed approvingly, "You'll be friends in no time – he doesn't usually take to new people so quickly." Barney continued to scratch Ralf's ears.

"–Eugene! I was starting to worry," she said, as a young man in his early twenties appeared in the doorway. He wore standard student gear of jeans and baggy pullover. The only clue to his artistic studies was a pair of paint-spattered old canvas trainers. He kissed her cheek.

"-Sorry I'm late – some bitch was on heat in Stanley Park and Ralf took off after her – it was love at first sight," he laughed indulgently.

"Oh, Ralf," admonished Rozalin. Ralf looked unrepentant. "Eugene, this is Barney Roper –" she turned to Barney, who was straightening up. The two men shook hands.

"Nice to meet you, Mr. Roper," said Eugene deferentially. They all followed Ralf into the kitchen where he stood expectantly beside a low cupboard. Rozalin bent down to open it.

"This is where I keep all his stuff," she said, taking out a bag of chews and giving one to Ralf. "– He likes a treat when he comes home."

"-Me, too," said Eugene.

"I brought some croissants, Eugene. Would you like one heated up?" He nodded and she took one from the bag on the counter and put it in the microwave. "– Barney has offered to drive me to the airport. Would you mind very much eating it on the way? – You could get a coffee at the terminal."

"Sure thing," said Eugene, "-no problem." The microwave pinged and she removed the hot croissant and wrapped it in a paper napkin for him.

"Good, I'll just use the bathroom and then we can go. – There's a spare set of car keys on the coffee table."

Barney went to retrieve his jacket from the bedroom and found the key ring she had sent him in his pocket. He added the car keys to it while Eugene and Ralf looked on, munching their treats. Rozalin reappeared with fresh lipstick.

"Eugene, could you manage that big case down to the car?" She picked up the smaller of the two bags and Barney took it from her.

"Here, let me," he said. She smiled and relinquished the case and then turned to crouch down to the little Yorkie. "Bye, Ralfie. I shall miss you – behave yourself while I'm away – no more 'liaisons dangereuses'." She gave him a last pat and stood up. "Right. 'Allons'," she said and they all trooped out the door to the elevator.

On the way to the airport, Rozalin drove her little yellow Peugeot compact and showed Barney the fastest route down Oak Street to Marine Drive. Eugene spread his long gangling frame out in the back seat and gazed out at the tugs on the Fraser River as they passed over the half-empty bridge.

Used to London traffic, Barney was struck by the wide quiet streets of Vancouver. In no time, they were at the airport terminal and Rozalin wheeled into the short-term car park near the departures' entrance.

"You don't need to bother coming in," she said. "–I'm used to airports on my own." – But Barney insisted and Eugene said he wanted a coffee so they found a trolley, escorted her to the Air France check-in counters and Eugene went off to find a

Starbucks. By the time he had returned Rozalin had her boarding pass and the three of them headed for the departure lounge entrance. She hugged Eugene and kissed him on both cheeks. She turned to Barney and he stuck out his hand. "Eugene knows where everything is," she said shaking his hand firmly "– I hope you enjoy your stay."

"You, too. Have a good trip and paint lots of pictures. Send me a postcard from the Jeu de Pomme." – On impulse, he leaned forward and kissed her cheek. She smiled and took her battered shoulder bag from Eugene.

"Take care of Ralf," she said to them both and disappeared down the corridor.

"She seems pretty fond of you," remarked Barney, as they made their way back to the car. Eugene shrugged and smiled.

"Yeah, she treats me like a son, sort of. She hasn't got any kids of her own," he offered by way of explanation. "– But she's got something a lot better. Talent. You got any kids, Mr. Roper?"

"Barney. Call me Barney. Yeah, I've got three. Not kids, though. All grown-up and gone – older than you, probably." He steered the little yellow car back onto the main highway, pleased that he was remembering the route Rozalin had shown him. "– So you think her paintings are pretty good, eh?"

"They're very good," said Eugene. "If you ask me I think Roz is probably one of the best artists in Vancouver – on the West coast even."

"High praise," smiled Barney at the young man's enthusiasm.

"You should see them," said Eugene. "Nobody out here is doing anything like them. She's streets ahead of anyone else."

"I'd like to," said Barney. "Rozalin said you might show me some of them. I gather you have a few yourself."

"Yeah, we worked out a deal – I look after Ralf and Roz pays me in paintings. I only have a handful of her minor pieces, of course. Her best stuff is stashed away in her storage lock-up in the basement. I keep after her to get a show together but she says she's tried and no-one's interested."

"Has she tried recently?"

"I don't think so – she seems happy to just do them for her own pleasure. She says she doesn't really need the money – her other stuff gives her a decent living, so why bother."

"Recognition? Communication? Fortune and fame?" said Barney."– Most of us would like a bit of that."

"That's what I say but Roz just says what's wrong with self-expression. Bobbi, my girlfriend agrees with her. She thinks all that stuff is just a distraction and only sidetracks you from your own development as an artist."

"-And you don't agree with her?"

"We're always arguing," said Eugene glumly. "– Bobbi says I've been suckered by the whole Western materialist con."

"She may have a point, there," said Barney. "- I guess most of us have in one way or another."

"I tell her she's an ivory tower idealist. That's all passé. – Once she got so mad she jumped out of bed, grabbed her coat and started to walk home to her place in the middle of the night. I had to chase after her in my underpants halfway down the street before I could persuade her to come back."

Barney laughed. "She sounds like quite a girl."

"I'm crazy about her, that's the trouble," said Eugene. "– I know we're totally different and it will never work out – but I can't bear the thought of losing her."

Barney glanced over at his downcast face. "– Hey, don't be too quick to give up, pal. You know what Shakespeare says and he's never wrong. –'The path of true love never did run smooth.'

"Well he was right about that alright," agreed Eugene.

"Bobby," said Barney, trying to lighten the mood. "Unusual name for a girl."

"Bobbi – with an 'i'," said Eugene. "–Her real name is Roberta. Roberta Michaels."

"What's she like?"

"Beautiful. Short dark hair and green eyes. Slim. And tiny – she only comes up to my chest." – Eugene indicated a spot on his ribcage that was obviously very familiar. "– Right here."

"-And she's at art college, too?" – Eugene nodded. "– And you live together?" Eugene shook his head.

"–No. Sometimes – weekends, mostly. We're at Emily Carr College on Granville Island and her folks live over in the West End. She takes the little tub ferry across in the mornings but it stops running after ten p.m. so she uses that as an excuse to stay over at my place."

Barney pulled up in front of the apartment building. "I never thought to ask – did you want to be dropped somewhere else?"

"No, this is fine. I'm meeting Bobbi in about twenty minutes and she only lives a few blocks away from Roz's." He opened the car door.

"Maybe we could have a look at those paintings one day," said Barney.

"Sure thing. I've got a key to the lock-up. Maybe see you tomorrow when I collect Ralf."

"Say hello to Bobbi for me. I'd like to meet her." Eugene gave him a thumbs up, closed the door and loped off down the street with long strides. Barney watched him go, smiling and gently shaking his head, thinking of his own son, Hunter. He drove down the ramp, fiddled with the fob until he got the electronic garage doors to open, and then drove slowly in long descending loops, down into the bowels of the building until he found Roz's parking bay.

He locked the car and noticed a large wire cage blocking off the corner of the garage. Crossing over to it, he peered in at the numbered lockers but couldn't make out which one was hers. He headed for the lifts. Back on the ninth floor, Barney opened the apartment door to be greeted by Ralf, wagging his tail and cocking his head as if expecting something. Barney crouched down to pat him.

"Hi Ralf, how you doin', boy? You want a treat?" – He rose, followed the little dog into the kitchen and got out the bag of chews. "–There you go."

He wandered around the flat for a while and then went out on to the balcony. Rozalin had cleared all the coffee things away and he stood at the railing looking out at the harbour. What had appeared last night as an undifferentiated mass of coloured lights now revealed itself as a sprawling marina in the foreground, with a long restaurant pier to the left. Out in the bay was anchored a large fuelling bunker with a tugboat moored alongside. Above it was the flashing red PetroCanada sign he had noticed the night before.

In the distance on the far shore was a jumble of docks and buildings that a squat ferry was moving towards. Some sort of circular red sign showed above them but he couldn't make it out. He went back into the bedroom, retrieved his bird-watching binoculars from his rucksack, and went back out on the balcony. He swept the shoreline and the red circle jumped into view as a huge letter Q.

He sat peering through the glass panels of the balcony with his binoculars at the busy traffic in the harbour for several minutes, sweeping the glasses back and forth. They came to rest on the big red Q again. Lonsdale Quay –

"Trish!" he said aloud. "–Oh my god –" He had totally forgotten about her. He fumbled in his pocket for his watch and snapped open the case. –Two o'clock.

He began emptying his pockets on the balcony table, searching for the phone number the flight attendant had given him for the airport infirmary. Finding the scrap of balled-up paper, he hurried into the phone in the kitchen and dialed the number. A woman's voice answered.

"Oh, hello. Listen, I'm a friend of Trish – Patricia White – she was brought in to you last evening off a flight from Gatwick. Is she all right? They told me to call this number."

"Miss White was released at noon after the doctor's visit. She left straight away."

"So she's okay then?"

"A bit hung-over but otherwise fine, the doctor said. He told her to check with her own doctor when she got home if she felt unwell again."

"Did she leave a message for me, by any chance? Roper – Barney Roper?"

"Just a minute, Mr. Roper and I'll check," said the nurse. A moment later, she told him, "-There's nothing here on the desk. Have you tried her home number? She should be back by now."

"I don't have it. – I uh, seem to have lost it," fibbed Barney weakly. "– You must have it there on her notes."

A distinct coolness entered her voice. "–We never disclose personal information, sir."

"Yes," said Barney. "–Of course." Putting down the phone, he went back out on the balcony to stare across at the big red circle. A ferry was just pulling away from in front of it. – Lonsdale Quay. He remembered Trish telling him she worked right next door to the big covered market. He racked his brain for an office name but nothing presented itself. I could take the ferry over and look around, I guess, he told himself. – Maybe I might recognize the name. He fetched his jacket from the bedroom and picked up his set of keys. Ralf. Damn. He looked for the little dog and saw him asleep in his basket. Rozalin had told him Ralf was used to being alone in the flat and he had already had his walk.

Barney let himself quietly out of the apartment. Down in the street he re-oriented himself and struck off down Georgia towards the Harbour Centre tower, which he could glimpse between the high-rises. Passing a newspaper shop, he went in, bought a pocket map of the city, and continued down the street. He knew the ferry terminal was near the tower, but he couldn't remember the street name. He stopped to examine the map.

"Spare any change for a coffee, mister?" Barney looked up from his map into the crumpled face of a man in his thirties with a scruffy beard and a front tooth missing.

"-Oh, yeah, just a minute." Barney fished a handful of change from his pocket and picked out a coin. "–Here." The man took the coin and then frowned, turning it over.

"This is no good," he said.

"What? Oh, sorry." Barney took it back, realizing he had given the man a British pound coin. He sorted through the mixed currencies in his palm and picked out a Canadian dollar coin. "–Here, try this." The beggar eyed the largish handful of change in Barney's hand.

"How about a tooney, mister? – I haven't eaten today yet."

"-Oh. Yeah, I guess so," said Barney pawing through the change and picking out the two-dollar coin with its brown centre. "–Say, can you tell me what street the ferry terminal is on?"

The man pocketed the pair of coins and pointed over his shoulder. "Straight down the hill and turn right – great big place."

"Thanks," said Barney.

"Any time. You have a good day, mister." He grinned, nodding his head and walked off.

Inside the handsome terminal building, Barney followed the crowd to the ticket machines and fed a tenner into the slot rather than sort through his change again. Pocketing the handful of coins, he felt the familiar weight that always accompanied his trips abroad, when he would continually accumulate change by breaking notes rather than puzzling over coins.

Passing down the concourse, he entered the waiting ferry and found a seat in the front row to enjoy the harbour view. While he waited, he decided to separate his British money from his Canadian by putting them in his right and left pockets. He made a mental note to find a currency exchange place to convert his British pounds. He wouldn't be needing them for the foreseeable future, he thought.

When the ferry docked at Lonsdale Quay, Barney wandered aimlessly around the market for a while before buying a bowl of fresh chowder from a seafood stall. While he ate, sitting at the counter, he reviewed his game plan. It didn't amount to much other than vaguely looking at office door signs hoping he would recognize the name of Trish's medical surgery.

He finished his chowder and left the market to begin searching. After systematically walking up and down the street on both sides for two blocks in each direction, he had found nothing that rang a bell. He decided to ask someone – but who? Would passersby be likely to know? – He entered a florist's shop that looked empty instead and approached the elderly woman making up a bouquet.

"I'm trying to find a herbal medicine place," he told the woman. "It's supposed to be right near Lonsdale Quay." She continued with the bouquet, arranging the sprays of chrysanthemums in descending rows.

"There's a holistic centre across the street on the second floor," she indicated with a nod towards the door, "- Is that what you mean?"

"Maybe," said Barney. "–Do you know what it's called?" The woman shook her head and tied some raffia around the flowers. They both admired the result for a moment.

"– Second floor, eh? Well, thanks very much –" He left the shop and crossed the street to look at the building opposite.

There was nothing to indicate any offices outside and Barney entered the foyer. A plaque on the wall held a row of names and he ran his eye down the list. 'The Lonsdale Clinic' – could that be it? Second floor. – He climbed the stairs and found the office door. A 'Closed' sign faced him.

"Shit," said Barney. Still, she was probably in no state to come into work anyway. He stood for a moment, unsure what to do next. – I could leave her a note, he decided and pulled out his small pocket diary and tore a page out of the back. – *'Trish,'* he wrote – *'sorry I missed you – call me a*t 604' – He stopped to flip back through the diary for Rozalin's phone number – *'544 - 0765. Barney Roper.'* Better not say too much, she may not be the only one here, he thought. He re-read the note and decided it was a bit curt. He added a P.S. – *'Hope you're feeling better'* – He folded the page and slipped it under the door. Walking back to the ferry terminal in the autumn sunshine, Barney felt his euphoric mood returning. He smiled at the other passengers waiting for the boat and some of them returned his smile. If Trish had been seriously ill they wouldn't have released her, he reasoned. I can't see what else I can do at the moment.

He boarded the ferry and rode back across the bay feeling his conscience was clear. It was far too nice a day to think of going back to the apartment and Barney dawdled along the waterfront streets until the huge white sails of the Canada Place conference centre loomed up. It jutted out into the water like some giant ocean liner and he walked along the concrete decks that encircled it – pausing to watch the wasp-shaped little helicopters taking off and landing from the helipad below him.

He continued along the waterfront past the gaping holes where huge cranes lowered hoppers of concrete down to small toy figures with yellow helmets and preying mantis scoop shovels bit into the earth.

Everywhere he looked, he seemed to be witnessing renewal and growth. The whole city appeared young and vibrant to Barney – what a contrast to London, with its dismal grey buildings and endless hurrying crowds of people with downcast eyes, avoiding any risk of contact with a fellow citizen.

"Any spare change, mister?" – Barney was jolted from his pleasant reverie by a grimy-looking girl in an assortment of faded sweaters and coats. She thrust her hand at Barney and gave him a challenging look. There was nothing of the supplicant about her and Barney hesitated a moment, taking in her green-streaked hair and studs through her nose and eyebrow.

"C'mon," she said. "You can afford it."

Barney reluctantly put his hand in his pocket and withdrew a sheaf of twenties and some change he had exchanged for his English currency at the airport. He looked through the coins for a dollar but couldn't see one.

"I've only got quarters," he told her. She glanced at the change, then in one practiced gesture grabbed the notes with one hand, pushed him backwards with the other and fled along the seawall. Barney stumbled back on to the curb and regained his balance. "- Hey!" he shouted. "Hey! –"

But the girl was running faster now.

He started running after her, shouting. She turned to look at him and ran full-tilt into a wooden park bench. Barney watched as she cartwheeled over the seat and landed full-length on the ground. For a moment, the girl lay sprawled, not moving, and then struggled to her feet only to collapse on to the bench. Barney ran up, puffing.

"You alright?" he asked her, momentarily forgetting the pursuit with the surprise of her fall.

The girl rubbed her leg. "–My knee," she said, pulling up her trouser leg gingerly.

"– My fucking knee! Owhh!" They both peered at a raw scrape below the kneecap. It was starting to ooze blood in tiny beads and she touched it lightly with a grubby finger.

"– Owwhh!" she said again.

"Here," said Barney, handing her his clean handkerchief. "Wrap this around it." The girl took it and began unfolding it and covering the scrape. She still clutched the wad of bills in her right hand.

"– What's the big idea!" he demanded. "– Give me my money."

The girl said nothing, only holding out the twenties to him. He took them and shoved them in his pocket. "Here, let me do that –" He folded the handkerchief lengthwise twice and tied it firmly round her leg.

"Ouch!"

"Serves you right. – Can you stand up?" The girl hobbled to her feet and tested her weight on her injured leg.

"Fucking hell!" She clutched his arm and took a couple of hopping steps.

"Take it easy," he said, supporting her arm. They took a few paces.

"You going to report me to the cops?"

"I bloody well should. You do this all the time?"

"No, that was my first time. Honest."

"Liar."

"Maybe once or twice," she conceded. They continued walking with the girl hobbling beside him, leaning on his arm. "–Well. Are you?" she persisted. Barney appeared to consider.

"Not sure," he said. "–What do you think?"

"Just forget it eh? I gave you your money back, didn't I?"

"I might – on one condition."

"What?" she said suspiciously, stopping. "– Whaddya want?"

"What do you think?" asked Barney, stopping too.

The girl gave him an appraising look. "I dunno – you old guys –"

"It's not what you're thinking."

"What then?"

"You can't guess?"

"I already did," she said.

"I'll give you a hint. You come up to me and demand money; then you try to push me over, steal my cash and run away."

"Okay. I'm sorry. I apologise."

"That's better," said Barney as they continued walking. "– I was going to give you something, you know."

"A lousy quarter," she said. "– Big deal."

"What do you want? A meal? A drink?"

She shook her head. "I just needed some money, is all."

"To spend on drugs," he said. "-No deal. If you want to get some food or shelter, okay. I'll lend you some money for that."

"Lend me! – How am I supposed to pay you back? – I'm livin' on the street, man, not the fuckin' Bayshore –" she nodded in the direction of the big hotel they were passing.

Barney took out the roll of twenties and peeled one off, carefully putting the others back in his pocket.

"–Call it a long-term loan. You can pay it back when you get a job. There's only one condition."

"Now what?" she said.

"You pay it back to someone else."

"Someone else – who?"

"-Someone like you, maybe –"

The girl studied him for a moment. "Are you some kind of fruitcake?" she said finally.

Barney shook his head. "I've got a daughter about your age."

"-I see. An' she's on the street, too," said the girl, nodding.

"No, she's at university – in Paris," he added.

"Huh. Nice for some –" She held out her hand and nodded. "– You gonna give me that or not?"

"I'm still waiting," said Barney.

"For what?"

"You haven't agreed to my condition."

"Oh that. Yeah, sure –" she tried to take the bill but he held it out of reach.

"Promise?"

She looked at him. "I promise." – He handed her the twenty. She placed it carefully in her cloth shoulderbag. "Look, I gotta go meet some people. Thanks, man." She smiled at him for the first time, revealing even, nicotine-stained teeth.

Barney grinned back at her. "Don't take any wooden nickels." The girl limped away, shaking her head and Barney watched her go; then turned off the seawall towards Rozalin's apartment building.

# CHAPTER 4

By the end of the first week Barney had begun to formulate his plan. Old men should be explorers, T S Eliot said. So, okay, he would become an explorer – a Third Age Explorer. His first mission was to visit the central library. The massive coliseum-style structure swallowed him up at ten in the morning and he didn't surface again until hunger drove him out after seven in the evening.

Barney scoured the college and further education brochures compiling an impossibly long list of 'seniors' courses, many of them duplicates in different locations. He divided them up under days of the week including the weekend, to see which days were overloaded and which times clashed. He spent another happy couple of hours agonizing over what to include and what to drop before leaving his things spread out to reserve his place. He descended the escalators to the atrium for a coffee and a poppy seed muffin.

He sat amidst groups of young foreign students chattering incomprehensibly or poring over laptops at their tables. Most of the city's cafes seemed to have its quota of students nursing a latte and bent over their portable computers. Barney felt a companionable sense of camaraderie now that he was practically a bona fide member of the city's student body. He finished his coffee and bought some large sheets of paper from the bookstore in the concourse before returning to his desk.

Using one of the large sheets of paper, Barney ruled up the page into a monthly grid with the help of his little pocket diary. He began transferring to it all his selections with their dates and times and durations, then sat back and admired his efforts. It was a nice balance, he decided, of activities and studies – *'mens sana in corpore sane'* with the weekends providing most of the outdoor action.

For years Barney had banged on to his own adult education students about the importance of life-long learning – there were no more jobs for life – if you were in work now, then your next move would be out of work – so keep learning new skills. Some of his students adopted this credo; many more didn't – refusing to believe that they would ever have to change direction, no matter how long they were unemployed. He liked to keep a toy dinosaur on his desk to show to all his classes as a warning.

Now he was determined to apply those lessons to himself – he would equip himself with new skills for his role as Third Age explorer. He put all his things in his shoulder pack and returned the brochures to the counter. Reluctantly he left the warm confines of the library and headed for home.

Walking along Robson back to the apartment he was panhandled by a series of people begging on each corner. They had cleaned him out of change long before he reached the safety of Rozalin's building. Ralf was waiting for his treat and Barney gave him his chew while he made some tea. He had started giving one each day when he came home, feeling guilty about leaving the little dog on his own for so long. Eugene had assured him Ralf was used to it and that he made sure he was worn out before he brought him back each day. Barney had also broken Rozalin's rule about allowing Ralf on the furniture, but he liked having the little Yorkie curled up beside him on the sofa while he read.

He approached Eugene about the begging next morning when he came to collect Ralf. He had been experimenting unsuccessfully with a number of different ploys for dealing with the street people. "How do you handle it, Eugene?"

"I'm broke myself most of the time, so it isn't a big problem. But occasionally I give to someone I think is desperate – not the druggies though, it's a waste of money."

"How can you tell who's who?"

"Yeah, it's a tough call," said Eugene. "– Stick to the old guys – and the bag ladies," he advised.

"Isn't there some kind of backup for these people? I mean there's an awful lot of them sleeping in doorways."

"Oh, there's night shelters and soup kitchens," said Eugene, "– and the food banks."

"How do they work?" asked Barney. "Are they run by the city or charities or what?"

"The city, I guess. I don't really know. – There's one just over on Granville – why don't you ask? - I see them lined up outside the church hall by St Stephens every Wednesday morning."

As it was Wednesday the following day Barney went along to see how it worked – he had some vague notion that he might be able to pass out chits to all the street people he met for food instead of money. It wasn't quite that simple, he discovered.

Inside the hall, a dozen people were arranging tables and stacking boxes behind them. Others were wheeling in trolley-loads of potatoes and onions from a truck parked outside. He was directed to a young woman leaning on a crutch ticking things off a checklist as they were unloaded.

"Hi," Barney said, introducing himself. "–They said you were running the show."

"I don't know about that. I'm in charge though –" she smiled and pushed her hair back behind her ear. She offered her free hand.

"–I'm Maggie."

"Looks pretty hectic," offered Barney.

"Two hours to set everything up, unload all the stuff, work out the rotas for the volunteers and figure out how much food everyone can have so we don't run out or send too much back. – It's like trying to stage manage a road accident." She limped over to one of the tables and began to count boxes of apples. Barney followed her.

"Can you tell me how the food bank works? We don't have these in England but it seems like a great idea."

Maggie moved to the next stack of boxes and did a quick tally. "Sure, but you'll have to follow me around. – I can't stop to talk now or it will be pandemonium." Barney nodded agreement.

"Maybe I can lend a hand – as long as I'm here anyway."

"Okay. You count and I'll check off. You can start with the soup," she explained. "Put one open box on the table and then count all the ones here behind the table."

"Does everyone get the same things or do families get extra?"

"I wish it was that simple. – No, singles get one, couples get two and families get three or four – depends what it is," said Maggie pointing to the boxes of canned fruit and vegetables.    They worked their way round the tables checking and tallying, while around them the volunteers gradually dispersed the stacks of boxes from the mountain in the middle of the room amidst much banter and good-natured pushing and swearing. Barney counted cartons of soya milk, baskets of sliced bread and bagels, crates of eggs and boxes of packaged fruit juice. They came to a stack of boxes labeled miscellaneous. Maggie groaned audibly.

"Oh god," she said, "Nobody wants to do these – there's always arguments."

Barney looked inside one of the boxes, which appeared to be an assortment of candy bars, gravy mixes, shampoo sachets, bars of soap and a bundle of ballpoint pens.

"We're not supposed to offer them a choice but they never want what they're given and it always holds up the line every week."

Two female volunteers were piling heaps of baby food and diapers and powdered milk onto the tables and checking it off on sheets.

"Rose and Doris have the hardest job, figuring out who's entitled to what," said Maggie. "– The babies and kids and single mothers all get different allowances."

"How do you remember who is who?"

"Everyone gets a different coloured ticket or tickets and they have to show them at each station around the room – no ticket, no goodies." She hobbled over to a row of tables near the entrance.

"Everybody has to check in first and show their ID and we find out if they are on our list. Cuts out double dipping."

"Double dipping?"

"Doing the rounds of the other food banks and getting multiple loads of supplies each week. It's all here in these ring binders – anyone who shows up in two different places gets a warning. More than two warnings and you get banned. – 'Scuse me, I've got to assign the volunteers." She limped over to the table with the binders, called for attention and began reading out names from her list and what they were handing out. "Rick, you're on miscellaneous –" An exaggerated groan from Rick and hoots and catcalls from the other volunteers - "Nice one, Rick –" "Way to go" "– Yesss!"

Maggie finished the assignments and turned towards Barney. "New volunteer today guys, this is Barney. Be nice to him, maybe he'll come back. – I'm putting him on meals in a can – nice and simple to start." She looked up at the wall clock. "Five minutes to doors open and remember – no arguments, just keep the line moving – we're expecting three hundred and fifty today, – any questions? – Okay, let's do it. Mike, you're on the door; make sure they've got their ID ready–" She swung her crutch in the air and the volunteers took up their stations.

"I'll be over by the front tables," she told Barney. "That's where most of the problems are, but I'll be floating as well – if that's the right word." She made a face at her crutch and limped off.

Barney took up his post next to a native woman called Mary who was doing pasta. When he lifted a second box on to the table, she shook her head.

"Only one box at a time or they'll ask to see the other one – and don't let them choose or they'll go through the whole box," she advised. Barney nodded and replaced the second box.

People in motorized buggies and wheelchairs poured through the door first, followed by young mums with pushchairs and soon the room was filled with voices calling out to each other and greeting the volunteers familiarly.

"How long have you been doing this, Mary?" asked Barney.

"Too long. Eight years about."

Barney handed his first customer a large can of chili.

"Hey, great. I love chili."

The next person held out a red ticket and Mary nodded and said, "Couple – two tins," and Barney gave the man two cans of stew. The man nodded and put them in his bag. A young man in a motorized wheelchair waved his hand, clutching a white ticket in a twisted jumble of fingers. He reversed his wheelchair expertly round so Barney could deposit a can in his bag behind the seat. The young man grinned lopsidedly at him. "Have a good day." – He wheeled round to Mary and she slipped an extra packet of pasta into his bag.

As the line shuffled past slowly and Barney handed out his selection of stews and chili and pork and beans, he noticed Mary handing out extras to some people in the queue. She caught him studying her. "Not supposed to – no favourites – not fair. But," she shrugged, "I know some of these people – very poor."

"New volunteer, eh?" said a tiny man with a woolly hat partly covering what looked to Barney like a skull covered in scars extending down his neck and scrawny arms and ending in stubs of hands with no fingers. He had a white singles ticket tucked under the remnant of a thumb and a cloth bag over one scarred arm. "Whatcha got in there?" he said.

Barney smiled, struggling to regain his equanimity. "Chili or Irish Stew?"

The little man looked at him through eyebrow-less beady blue eyes. "Tough call. Irish Stew, I guess."

"Have the chili as well," said Barney; quickly tucking the extra can in his satchel.

"Hey, Christmas! – I like new volunteers," he said to Mary. She looked at Barney but said nothing.

For the next hour and a half a steady stream of Vancouver's less-celebrated citizens eddied  round the food bank  tables; some sullen, some joking, some pathetically grateful, some demanding; each clinging to the remaining shreds of their dignity. Dealing with them in turn, Barney felt as if he were walking on eggs, careful lest he offend anyone by inadvertently patronizing them.

Beside him, on his left, Steve dealt with them in his own way – joking with the men, leaning across to hug all the snaggle-toothed old women, and occasionally demanding a kiss from some of the younger women he knew before he would surrender his wares.

At last, the remaining stragglers went through the line and the volunteers moved into clearing up mode, reloading the remaining goods back onto the truck and folding up tables. They took their own previously collected groceries and quickly departed, calling out goodbyes to the others, everyone seemingly uncomplaining and happy to be doing a job even if the wages were only groceries. Being on the other side of the tables apparently made a huge difference to them. Maggie came over to Barney's table.

"Looks like you slotted right in no problem," she smiled, brushing her hair from off her face with her free hand.

"Quite an experience," he said. "–Anything else I can do?"

"Only sweeping and swamping left, I'm afraid. I'm still doing paperwork but if you wanted to talk after that, I'm free."

Barney joined one of the other sweepers in the hall and then switched to a mop and wringer trolley for the final cleanup. Maggie was stuffing folders into her battered briefcase when he finished his chores.

"Is there some place near we could have a coffee?" he asked her.

"Blenz around the corner on Granville has nice leather armchairs," she said. He took her briefcase while she locked up the hall. She pointed with her crutch. "This way."

Barney walked slowly beside her as she hobbled along supporting her weight on her left foot. "What happened to your leg? – Accident?"

"Broke it in two places. –Falling down stairs. And a minor concussion, too."

"That's terrible. I'm sorry."

"Could have been worse. If I'd broken my arm and couldn't write, I'd be out of a job. This way, I can still earn a living."

"When did it happen?"

"About a month ago. – Still hurts like hell at night. I stump around all day no bother and then when I lie down in bed it starts to ache." She gazed ruefully at the plaster cast as she took a seat in the coffee shop armchair and lifted her leg up onto the low table in front of her. He went off to order and when he returned with the coffee, she was looking through a packet of photos.

"Picked these up on my way in this morning - my son's birthday party – six years old." She held one out to him.

"Six! I don't believe you – you don't look a day over twenty-three."

"Huh - more like thirty." She handed him another photo of a homemade-looking cake with six candles. "Proof of the pudding. His name is Marlon," she said, showing him more pictures of kids in paper hats chucking food at each other.

"Some things never change," smiled Barney, remembering his own kids' parties.

"– Marlon, eh?"

She shrugged, "Not my idea – his father is a biker and 'The Wild One' was his favourite film. I prefer 'Bambi', myself." She eased her leg gently to reach her cup.

"I don't think your son would have thanked you for calling him Bambi. – Thumper, maybe." He stared at the scrawl of signatures and cartoons spreading over the cast on her leg.

"All the volunteers," she explained, "- my first day back at the food bank. They've been great – saved my bacon more than once. – Look at this." She showed him another photo of Marlon opening a present. "They all clubbed together and bought him a toy truck – painted 'Food Bank' on the side. Can you believe it? None of them has a job and they go and do that. I bawled like a baby when he opened it. He brought it in to the food bank and drove it around under their feet all morning. They loved it."

"Mary doesn't say much but she seems a bit of a softie," said Barney.

"Oh, everybody loves Mary. She's always getting told off for giving extras – strictly forbidden, but–" she shrugged. "– She's been there for years – never misses – gives all her own groceries away as well, usually, or else passes them on to her grandchildren." She put the photos back in the folder. "If it wasn't for the food bank I'd be on the other side of the tables joining the line."

"You're not a volunteer, too?"

"Nope, paid employee. Full time. I started out in the warehouse sorting cans but they needed somebody here when the regular volunteer organizer went into hospital with lung cancer."

"Who runs it anyway – the city?"

"No, it's a charity – eighteen depots all over the city."

"Are there many of you working full time?"

"Just enough for a core team – admin, drivers and a couple in the warehouse. All the rest are volunteers."

"And the food – where does that come from? Donations? – I've seen those bins in the supermarkets sometimes."

Maggie nodded, "Yeah. And the food and catering industry – we get all the damaged pallets and insurance write-offs and perishables near their sell-by date. Plus we do campaigns to buy fresh stuff like milk and eggs. You should come and see the warehouse – it's heaving at the moment – not enough volunteers to sort stuff."

"I'd like to," said Barney. "– Maybe I could give you a hand while you're laid up."

"Any day. I'm not really pulling my weight in the warehouse so you'd be really appreciated. - People prefer to volunteer in the depots rather than the warehouse so they can meet the clients, but the warehouse is more important – if we can't fill the orders, the trucks don't go out. Sometimes we're there till midnight."

Maggie pulled up her trouser leg and pulled out a plastic knitting needle from her handbag. She poked it down inside her cast and started scratching with it.

"– Ahhh – the itch is the worst part now – drives me crazy sometimes."

"How did you manage to break it in two places?" asked Barney.

"My ex-partner shoved me and I fell awkwardly, caught my ankle in the stair rods and sort of twisted backwards – banged my head on the wall on the way down."

"He pushed you downstairs?"

"Yeah, we were having an argument over Marlon in the bedroom and it got a bit heated – turned into a shoving match and he won."

"So you left him."

"When I came to in the hospital he was there and I told him it was over – that was the last straw. Told him I wanted him out by the time I got home or I'd tell the police what really happened."

"You sound as if you meant it."

"It's not as if it was the first time – every time we had an argument, he'd lose his temper and start pushing me around. No more. It's finished."

"What about Marlon?"

"Marlon's with me, and that's where he stays," she said firmly. –"My mum looks after him while I'm at work – takes him to school and picks him up."

"Doesn't he see his dad?" Maggie shook her head.

"Sounds a bit hard on him."

"I don't give a damn about him after what he did to me."

"On Marlon, I mean."

"Yeah," Maggie conceded, "- he misses his dad – but I don't trust Zeke anymore – maybe one day." – She finished her coffee. "I better get going; I promised my mum I'd pick Marlon up today." She pushed herself up out of the armchair and Barney picked her crutch up off the floor for her.

"Can I give you a lift to his school? My car's just around the corner by the food bank."

"Thanks, that would be great. The bus only goes within a couple of blocks of the school so I have to walk. I'm pretty slow with this thing–" She hoisted her crutch.

They walked back to the car and Barney noticed again how heavy-set she was as he opened the car door. It was odd how women put on weight around their hips after they had a child. He thought how often his wife Alice had tried unsuccessfully to 'get her waist back' as she referred to it.

Maggie directed him to an old Edwardian downtown school where the children were only just starting to come out into the playground. A row of moms with parcels and pushchairs stood by the front gate as Barney pulled over to park.

"Do you think I could meet Marlon?" he asked. "My kids are all grown up and gone long ago."

"Sure, if you want to. – He doesn't meet enough men. He's with me or my mum – his teacher's a woman. So is the principal." They joined the other women by the gates and Maggie spoke to one or two of them. Barney watched knots of children emerge from the school and race around swinging their schoolbags and releasing pent-up energy. How many years had he stood at school gates, he wondered, remembering that camaraderie with other parents that occasionally blossomed into friendship.

A small boy detached himself from a group and raced up to Maggie. He hugged her impulsively and then remembered himself and glanced round to see if any of his friends had noticed.

"We played soccer today, Mom." He handed her his satchel and coat.

"Did you score a goal, sweetheart?"

"I was the goalkeeper. They got six goals. Can I have a coke, Mom?"

"We'll see. – Marlon, this is Barney. He's helping me at the food bank." The boy retreated to the far side of his mother. He had blond hair, unlike hers and blue eyes with long lashes. His expression was non-committal.

"Hi Marlon," said Barney. "– Your mom said you just had your birthday. Are you really six?" Marlon nodded, gripping Maggie's hand. "And you got a special truck for a present, too? With a sign on it?"

Marlon nodded again. "It says 'Vancouver Food Bank'. – And you can open the back doors."

"I'd like to see that, sometime. – Open the back doors, eh? Do you want to see my friend's car? – It's a yellow one." Barney turned to Maggie. "Can I give you a ride home?"

She hesitated briefly. "We live over on Cardero - are you sure it's not out of your way?"

Barney shook his head. "I'm in no rush. Come on, Marlon. You can sit in the front seat–" They piled Maggie in the back along with her crutch and Marlon's things and drove along Davie Street. He pulled over to the curb.

"We could get some pop in here. I'd like a can of lemon-lime, myself. Maggie? Marlon?"

"Not for me, thanks –" She opened her purse and handed Marlon a coin. "– No coke, okay?" The child nodded agreement and he and Barney went in the shop.

"I've been in here before," said Marlon, "- with my dad. He lets me buy coke –" He opened the cooler door to make his selection. Barney only nodded and said nothing, taking out a can of lemon-lime. Marlon chose a Pepsi.

"Isn't that the same as coke?" said Barney. Marlon considered for a moment and then put it back and took a can of orange instead.

"Good choice. Don't want to cook the goose that laid the golden egg, eh?" Marlon gave him a funny look and went over to the counter to pay. Back in the car, he held up his pop for inspection and handed his mother the change. She guided Barney down the hill towards Cardero and they stopped outside a dingy-looking older style block of apartments.

"Thanks for the ride and the help today –" She took a business card out of her bag and handed it to him. "– If you decide to come out to the warehouse, that's the phone number and address. Just ring and let me know – any day you want." She and Marlon climbed out of the car.

"You could come up and see my truck," offered Marlon. Barney smiled and shook his head.

"Maybe next time, pal." He smiled and waved to them as he drove off, watching Maggie limp into the building holding Marlon's hand.

# CHAPTER 5

Alice walked her new bike to the train station in the early morning as it was only a few streets away and she had to balance her smaller daybag as well as her heavy backpack. She had been staying at her friend Stevie's for the past week since the sale of the house had finally gone through and she insisted on saying goodbye at the front door. Her new spade she left behind so Stevie would have an excuse to visit her soon in Oxford.

She struggled on to the train and wedged her bike in the rack, stashing her bags on the empty seat beside her. The Saturday morning train was quiet and she had half the carriage to herself. From her daypack, she fished out her new copy of 'The Enemy Within – A Closer Look at The Roman Occupation of Britain' by Hector Savage, Professor of Archaeology, Oxford University. He was to be her tutor so she felt she'd better bone up on his work. The jacket photo showed a craggy weather-beaten face, scowling at the photographer – obviously a man not fond of having his picture taken.

A compulsive reader of blurbs and forewords, Alice scanned them for some hint of the man but found nothing personal – only a list of his academic credentials, which were considerable. He had honorary degrees from three different foreign universities and had written a string of articles for learned journals as well as two other books on his specialist subject – this was his third. Alice felt a bit daunted by the skimpiness of her own qualifications and she turned to the main body of the book and began to read. The style was a tad racy for an archaeology book, she felt, almost written like a thriller. Maybe the influence of his stint as visiting professor at the university he had taught at in Arizona.

For the next hour, she was engrossed in it and only stopped when the refreshment trolley arrived at her seat. The coffee was instant so she asked for tea instead, easily resisting the limp Danish pastries on offer. The countryside unrolling beyond the window made her wistful at leaving Gloucestershire with its grey stone villages. The Cotswold's with their toffee yellow stone cottages were too pretty-pretty and unreal for her taste; she liked the more rugged, less manicured look of the Welsh border counties. Not that they had ever lived in a stone cottage – yellow or otherwise – Victorian red brick was all they had ever been able to afford.

Alice's dream of a Georgian townhouse seemed destined for oblivion since she and Barney had chosen to go their separate ways. She thought of the mouth-watering Georgian terraces of Bath; her favoured choice of town with its

Roman remains and peopled with Jane Austin characters in Alice's mind.

"You can't have everything, my girl," she told herself. "Be grateful you've got Oxford."

She tried to picture what her tiny student flat over a second-hand bookshop would be like. The accommodation office had assured her over the phone that it was in a quiet side street and only walking distance from St Swithens College. They had originally offered her a room in Halls and although Alice was tempted at first by the romantic idea of it, experience of her own teenagers' noisy gangs of friends swarming in and out of their house, told her the reality would be rather different.

She opted for the small one-bedroomed flat and decided to take her chances with being lonely. She was here to study, not socialize she reminded herself. Still, if there was a decent-sized cooker in the kitchen, she could always invite her fellow-students around for a curry and a beer. There was no need to be unnecessarily Spartan and she would be making most of her own meals anyway – years of canteen cooking at work had been another factor in declining the offer of Halls.

The half-empty train was just passing through Didcot and Alice started to gather her things together. She had prided herself on the slimmed-down wardrobe she had chosen for her new life as a student – almost nothing apart from her underwear and a few favourite items of casual clothing had survived her ruthless clearout of her cupboards. There was to be no hint of her former career-woman apparel, she decided. At the same time she wanted to avoid any accusations of appearing like mutton dressed as lamb and steered clear of anything that seemed too obviously student-y or currently fashionable.

She had enjoyed trying on the figure-hugging gear favoured by the younger women in her office, but restricted herself to admiring them in the privacy of the shop changing cubicles. The safest bet had been to buy clothes which she calculated might be worn by staff and faculty members – that way she could remain relatively inconspicuous and the worst that could happen would be to be taken for one of the lecturers.

In fact, she bought relatively little, not wanting to turn up to class in obviously new clothing. The Oxfam shops were a more fruitful resource for a prospective student – definitely a better class of donor, she decided, trying on an armload of skirts and tops she could never have afforded to buy when they were new. It was no hardship for Alice, really. Years of scrimping and patronizing charity shops and jumble sales to clothe herself and her family had blunted her desire for the latest fashions. Now that the children were gone and she could afford to buy what she wanted, the appeal had gone. Occasionally the urge would return and she would bring home a fashion item to model for Barney, only to return it to the shop a day or so later.

His incredulous reaction to the cost of women's clothing had never varied –shaking his head, mystified how anyone in their right mind could pay that kind of money just for something to wear. He hated shopping for clothes and wore the same things until they were threadbare and then went looking for similar, preferably identical items. It must be some male gene, Alice assumed, thinking of most men she knew. With one or two exceptions, they all had similar attitudes to her husband.

"Ex-husband," she said aloud, trying the word out to hear how it sounded.

At the train station in Oxford, Alice showed her map from the college to the ticket-taker and he pointed her in the right direction but she was soon lost, as she had to keep stopping to refer to the map, which only showed the main streets. She spoke to a girl on another bike waiting at a red light to see if she was a student. Not from her college it turned out but she offered to lead Alice there anyway.

She cycled off and Alice found it difficult to keep up with her loaded bike. When they arrived at last at St Swithens, the girl simply pointed to the main gates, waved and rode off. Alice wheeled her bike up to the keeper's gatehouse and dismounted. A thin, wiry man in a security uniform came out of his cubbyhole at her knock. Alice introduced herself.

"I'm supposed to be going to a graduate student get-together here later," she said. "But right now, I'm trying to find my flat so I can leave my things. My name is Alice Roper."

"Hang on a tick," he said, "I'll check my list." He dived into his little room and reappeared with a clipboard. "Here we are, - Roper, Alice, Mrs. -You could leave your kit here at the lodge with me, if you liked, missus. But the grads' do isn't for another couple of hours. Where's your digs?" She showed him the map.

He nodded. "I know it – over Nolan's old bookshop. It's not far from here. You'll have plenty of time to go home first, missus."

"Please, just call me Alice. – What's your name?"

"Everyone calls me Sid, missus." He showed her the way to her street, coming out from his lodge and through the college gates to point her in the right direction. "Remember -

three turnings, two to the right and one left. Nolan's is on the corner – can't miss it."

"Thanks, Sid. If I don't reappear in two hours, send out a search party, will you?"

"You'll be fine, missus. Ask anybody, they all know Nolan's."

Alice cycled off again, counting off the turnings. Sure enough, there was the corner bookshop, right where Sid said it would be. She was always surprised when she found a place first time - directions were not her strong suit. A narrow alleyway led to the rear of the shop and she leaned her bike against the wall and padlocked it.

Returning to the front of the building - yet another Victorian brick, she tried the shop door. Locked. A small notice, hand-written, was stuck to the glass. 'Sorry, closed. Back soon.' Alice looked up to the windows above the shop and noticed a strange turrety-looking projection over the corner – some Victorian builder's fantasy – seen too many Oxford oriel windows and decided to add one of his own, she thought. I wonder if it's part of my flat? Walking around the corner, she saw that a doorway was set back next to the shop window with a small door buzzer. 'Flat 1A' was written on the little tag.

1A Hemlock Street was her address, according to her map from the college. She tried the key and opened the door to face a steep flight of stairs. Hefting her packs, Alice climbed the steps and turned right into a small bedroom overlooking the alleyway. She deposited her rucksacks on the bed and crossed the landing. Opening another door, she found a small windowless bathroom with newish-looking fittings – a bit grubby, but she would soon get them shining. She loved cleaning her bathroom and hated cleaning her kitchen – definitely Freudian, Stevie said.

Pleased with her find, Alice opened the last door into the living room. The projecting corner window had a comfy cushioned window seat. She kneeled on it to look out the window. I can sit here and read and look down two different streets just by turning my head, she thought. A row of tall old trees lined the side street, spattering the pavement with their autumn foliage. The room was what country cottage brochures described as 'snug' – estate agentspeak for small, with a battered sofa and non-matching armchair, a round table with two wooden chairs and by the other window a student desk, chair and floor lamp. An open doorway led to the kitchen alcove with apartment-sized fridge and cooker and a modern tilting skylight that opened with a sash-cord.

An electric kettle stood on the counter and Alice realized she hadn't had a cup of tea since the rather insipid lukewarm one on the train. She switched it on and went back into the bedroom for her daybag, found the polythene bag with the Earl Grey tea bags and three little catering portions of milk she had pinched from work for just such an eventuality. She was too fagged to go out hunting for a corner shop. With her cup of steaming tea and a small packet of sesame seed wafers, Alice returned to the window seat. She kicked off her shoes and curled up on the cushions, feeling pleased with herself. She wondered if she had time for a bath before the drinks party and decided she did have.

"You have landed on your feet here, my girl," she said aloud, taking in the all-white walls, which added to the light from the three windows in the room. "No magnolia – amazing."

Over the years, Alice had come to believe that there was only one colour for walls – the ubiquitous cheap-and-cheerful magnolia. She longed for a strong regency green or burgundy to go with her fantasy Georgian house, set off with those lovely striped wallpapers. But they needed big rooms and Victorian terrace row houses never had any – at least not any Alice and Barney had ever lived in.

She carried her cup of tea into the bathroom and proceeded to clean the tub before filling it. She had no bubble bath so she used one of her shampoo sachets instead. As she lay soaking in the hot water, she wondered who her fellow grad students might be. Probably all – no, definitely all of them would be younger than her – much younger. A momentary panic struck her – god, this could be embarrassing – she allowed the wave to sweep over her and pass off. What was the worst that could happen? They would think she was some elderly tourist who had wandered into the college by mistake and kindly lead her back out into the street. - Nonsense, I don't look that old – they wouldn't dare. Her eyes ran down her body critically, assessing the ravages of fifty-nine years of working, child rearing and bouts of hard living and over-indulgence. Lying on her back, she noticed yet again how her breasts lost their downward sag but compensated by sliding sideways towards her armpits. Her stomach flattened out wonderfully simply by changing the direction of the pull of gravity. She raised one leg clear of the bath water and stretched it out turning her foot to get the best angle. Her legs were still her best feature, she decided, although the stretch marks at the tops of her thighs and the dread orange-peel effect were becoming more pronounced each passing year.

Lying back again and closing her eyes, she recalled what Barney often said. He told her that when she lay on her back she looked twenty years younger. He had meant it as a compliment of course but Alice took the converse to be true and that when she lay on top of him, she looked twenty years older. He once joked that if she ever had an affair to be sure to take the missionary position.

In the privacy of her new empty flat Alice decided to test this theory, carrying a narrow three-foot long mirror from the hall and holding it at arm's length above her, as she lay naked on the bed. It was true the lines on her face magically disappeared and she smiled and mugged at herself delightedly for several minutes. Next, she laid the narrow mirror lengthways down the bed and kneeled over it pretending she was on top of Barney.

What she saw appalled her. The younger woman of the moment before had become her mother, with sagging breasts and belly and face collapsing into deep wrinkles. She forced herself to continue looking at this semi-stranger for several minutes imprinting the image on her mind before rolling off and onto her back, once again lifting the mirror and holding it above her. The younger woman reappeared, this time frowning unattractively. Alice quickly smiled at her and the woman smiled back, her face as free from wrinkles as one of those ads for Botox treatments, which plastered the billboards with middle-aged women grinning maniacally down at her.

Alice thought of that story of Oscar Wilde where the young man's portrait ages horribly but the man stayed forever youthful – except she couldn't recall how it ended – something about the situation being reversed suddenly, she thought. It had saddened her unbearably, like so many of Wilde's fairy stories which she had bought for her children and could never finish reading without her eyes filling with tears.

'The Giant's Garden' had the same effect on her daughter Netta and 'The Star Child' always made Hunter, her step-son gulp and dab at his eyes, especially at the sardonic world-weary last line where the wicked king continued to rule cruelly over his people for many long years.

It was all so unfair, Alice thought, staring at the younger woman hard. She stared back inscrutably and Alice set the mirror aside - Which one is the real me? she wondered. –Will the real me please step forward - Putting the mirror back on the wall, she began to dress carefully for the drinks party, choosing and discarding items from her limited student wardrobe and trying to adhere to her imaginary faculty member dress code.

She settled for a tweed skirt and a high-neck pullover topped with her all-purpose favourite jacket and studied the result in the now vertical mirror. Once again gravity presented her with a new image of herself. At least with her limited wardrobe, there was no danger of being over-dressed and the high-neck jumper took a few years off, she hoped. She resisted putting any makeup on, apart from a slight touch of mascara on her eyelashes and the merest lick of lipstick.

Her handbag had proved to be one of her most difficult choices – nothing she owned seemed to match her new image and her strict rule of only one of each accessory. She had finally settled on a soft brown suede leather shoulder bag just big enough to hold her wallet and a paperback-sized book. With a last look in the mirror to make sure there was no lippy on her teeth, Alice left the flat and headed off down the leaf-strewn pavement towards St Swithens. She had considered taking her new bike but decided against it – too limiting if she were asked back to someone's place, and anyway she would arrive too early – another gaffe she constantly guarded against.

Often in the past she had made Barney drive aimlessly around until they were at least five minutes late – ten minutes was her preferred length but Barney insisted that was rude.– Totally wrong, of course, - fifteen minutes was borderline; twenty was rude. Alice dawdled along, absorbing the atmosphere of the ancient city, relishing her new unfamiliar role of student and arrived at the college gates at ten minutes past the appointed time.

She smiled at Sid, sitting reading his tabloid in the gatekeeper's lodge. "Hello Sid. I found my flat, thanks to you. I'm back for the grads' meeting."

"You're late, missus," he said, pointing to a hallway. "They're all here – in the Faculty Common Room at the end of the hall. Go straight in," he advised.

"Damn. Thanks, Sid." She followed his pointing finger down the hall, hesitated a moment outside the closed door and pushed it open. A buzz of voices filled the large oak-panelled room and a cluster of people clutching wineglasses hovered near the drinks table. Someone, a stout, bald middle-aged man was holding forth in the midst of another group who were nodding sagely. Alice made for the drinks table. A tall man in a rumpled corduroy jacket turned as she approached. She recognized the face from the book cover earlier.

"Hello. You made it then. –You must be Mrs. Roper," he said, holding out his hand. "Hector Savage – I've been waiting for you." She took his hand and nodded.

"Alice, please. Sorry I'm late. I didn't think anyone would be here this early." She glanced at her watch.

"You're back in school now, Alice. Things start on time – especially when there's free drinks on offer. What can I get you - red, white or sherry?"

"Red, please – What do I call you – doctor – professor – sir?"

"Heck will do," he said, handing her a glass of red wine. "It's only the college house wine but it's not bad stuff. The white's pretty good as well -I'm on the wine committee so I get to taste it all."

"Lucky you."

"Perks of the job." He raised his own glass. "Cheers. Come and meet some of the others." He led her over to the group around the stout bald man who turned out to be the Head of the Archaeology department. Most of the students grouped around him were in their mid to late twenties but one woman was in her thirties and a couple of the men wearing wedding rings looked older as well. As Alice had anticipated, she was the eldest member of the group, including the Head and her tutor.

"I look forward to talking to you about your thesis topic, Mrs. Roper – but not tonight. These occasions are mainly social – a chance for everyone to get to know each other. I've asked Professor Savage to make sure you meet all the other students and faculty." The Head nodded his shining bald pate as he spoke and the light bounced off it from the ceiling spotlights. "It's important we all share information and keep abreast of colleagues' work, so these little informal get-togethers serve a dual purpose." He smiled and turned to resume his conversation with an earnest-looking young man poised at his elbow. Hector Savage gestured towards another group and led Alice over to them.

"I don't really know half these people very well myself and I can never remember their names unless I've tutored them or been out in the field with them," he told her. "So I'll start with the ones I know." He stood a head taller than most of the students and they all turned to look at him as he approached.

"Some new blood for the department, everyone. This is Alice Roper from Gloucester and she's researching family rituals so I thought she could start with us. This is Sally," he said, introducing an athletic woman with muscular bare arms and a tanned face. "She helps me organize my digs, or perhaps I should say I help her – anyway, they wouldn't happen without her. Keep in with Sally and you'll sail through your year."

Sally smiled and shook Alice's hand warmly. "Nice to have another woman in the department - we're a bit thin on the ground here - at least at the post-grad level."

"Yes," nodded Hector, "I'm hoping Alice will have a civilizing effect on some of our more Neanderthal members. – Speaking of which, this is Auberon, another useful person to know when you're in the field. He's our geo-physics expert – if he was half as good at writing thesis papers as he is with interpreting sonar squiggles, he'd have my job. As it is, however, judging by his latest effort, I'm safe for another year."

Auberon grinned at Alice through an unruly beard showing perfect white teeth. "Are you any good at organizing material? I'll gladly help you with the technical stuff if you'd take a look at my thesis – my English style is pretty hopeless. Professor Savage describes it as Early Stone Age."

For the next hour, Sally and Auberon took it in turns to introduce Alice to everyone in the room and fill her in on what most of them were doing. Despite the Head's ban on shoptalk it was difficult for them to keep off their subject for long and her head was reeling trying to follow much of what was being discussed. Hector Savage finally rescued her from a heated debate and steered her back to the drinks table. He indicated a handful of faculty members with their partners gathering near the doors to the Common Room.

"Some of us are going for a bite to eat at Oscar's and I wondered if you would like to join us," he said pouring himself another glass. "Or would you rather stay here and help this lot polish off the wine? They won't leave till it's all gone," he said, pointing to the unopened bottles on the table.

"My drinking days are pretty much over," said Alice, "especially on an empty stomach. I'd love to come."

"Good, I'm always odd one out at these evenings, being an old bachelor. - One for the road?" He held out a bottle but she placed her hand over her glass and shook her head.

"Two's my limit, at least until I've eaten."

He finished his drink and they joined the others who were starting to leave. Alice turned and waved to Sally who was collecting empty glasses and wine bottles from around the room. The debate raged on in the corner as she left with the others and emerged into the early September evening. Apparently Oscar's was within walking distance as they all set off down the street with Alice and Hector following. She probed gently.

"You have no children, then?"

He shook his head. "No, unfortunately – never stayed married long enough. – You?"

"Three. Two of my own – girls, and a step-son. All long gone, of course. That's partly why I'm here."

"What's the other part?"

"Going back to my first love – I always wanted to do archaeology."

"Why didn't you?"

"It was a long time ago – nowadays it's very fashionable, TV programs, news coverage, Family Digs, popular books in thriller formats" –The words were out before she could stop herself. Hector winced visibly. – "Sorry, I didn't mean yours" – Alice felt her face flush.

"If the shoe fits," he said. "I guess I did stray a bit over the line from pure fact – I take it you are referring to 'The Enemy Within.' Do you think I went too far, dramatizing the characters?"

"Not at all. Anyway, I love thrillers. If I ever wrote a book, that's what it would be."

"It was kind of fun," he admitted. "I was tired of writing for the academic journals and thought I'd try something with more general appeal. A lot of people here agree with you, though – think I'm damaging my credibility. The Dean even implied it could affect my career if I did it again."

"Why, that's outrageous," said Alice. "I hope you told him where to get off."

Hector shrugged philosophically. "He's probably right. Fact of the matter is, I don't much care about my so-called career prospects. I prefer teaching and doing fieldwork. Politics doesn't interest me – too old, I guess. I enjoy writing though."

"You could always use a pseudonym – Have your cake and eat it too."

"Yes, I thought about that. Truth is, I didn't really expect it to be so popular. You're right about archaeology being flavour of the month."

"I blame 'Time Team'," said Alice, referring to the frenzied TV show with its calculated imposing of a race against the clock to inject artificial excitement into what was essentially, about as exciting as watching ditch-digging for ninety-five percent of the time – at least for the general public.

"The Dean loves it," said Hector. "Says applications for archaeology are up twenty percent since it started running. – Ah, here we are – Oscar's – do you like seafood? Best fish in Oxford." He held open the door and they joined the others in the crowded restaurant. They were obviously regulars and the head waiter showed them to a reserved table.

After the meal, one of the faculty wives offered Alice a lift home and invited her over for coffee the following week. Back in her tiny flat again, she went round turning on all the lamps and lights in every room to see what it felt like to be alone in a strange house in a strange city. Pretty good, was her verdict.

She poured herself a glass of mineral water from the bottle she had bought at the train station and added a couple of ice cubes from the fridge. Crossing to the window seat, she kicked off her shoes and settled herself comfortably among the cushions. She looked out at the darkened street and then closed the curtains. Picking up 'The Enemy Within', she began to read, a smile spreading across her mouth.

# CHAPTER 6

When Alice opened her laptop that morning, she saw there was an email from her elder daughter Netta. She had become so enmeshed in her new student life that her own family had hardly impinged on her consciousness these last few weeks. The lectures, seminars, field trips and research at the Bodleian library had swallowed her days and weeks up in huge bites.

She had carried the laptop over to the window seat, planning to make some outline notes for her thesis. The autumn sunlight made her sneeze and she pulled the curtain across the oriel window slightly so she could read the screen more clearly.

'*Hello Mother* – I've become so used to putting my ideas on a computer that it seems easier than phoning somehow. Some days I don't speak to anyone at all – just sit here in my room, endlessly writing reviews and then going out in the evenings to sit in a darkened cinema to watch more films, so I can go back and write more reviews....

I am becoming all pale and wan like the Lady of Shallot – you know the one in that Pre-Raphaelite painting Barney used to keep over his desk at home. I think she sort of became my role model when I was a little girl – such a hopelessly romantic woman – I keep comparing her to all the female characters I see in the films I review and naturally they're not a patch on her, so I slag them off and the students eat it up. They're so predictable in their anti-establishment poses.- 'épater le bourgeoisie.'

I've become a minor celebrity with my 'biting, acid English wit' – I've even had offers to do reviews for some of the big newspapers and monthly magazines – enough to turn a girl's head. –Trouble is, they want exclusives and that means I can't use the stuff in the student paper and I can't be fagged to rehash them a second time.

If I sound a bit jaded it's probably because I am – it's been great being here for a whole year with my father and my new family – they've been very kind to me – but all the same I've been thinking of abandoning the groves of academe at long last and entering the real world – I guess it was partly to do with hearing about your decision to go to Oxford that made me decide it was time to move on.

Philip finishes his fellowship here in another couple of months and has been offered a teaching job at one of the Further Ed colleges in North London. He wants me to come back with him and get a job in London – he says I could easily find freelance work on the strength of my experience here, but I'm not so sure I could make that smooth a transition from big frog to small frog –

Anyway, that's only partly why I'm writing – it's Hunter. Have you spoken to him lately or seen him? He's just dropped from sight – one minute he's badgering me to come back to England and the next he's vanished – not a dickey-bird from him for weeks now. He used to write to me in longhand every week – said he couldn't afford a computer and too many people staring over his shoulder in the public library.

I told him he could at least go there to read mine – I haven't used a pen for so long I've probably forgotten how – so anyway, that's what we did – until he stopped – no reason, just stopped answering my emails and I don't have a phone number or an address – he wouldn't give me any – said it was no use, they kept changing. Part of me was relieved that he had finally stopped badgering me to come home – I told him, what home? - there is no home – it's sold. - Barney's gone to Vancouver, you've moved to Oxford – it's time to grow up, stop living in the past – it's over. Done with.

He used to write me these long rambling letters - at first it was mostly just reliving all the old days together with you and Barney when we were kids. Hunter has the most amazing memory – he remembers stuff I'd totally forgotten – Saturday morning pictures with Barney at first and then later just the two of us – he'd tell me the entire plot from the previous week's film while we watched the trailers.

And how we'd keep some of our popcorn to play Hansel and Gretel when we walked home, watching the pigeons eating up our trail and pretending you and Barney would never be able to find us. And then sneaking into the house and hiding for hours in my big closet like the lost babes in the wood - telling each other stories while we waited for you to come home.

That's how I actually got started in this film reviewing business – from those Saturdays at the pictures and then retelling the stories after in my closet.

Anyway, please– just email me as soon as you find out anything about him.

*Love, Netta xox*

Barney and Alice had been delighted that their two children hit it off from the beginning, when they had anticipated a long awkward period, which might ultimately split them apart if Netta and Hunter couldn't adjust.

They had been inseparable from the day they met. When it came time for them to go to school and Alice had suggested an all-girls school because statistics showed girls performed better academically in a single-sex environment; Netta had flatly refused to go. She told her mother that if Hunter couldn't go to her school she wouldn't either.

Barney stayed out of it although he disapproved of single-sex schools in either the public or the private sector. Netta was Alice's child – it was her choice, he said. His decision would come later when Hunter was old enough for school. In the end, Netta won and Alice settled for a state school nearby where she knew the headmistress was a staunch feminist.

Barney's decision was pre-empted because Hunter automatically adopted Netta's school when his turn came; the two of them heading off each morning, hand in hand like the Start-Rite kids in the shoe ads.

Netta had persuaded Alice to tell her about her real father and she had been able to trace him to a small college in Pennsylvania where he lectured in medieval history. He had moved about a little after he returned from his post-grad year in England but she had found him through an alumni tracing group at his old college. American colleges were relentless in sniffing out old students for funding, she discovered and had little difficulty locating him

He and Alice had already split up and he had returned to the States when Alice realized she was pregnant. She had determined to go it alone and her parents rallied to support her. They owned a big old mansion flat in Highgate with endless rooms including a maid's quarters, which they cleared out to make into a nursery for Netta.

Alice had given up her student room to return home for the last few months of her pregnancy and her parents, Martha and George, were delighted to be having a child to brighten up the echoing flat. Martha was older than her husband and had already retired but George still had two years to go. They were both ardent Hampstead socialists and having a single-parent mother for a daughter was almost a badge of pride for them – an opportunity to put their ideals into practice and they fell to with a will.

Netta lacked for nothing and her grandmother read to her constantly and lulled her to sleep with Chopin and Brahms LPs playing on Alice's old record player, which her grandfather resurrected from one of the lumber rooms. George took her to puppet shows and children's theatre plays every weekend and even to see some easy Shakespeare in Regent's Park when she was five.

By the time Barney and Hunter arrived on the scene Netta was six years old. Alice had moved out as soon as she could after graduating, despite her parents' protests and she and Netta lived in a cramped one-bedroom place in the back of Kentish Town. Netta still spent weekends with her grandparents as they had a large garden and Alice had none. It had suited everyone and Alice was relieved to escape from the constant demand for attention from her precocious daughter.

But Hunter changed all that. He was four at the time Alice and Barney met and only spent weekends with his father. It all became very complicated for them. When Barney was free during the week, Alice had Netta, and when she was free at the weekend, Barney had Hunter with him. They triangulated about between her parents' big mansion flat and hers and Barney's pokey little ones for nearly a year.

Hunter demanded to play with Netta every weekend and George and Martha gathered him in. George restored an old train set which Barney had saved until he would have the space to set it up one day. The two men spent a happy weekend clearing out yet another spare room in the big old flat and fiddled for hours making bridges and platforms and cleaning the rusty tracks.

Hunter and Netta soon lost interest in the minutiae of this business and went off to bake chocolate cupcakes with Martha and Alice. The children were becoming inseparable and Barney and Alice decided it was time to take the plunge and move in together. They rented a two-bedroom flat in which they put some bunk beds for Netta and Hunter.

There was no room for the train set and it stayed as a consolation prize for George and Martha who had fought a strenuous rear-guard action to maintain the status quo. The children still spent occasional weekends with them and the grandparents did a regular Saturday night baby-sitting session so Alice and Barney could see a film or go out with friends for a meal.

Occasionally Netta would grill her mother about her missing father but when he never appeared she gradually stopped asking, accepting Alice's brief explanation that he had gone away before she was born and didn't know about her. She took to Barney instantly and never wavered in her affection but she hesitated at calling him Daddy; some part of her reserving that powerful word for the lost father who never realized he had a daughter waiting for him.

So Barney remained Barney; father in all but name. They were a mutual admiration society, defending each other loyally whenever Alice launched an attack over some neglected domestic task. Netta and her mother were too much alike and their relationship often flared into stand-up rows. Alice complained that Barney always took her daughter's side and he discussed his problem with Netta after one of these contretemps. She loved it when he treated her as a grown-up.

"Netta, I need to talk to you."

"Man to man?" she asked, climbing onto his lap.

"Man to man. – We have got a problem here and I need your help."

"Okay," she said solemnly, putting on her serious face and pulling down the corners of her mouth with her fingers the way he had showed her. "–What is it?"

"Well, you know how you and your mother have these bad arguments sometimes?" – He felt the child stiffen slightly. "–And how I have to kind of referee?" Netta nodded.

"And don't I always stick up for you?"

"Yes, you do – because you're my friend." – She gave him her best friendly hug.

"Even when you're wrong," he persisted. Netta had to agree this was so – had even come to expect it, in fact; which had led her to become careless in her rows with her mother, protesting her innocence too loudly sometimes.

"–And that's my problem, you see. Your mother says I'm not fair and then she gets angry with me, too. So what do you think I should do?"

"Maybe we should stop arguing," said Netta, stalling for time.

"You will, one day, when you're older - but in the meantime?"

"She's always picking on me, though. – You could tell her to stop picking on me."

Barney considered this for a bit. "–Yeah. Okay. – Anything else? – I really hate for your mum to think I'm not fair."

It was Netta's turn to ponder. "–I suppose you could take her side sometimes – but not all the time."

"Sounds good to me," said Barney. "– And fair. Once on her side and once on your side." He stuck out his hand. "– Deal?"

"Deal." She shook his hand and then burst into a fit of giggles, unable to maintain her serious demeanour any longer. He gave her a bear hug to clinch things.

She had a sudden inspiration. "Maybe you could give me a secret sign – when you're going to take her side, I mean."

"I'll tip you a wink, he said, blinking owlishly, and the two of them fell about laughing.

"What's so funny?" called Alice from the kitchen.

"Nothing," Netta called back, winking at Barney conspiratorially. She slid off his lap and went out to see her mother in the kitchen. "We were just talking. – Man to man," she couldn't resist adding.

When Netta tracked her father down at last, she then had to consider how to approach him. She mulled over the possibilities but could not decide – a certain shyness had overtaken her at the thought of facing this person whom she had kept secretly hidden in the back of her mind. What if he refused to acknowledge her – then what?

She studied her face in the mirror trying to picture his, but saw only her mother staring back at her. What if he didn't look like her at all – maybe he was fat and bald and wore a medallion. In her fantasies he had always been alone – a lean, impossibly good-looking man with dark hair and strong hands with long artistic fingers – he might have been a concert pianist – his career had mutated through several different occupations as she had grown up and her interests changed, but always he remained a benign talisman watching over her and smiling his sad little half-smile.

Her periodic updatings of her father's image had slowly been abandoned as she reached her later teens and now that she was confronted with reality, she prepared herself for the worst. She consulted with Alice as to tactics and her mother advised a softly-softly approach –a short, introductory letter at first, maybe enclosing a recent photograph and await results.

Netta was relieved to be removed from the decision-making and wrote accordingly – but without the photo. She had none she liked well enough and decided to wait until they met face to face. They would both just have to take their chances. An agonizing fortnight passed before the airmail letter with its American stamp arrived.

It spoke of his astonishment and delight and sadness all mixed together. It revealed that she had a whole ready-made American family; step-mother and two half-sisters and a half-brother who were curious to meet their English relative. Would she consider visiting them so they could start making up for lost time?

Several possible dates were suggested and an offer of an airline ticket. It ended with the inclusion of a telephone number. Netta was stunned. She had not bargained on having to take on board a completely new family. She toyed with abandoning the whole project but Alice urged her to go and settle her demons once and for all. And so she went.

Although not the semi-tragic figure of her imaginings, her father measured up surprisingly well. Neither fat and bald nor tall and strong, he was somehow just right – a slight, scholarly man with dark-rimmed glasses and a thatch of unruly hair which fell over his forehead and pushed back with a shake of his head.

Netta recognized him instantly by his smile – she had seen it every day in her mirror – not sad or wistful, but warm and welcoming and full of gleaming white American teeth. The whole family had turned out to greet her and she was enveloped in a tide of affection that swept her out of the airport and into her father's capacious station wagon; everyone talking excitedly and quizzing Netta with a hundred curious questions.

Their house was in a large university town in one of the older leafier suburbs and Netta was given one of her half-sisters' rooms who had long since moved out to her own place. After the initial flurry of excitement and orientation tours of the area, it was quickly decided that Netta would stay with them. She could find a job at the university where her father assured her he could swing her a position on the college newspaper.

He was a senior lecturer in the history department and the editor was a student of his. She gave herself up to this sudden change in her circumstances gladly. She filled in at the college paper for someone who was leaving the arts section and quickly carved out a niche for herself as the resident arts critic covering all the bases – music, theatre, books and especially films.

She developed a wickedly sardonic style of reviewing the latest Hollywood releases and championed foreign films and classics. Her student readers ate it up and wrote glowing tributes on her insights in the letters to the editor. She was lionized for her sophisticated European views and was widely quoted in the student union bars.

A lone voice dissented. An English voice. Philip French was a visiting lecturer from Bristol who had won a student fellowship for one year to teach Anglo-Saxon. He took Netta to task publicly via the letters column of the college paper, accusing her of being a snob. This was a red rag to a bull and Netta snorted her rage in acrimonious replies. It culminated in a visit to her office by her accuser.

Philip French recognized her, as one of his students had identified her for him. He approached her at her desk in the cluttered editorial office. He had not yet figured out why he was seeking to confront her in person but had decided only after she was pointed out to him.

"Good morning, Miss Roper. My name is French, Philip French. We've been corresponding - sort of." He held out his hand as a peace offering, which Netta took after a slight hesitation.

"So we have." She removed her reading glasses which had slid down her nose. "-P. French – but you're English. Student or staff?"

"Both. I'm over here on a fellowship but there's some teaching attached – Anglo-Saxon."

"I wouldn't have figured Franklin College was a hotbed of Beowulf studies, myself," smiled Netta.

Philip waggled a finger at her. "–Uh, uh, - more English patronizing."

"It was only an observation. - And anyway, you're a fine one to talk about being patronizing – your letters were thick with it – lecturing me on how to behave –"

He held up his hand. "–Actually you're quite right – most of my students think the Anglo-Saxon Chronicle was a newspaper. - The main reason I wrote in the first place was because your pieces were head and shoulders above most of the trivia that passes for journalism here. I was hoping to get a rise out of you, but I hadn't reckoned on being quite so heavily trampled -" He smiled again.

"Sorry. I guess I was a bit fierce. Probably over-reacting when you got a bit near the knuckle. Truth is, nobody ever challenges my stuff over here. Back home, I'd be shot down regularly for some of the things I write. They let me get away with murder, here. I began to believe I was infallible – till you stuck your oar in. Can I get you a coffee or something?"

"I was hoping maybe you could spare a half-hour away from the whirring presses to go to the coffee shop. I could introduce you to the delights of honey crullers."

"They sound ghastly – more American junk food, I bet."

"Uh, uh, - prejudices are showing again – wait and see. Personally, I think fast food is wonderful. – It's not far, you won't need your coat."

Netta slung her bag over her shoulder, shaking her head. "How can you even begin to defend something as obscene as junk food? Some of the crap on offer over here makes our fish and chips seem like haute cuisine."

"I make an exception for honey crullers – and so will you, you'll see."

"Never," said Netta.

The coffee shop was half-empty when they entered and they found a quiet booth by a side window. The waiter brought them coffee and Netta declined the crullers – it seemed they came in a variety of guises besides the honey ones Philip championed.

"At least, try a bite," he coaxed. "– If only to show how unbiased you truly are." She stuck out her tongue at him, then took a small mouthful from the one he held out to her.

"–Well?"

"You want my unbiased opinion?"

"Absolutely," he grinned.

"Disgusting."

He laughed aloud and pushed the rest of the cruller in his mouth. "You're so predictable. I knew you were going to say that."

"I'll bet you're a public-school boy – that's why you like all that sweet stuff – you crave all that horrible yellow custard and treacle pudding and tuck-shop pap - regular little Billy Bunter."

"Do you want another bite?"

"Yes."

The two of them polished off the remains of the crullers, licking their fingers and picking up the last few crumbs.

"I was going to ask you if you'd like to go to the pictures – but I don't suppose there's anything on you could bring yourself to watch," said Philip.

"Now who's being patronizing? I watch everything, as you know from my stunningly perceptive reviews. But that doesn't mean I have to like it all. What did you have in mind?"

Philip mentioned one or two, both of which she had seen, so he asked her to suggest something. She chose a Bergman film, 'The Seventh Seal' – something she hadn't seen in ages – the college was having a season of foreign films, thanks to Netta's urging and she could review it for the paper.

After it was over, he walked her home to her father's big wooden house. "–Well, what did you think?" she asked.

"Loved it – all that Scandinavian gloom and angst – especially that scene on the beach, playing chess with Death – very symbolic stuff."

"Very," agreed Netta. "The first time I ever saw a Bergman film I thought it was so profound I had to tell my English professor about it – I gushed on and on for ages and at the end all she said was 'caveat emptor'. I had to go away and look it up."

"'Let the buyer beware'," said Philip. "–What did you think this time?"

"I still liked it – in parts. Just a sneaking feeling it might be a wee bit pretentious. How about you?"

"A touch ponderous and I always take half the film to get used to the subtitles – great story, though. Can we go again?"

Netta and Philip fell into a routine over the following weeks and months, of covering the art scene together. She slowly mellowed towards the Hollywood output, conceding the occasional strong performance from actors and actresses she had previously slated. Philip had a modest teaching load and he worked on his own book on the Venerable Bede.

He taught Netta to recite Caedmon's Hymn and the opening verses of St Mark's Gospel in Anglo-Saxon. Philip became a regular at her stepmother's dinner table, regaling them all with episodes from Beowulf that he related like a thriller and reciting snippets in the original with the deep sonorous tones of the Nordic bards.

Netta spent more and more of her nights in his small apartment, reluctant to ask her father if Philip could stay over. In the end, she simply moved in with him and the two of them returned to her stepmother's table for Sunday lunches and walks round the campus with her father. Philip's fellowship was running out and he looked into the possibility of staying on, but with no job, there was no green card and with no green card, there was no job.

He applied for teaching work back in the UK and was offered a post in North London. He pleaded with Netta to come back with him. She stalled for time, torn between her father and Philip. In the end, Philip won out and Netta returned to London. Before she left she phoned Barney in Vancouver to get his blessing.

# CHAPTER 7

Barney? It's Netta - I need to talk to you."

"Man to man?"

"Yes."

"Okay, sweetheart, shoot."

"I'm going back to London – Philip has asked me to join him."

"I thought he was in Connecticut, too."

"He is, but he can't stay – no green card, so he's going home next month."

"Give me a hint, here, Netta. Is this supposed to be good news or bad?"

"I'm not sure, Barney. Good, I guess. That's why I'm phoning you. I was hoping you might know."

"Well, the details are a bit sketchy – but it sounds like good news to me. I'm assuming you've said yes."

"Yes."

"- and?"

"Well, it's just that I'm really happy here – happier than I've been for ages. My father and his family are terrific – they treat me like one of them."

"You are one of them."

"-And I've been offered some reviewing work with two different newspapers."

"They have newspapers in London, too," Barney pointed out.

"Oh, I know, but I'd have to start all over again."

"And you're so old."

"It's just that I kind of like being a big fish."

"And in London you'll be a minnow amongst all those big sharks."

"You know Philip and I have been living together for almost a year – I only see my father at the weekend –"

"You could swap him for your mother – go and see her at the weekend. – I'm sure she'd be delighted."

"When are you coming back, Barney?"

"Not for awhile, sweetheart. –Things to do, places to go, people to meet –"

"You could meet Philip – I want you to."

"And I want to, too. But I already approve of him, sight unseen. If you've chosen him, he must be something special - and anyway, don't I always defend your choice?"

"Even when I'm wrong."

"Netta –isn't that why you rang? To check?"

"I guess so. - Come back soon, Barney. Please, - I miss you."

"I miss you, too, sweetheart. Give my love to Philip. Maybe you could ask him to phone me – we could have a talk - "

"Man to man?"

"Right. - And remember Dr Johnson -"

"Mm hmm. 'When you're tired of London, you're tired of life'".

"Bye, Netta – lots of love."

"Bye, Barney. I love you."

When Barney hung up the telephone, a deep sadness engulfed him. Was it always going to be this difficult to make his family understand what he was attempting to do? He had discussed it all with them until his jaw ached but it didn't seem to make any difference. They still wanted him to be there – like some rock or anchor – in case they needed him. Now here he was – changing and shifting; rocking the boat.

He and Hunter had sat up one night till two-thirty, talking about change being the only thing you can rely on. Barney was reluctant to discuss his Buddhist philosophy with his children unless they asked, but he often used it without naming his source. Hunter had liked the Indian idea of the four stages of life – the student, then the householder; next the contemplative and lastly the wanderer seeking after truth.

It seemed so much more positive compared to Shakespeare's world-weary sardonic 'seven ages of man' with its bleak ending - 'sans eyes, sans teeth, sans taste, sans everything.'

Barney chose the Indian model and was determined to explore his Third Age wherever it led. Not for him the quiet life, keeping a low profile, not putting his head above the parapet, always choosing the comfortable easy option, sinking quietly into senility. Old men should be explorers, T.S. Eliot said. Barney liked that notion, having been all his life a traveller at heart. Now at last, he would be one of Eliot's explorers.

He tried to explain his feeling to his son by quoting him a passage from Tennyson's 'Ulysses' – how the wily, old seafarer had attempted to rouse his weary men for one final journey:

'Old age hath yet his honour and his toil;
Death closes all: but something ere the end,
Some work of noble note may yet be done...
And though we are not now that strength which in old days
Moved earth and heaven; that which we are, we are;
One equal temper of heroic hearts,
Made weak by time and fate, but strong in will
To strive, to seek, to find, and not to yield.'

But Hunter had his own heroes and Barney failed to make him understand what was driving him to abandon his comfortable home and puzzled family, leaving only hurt and bemusement behind him. This was not how he had imagined it at all. He wanted to go with their blessing and most of all their understanding.

Only Cassie seemed to grasp what he was doing and had wished him good luck – asking only that he keep her in touch by email. She had made no bitter accusations or demands for him to conform to social conventions – but she was the baby, the third child, the undamaged one. She had grown, like Topsy, benefiting from all the lessons Alice and Barney had learned from their first two children, in a laissez-faire atmosphere that suited her easy-going nature.

Cassie had been a dream to raise, they had often told each other, amazed at their good fortune. After the battles and conflicts with Netta and Hunter, they were content to let her find her own path; largely avoiding confrontations they would have blundered into with their first two.

So when Barney had sat Cassie down on one of her rare visits home from France, to tell her of his plans, she had accepted his explanations without too much questioning and wished him well. Perhaps it was the influence of her French university friends who sounded so politically involved and socially aware when she told him of her own plans. She wanted to go to Africa and be an aid worker when she graduated next year and Barney had applauded her decision. He might even join her there he said, if she could find him something to do.

Netta had been more difficult to convince, siding with her mother, as Barney had anticipated. He tackled her from a more oblique angle by first gaining Alice's reluctant consent to his plan. With his wife's objections dealt with, it should be an easy matter to win Netta's approval, he reasoned. But Alice proved a formidable obstacle, and fought a fierce no-holds-barred action, which left them both weakened and exposed.

In the end, his parting had been a painful tearing, ripping and sundering, leaving a bitter aftertaste in everyone's mouth with the exception of Cassie. He had won Alice's grudging consent but it had been a pyrrhic victory and he lay awake often in his rented apartment in Vancouver, high above the city, pondering over the wisdom of his choice .The words of Eliot and Tennyson rang hollow in his fretful dreaming.

'Fine words butter no parsnips,' his grandmother was fond of saying, which he had always taken to mean that talk's cheap - deeds not words were what counted. And wasn't that what he was doing – at last? All those years of dreaming of this time in his life when he would be free from family ties and obligations, free to follow his ideals, to be that seeker after truth, that explorer of the third age.

Did all those Hindu men agonize like him when they left their worldly life behind to take up their quest for truth and enlightenment? He doubted it. But they had a whole history and tradition to bolster them on their journey while he....

"Come on," he told himself, "get a grip. Stop being a wimp."

And he had plunged in, starting hares in all directions. He studied, joined groups, got involved. The city had so much to offer once he began his explorations and it was hard to know where to start. Theory *and* practice advised Marx, an early mentor of Barney's.

He worked out a judicious mix of astronomy, geology and physics; subjects of which he had only the sketchiest notions, but seemed important to attempt to come to grips with. To these he added community work - volunteering at the local food bank and doing a shift with a mobile soup kitchen, which fed the street people of this sprawling young city of eager entrepreneurs.

To Barney, used to an admixture of humility and sullenness in Old World beggars from London to Calcutta, the street people of Vancouver took him by surprise. For a start, they were nearly all young. And they seemed to have taken their cue from this thrusting new city of people on the make. They were all hustlers, operating a black economy, which shadowed and parodied even, or so it seemed to Barney, the shining, gleaming surface that Vancouver presented to the rest of the world.

He watched the 'dumpster divers' busily retrieving anything salvageable from the metal waste containers which dotted the back alleys; the Asian immigrant women touring the residential streets ahead of the recycling trucks, harvesting aluminum cans in black bin liners balanced on poles across their shoulders – a more profitable crop than rice by far.

Everybody had a business of some description or another – they were all self-employed. And they worked so hard! – pushing their supermarket trolleys loaded with contraband; spreading out their wares on the ground in front of their favourite pitches; busking with battered musical instruments at cinema queues and Skytrain entrances; or simply doing a one or two hour shift of panhandling by bank ATMs and liquor store exits.

These particular pitches were highly prized and fought over by the astute and experienced among them; judging to a nicety the chinks in the armour of their victims; openly demanding their cut of the takings. Only the hardest of hearts could resist giving some small change, with a bottle of good B.C. sauvignon tucked under their arm or a wad of crisp new twenties filling their pocket.

Barney especially admired the inventiveness of the beggars working the tourists window-shopping the smart stores and cafes of Robson Street. They were entertainers in a tradition stretching back into the Middle Ages; exposing their bodies ravaged by Aids, crack cocaine and binge drinking, for the edification of all

They had little hand-scrawled signs, like labels, identifying their specialty. Most employed the classical 'ad misericordium' approach to soften up the tourists. But some of the younger ones, learning the trade of sleeping rough, appealed to the hip, internet-savvy crowd with witty requests for funds for penis extensions, breast implants, Botox injections or drying-out clinics.

Begging seemed far too humble and inappropriate a term for all this bustling energy, which flowed through the streets of Vancouver, leavening the rich mix of Asian and European cultures drawn to this city filled with promise. Everyone wanted a piece of the action. A twenty-first century version of a gold-rush city but this time the lure was the 'good life' – Lotus Land, the denizens of Vancouver called it, with its jewelled location of mountains, sea and forest.

Barney plunged in, breathing in the heady aroma of the Pacific Rim – 'Life on the Edge,' the tourism brochures proclaimed. And he did feel on the edge of some great new adventure. The west coast lifestyle suited his new mood and galvanized him into further exploration of it.

He started joining Eugene on his dog-walking rounds and the two of them covered miles of the city's seawalls and beaches.   Eugene introduced him to some of his clients – wealthy widows in huge echoing condominiums with heart-stopping views of English Bay and the Coast Range. He was invited to join bridge clubs and for afternoon tea, and then lunch, by an array of older women whose husbands had paid the price exacted by the city in an earlier era – in return for giving up its riches; they had given up their lives.

Their women had been much stronger, often outliving a second or even a third husband. Barney was grist for the mill and they vied for his attention; appreciating his more formal, courteous English manners acquired at Hampstead socialist dinner tables. They became willing confidantes, contributing generously to his local food bank and cooking batches of cookies, cakes and casseroles for his soup kitchen rounds. They drew the line at venturing onto the streets with him, preferring to hear his stories from the sidelines.

Eugene they treated like a grandson, stuffing him with pastries and smoked salmon sandwiches after his rounds with their pampered animals. They paid him generously and were interested in his progress at Art College.

On fine sunny days, Barney and Eugene met up with Bobbi at one of the Granville Island cafes and drank coffee overlooking the busy throng of boats sailing up and down False Creek. Ralf stalked seagulls, keeping the area around their table clear of the strident squawking birds. Bobbi fed him corners of her pastry.

On their walks, Eugene had often spoken extravagantly about Bobbi and how she had changed his life. He was torn between his longing to travel the globe and see all the great art museums; and his passion for this wonderful girl who now dominated his thoughts.

Barney was unprepared for the actual person by Eugene's glowing descriptions. For a start, she was minute, especially when beside the long, ranging form of her boyfriend. She was thin to the point of boyishness with short, jet-black hair. Her hands, which moved continually and expressively, had fingernails bitten to the quick.

She seemed unaware of the spell she had cast over Eugene and hugged him enthusiastically whenever he said anything she approved of. Her attitude to Barney was deferential, as to someone of a great age and he supposed to her young mind that was how he appeared.

"Eugene has been telling me how fortunate he is to have met you and now I can see why," said Barney gallantly. Bobbi sent Eugene a dazzling smile and squeezed his arm. Barney understood then how the boy had been smitten.

"I'm the lucky one," insisted Bobbi. "He's the most talented student in the whole art school."

"I wish my teachers agreed with you – they think I'm wasting my time there."

"Only one or two of the old ones – most of them think he's hugely inventive."

"But I can't draw. Bobbi draws like Leonardo – they love her work."

Bobbi dismissed this with a wave of her nail-bitten hand. "All derivative stuff – not an original idea in sight. Good teaching potential – that's what they think of me. I'll end up in front of a classroom but I don't mind. I love kids. But not Eugene – he's head and shoulders above us all – I predict great things for him." She wrapped her thin arms around his neck and Eugene grinned foolishly at Barney. "Has he showed you any of his work, yet? I bet he hasn't – he's hopeless. What he needs is an agent. Maybe that's what I should be – I may not have talent but at least I can recognise it."

"My work's much more derivative than yours," Eugene protested. "They just don't recognize the source, that's all."

"You mean Rozalin?" asked Barney and they both nodded.

"Isn't she fantastic?" enthused Bobbi, "And she's even worse than Eugene for trying to show her work. - I should be her agent, too - put on a huge show and wow the whole city," she laughed.

"Why don't you?" said Barney. "I'll help you. –I've always wanted to stage an art show of new artists. I had this idea that instead of selling the paintings, people would borrow them – like library books. They would only pay a rental fee – so much a month and then return them and take out another."

"Like videos – and DVDs," said Bobbi.

"That's right and the best part is the artists get to keep their work – they retain the copyright, like writers and composers."

"It's a brilliant idea," agreed Bobbi. "How did you think of it?"

"Well, it's not my original idea," confessed Barney. "Years ago, where I lived in London, they ran a scheme like that from the local library. You could borrow a picture on your library ticket, try it out for a month or so and then get another one. I loved it – original new work on the walls of my scruffy old flat every few weeks."

"What happened to the scheme?" asked Eugene.

"Local government cuts – arts budgets are the first to go when times are tight. I used to fantasise about restarting it as an artists' co-op. I tried to interest some of my painter friends but they couldn't get it together. - I still think it would work, though."

"So do I," said Bobbi. "I bet I could make it work. I love that idea of art for everyone. We'd need to have a big launch party – someplace really different – not a gallery or library – too stuffy."

"Maybe we could showcase Roz's work," suggested Eugene. "I wonder if she'd let us?"

"You could email her and ask," said Barney. "She might like the chance of a big retrospective."

Bobbi was writing a list of names in her notebook. "I can think of seven or eight people at the college who are good enough to include - besides Eugene."

"And you, - you're as good as any of those," said Eugene, looking over her shoulder at the list.

"Why don't you ask them if they want to be part of it and meantime Eugene can try to persuade Rozalin by email? I hope she's as good as you say she is – you still haven't showed me her collection in the basement. Perhaps we'd better do that first before we go any further – and yours and Bobbi's too. I don't want to get involved with a bunch of amateurs," smiled Barney, trying not to appear too excited at the prospect of seeing one of his long-cherished ideas coming to fruition.

"You could come over to Eugene's place now and see his stuff - I'll go home and bring my portfolio over and meet you there in an hour or so," said Bobbi, closing her notebook and taking out her cell phone.

"I'm going to call some people," she hugged Eugene and held out her nail-bitten hand to Barney. "See you guys later." She headed down the ramp towards a little tub ferry just pulling into the dockside.

Eugene watched her go. "I told you she was amazing, didn't I?" He stood. "Well, I guess we'd better make a move if we're going to look at my pieces before Bobbi gets back."

He whistled Ralf back from seagull duty and put on his leash and the three of them headed off under the towering spans of Granville Bridge towards Eugene's crumbling old Vancouver saltbox, which he shared with a group of other students.

Eugene's 'pieces' as he called them, were collages of materials culled from his long dog-walking trips in the parks and beachcombing on both shores of English Bay. He never went out without his battered old rucksack in which he stowed all his finds and unused piles of them filled the corners of his cluttered room. Bobbi was right; they were highly inventive and witty too, in their clever juxtapositions and combinations.

"What do you call this one?" asked Barney, pointing to one which caught his eye with its conical heaps of multi-coloured tiny seashells, peeking like mermaids' breasts out of a tangle of old fishnet and bits of flotsam which might have been a boat.

"It depends – I'm still working on it – sometimes I call it 'Clinging to the wreckage,' other times it's 'Coming up for Air'."

Eugene's room had been the former living room of the old wooden house and piles of unframed pictures leaned against the fireplace while each of the four corners had further piles and collections of materials culled from his dog-walks. A lumpy-looking futon with a heap of bedding lay on the floor against one wall.

Barney roved round the room to stare in turn at each of the different pieces, which Eugene pulled out to show him. He tried to block out his conventional notions of how a picture should look and instead just let them work on him, not attempting to read anything significant into them, letting his eyes focus on whatever caught his attention. Aware that Eugene was watching him, he felt called upon to say something.

"Are you showing me what you think are your best pieces or…" Eugene shook his head.

"Not particularly. They all have some significance for me but I'd find it hard to say which is my best work. Usually, I think the one I'm working on is going to be it."

"Do you mean the 'wreckage' one?" said Barney, nodding towards the conical mermaid's breasts poking pertly out from the frame.

"No, I did that one a while ago – but I'm still messing around with it. This is my current piece." He pointed to a large work standing on its end like a dresser drawer with a ship's prow coming out of the center. It reminded Barney of that Magritte painting where the train locomotive emerges from the fireplace. The waterline bisected the painting at the ship's Plimsoll line and above and below it were fragments of birds and fish – a still life of actual feathers and tiny claws, fish skeletons and empty crab shells. High up on the ship's prow a tiny figure was tipping a sack of rubbish over the side – the contents flowed down like a cornucopia; from little painted objects near the top, graduating in size and becoming real items as they neared the water –opened tins, plastic containers, broken electrical appliances, cans of industrial chemicals – and as they entered the ocean, their contents spread a widening stain to the bottom of the picture.

"I like this one," said Barney. "Is it finished yet?"

Eugene laughed, "Oh no, I'm just nicely getting started – these are just some ideas I'm playing around with. It'll probably end up looking totally different."

"Not too different, I hope. I like it the way it is." Barney looked around the room. "So are any of them finished, then?"

Eugene shrugged. "Picasso said he didn't finish his paintings, he abandoned them. - I think that's how I feel. But I can't quite bring myself to abandon them so I keep revisiting them and messing about with them. I envy Bobbi – she finishes what she starts and then goes straight on to the next one – but she can draw and I can't. I just play about with ideas and materials."

"Is Picasso one of your heroes, then?"

Eugene nodded glumly. "It's no joke trying to be a painter after Picasso."

Barney looked at his pocket watch. "I'm not going to be able to stay to see Bobbi's drawings. I'm supposed to be at the Food Bank warehouse today – it's cheque week."

Once a month when the welfare payments were made, the food bank closed so he went to help out in the warehouse, sorting food for distribution to the depots around the city. "Why don't you both come over to my place for beer and chili and we can plan some more?"

Eugene nodded. "Can I see that?" he asked, holding out his hand for Barney's watch. Barney handed it to him. He turned it over in his hand. "How do you open it?"

Barney showed him how to push the stem to make the lid of the gold hunter pop open. "It was my grandfather's. His retirement present. They actually did give people gold watches when they retired in those days. – Look, you can unscrew the back and read the inscription – forty-two years of service and this is your reward. I've known this watch since I was a little boy. He left it to me in his will. My family think I'm odd because I still use it. They keep giving me new wristwatches but I like to use this – it reminds me of him.

"'The Persistence of Memory,' said Eugene. "You know that painting by Salvador Dali of the melting watch? – that's what it reminds me of."

"Well you can't have it to stick into one of your pieces if that's what you're thinking," said Barney, retrieving his watch from Eugene. "But, I'll see if I can find you one, if you like. Say goodbye to Bobbi for me – tell her I expect to see lots of plans when you come round for chili."

On the bus to the warehouse, he passed a pawnshop on East Broadway and Barney made a mental note to stop in there one day to see if they had any old pocket watches for Eugene. He was becoming very fond of the young man and enjoyed his avuncular role more and more.

At the food bank warehouse, he made a cup of tea in the bombsite that passed for a kitchen and carried it out into the cavernous chilly warehouse. He now wore a body-warmer to work in after the experience of the first time when he became chilled to the bone from the unheated building. He threaded his way through pallets stacked high with unsorted cardboard boxes of food, stacked by the forklift truck into rows near the packing tables. Maggie was inducting a group of Chinese high school kids and their teacher into the complicated sorting system. The warehouse operated with a skeleton staff and volunteers were always a precious commodity.

A grey-haired man with a ponytail was unloading cans of soup into a supermarket trolley. He nodded at Barney and smiled. "I'm Clive. Clive Russell. This your first time?"

"No, I've been here a few times. My name's Barney. Do you work here? I don't think I've seen you before."

"Just another labourer in the vineyards – I've been volunteering here for years. I've been away on a trip, that's why we haven't met. Looks like things have been piling up in my absence."

"Anywhere interesting?" asked Barney digging into the piles of cans.

"Cabo San Lucas." – Barney looked blank. "Tip of the Baja," said Clive. "Mexico."

"Ah – the Baja Peninsula. – I thought that was California."

"Yeah, it's confusing. It's called Baja California but it actually belongs to Mexico – although it's full of American snowbirds – and some Canadian ones too. Escaping the northern winters."

"Are you a snowbird?"

"More of an albatross, I'd say. I go sailing down there sometimes."

Maggie hobbled over to them. She had finished teaching her new volunteers and they were all busily sifting through the contents of a pallet of boxes she had assigned them.

"Good bunch?" asked Clive. Maggie sighed, easing herself down onto a stack of boxes and propping her crutch against the sorting table.

"If only we could get them to come once a week instead of once a year, we could really tackle this backlog."

"You'll just have to settle for us old boys," said Clive. "We may be slow but we're reliable." Maggie blew him a kiss.

"Thanks for coming on your week off, Barney," she said turning to him. "I see you've met Popeye already. He should be running this place but he keeps disappearing on his boat."

"How's your leg?" said Barney. "I thought you were due to have the cast off by now."

"It's coming off this week, thank God – I feel like I've been lugging round a ball and chain for months." She took out her knitting needle from the side of the cast, inserted it inside the plaster, and scratched vigorously. "The itches are driving me insane. I don't know which is worse, my cast or Marlon."

"Why – what's he doing?"

"Nothing really. He's just fed up because I can't go out and play with him with this thing on. He hates waiting for me all the time."

"Does he like dogs?"

"Like them! He'd swap me for one tomorrow – why?"

"Well, maybe he'd like to go out with me and Ralf along the beach one day. - You could sit and have a coffee at the beach hut and keep an eye on us," added Barney tactfully.

"Ralf's your friend's dog – right?" Barney nodded. "Marlon would love to go, but are you sure you want to? He's a bit of a handful."

"You could bring him over on the aquabus ferry to see my boat," said Clive. "If it's nice we might even manage a short sail around the bay."

"Yes please – it sounds wonderful. Wait till I tell Marlon. – When could we go?"

"This weekend if you want – weather permitting," said Clive. "Make a day of it – on the beach with Barney and his dog in the morning and on my boat in the afternoon."

"Would there be room for us all? I mean, the dog and everything?" asked Maggie.

"Plenty of space – I live aboard. I'll borrow a kid's life jacket for Marlon. I've got spare adult ones for you two. What about lunch?"

"Picnic?" suggested Barney. "Most kids like picnics. – I'll bring the hard-boiled eggs."

"Please. Let me do the picnic. I can use all the dented tins we're not allowed to hand out from here – they only go to the pig farm otherwise. I often take them home myself – my mum and I live on damaged stuff."

"Pig food lunch it is," said Clive. "That's settled then. At least the dog will like it."

"So will you – you'll see," said Maggie, hauling herself upright. "I'd better do some work – and thanks for the offers – both of you." She limped off towards the office. Barney and Clive watched her go.

"I'd like to get my hands on that guy," said Clive. "Pushing her downstairs – she could have been killed. He's been hassling her since then, too, according to the women in the office. Calling her up at work and demanding to see the boy."

"She told me she doesn't trust him anymore," said Barney. "She's worried he might turn violent with Marlon. Have you met him?"

"Yeah, a couple of times when he picked her up after work – he seemed an okay guy." Clive shook his head. "And then he goes and does that to her – not the first time, either. I'm glad she's not my daughter – I might do something I'd be sorry for."

"Six years seems a long time to find out something like that about him," said Barney. "Do you think it's been going on all along?"

"Wouldn't surprise me – nothing surprises me about women - they put up with a lot of shit for the sake of their kids."

"Have you got any yourself?"

"Kids? No, never stayed in one place long enough to have any. Probably just as well – I don't think I'd make a very good father. Besides, they tie you down too much – wouldn't have suited me at all. I'm a drifter – always have been. My ex said if I lived on land instead of at sea, I'd be trailer trash – she's probably right."

"But you said you've been coming here for years?"

"Oh, I don't travel that much any more – maybe once or twice a year – just live on my boat in False Creek – at the government fish dock. The harbourmaster's another old sailor come to anchor there – he lets me stay aboard as long as I leave once in a while – don't know where I'd go if he kicked me out – maybe Mosquito Creek or Steveston or Finn Slough. There's still a few places around Vancouver to hole up when the property developers move in and take over the fish dock for another flashy marina."

"I'd like to see your boat," said Barney. "I've been thinking that's just the sort of thing I could do – buy an old fishing boat and live aboard – right in the heart of the city and yet be able to sail off around the Gulf Islands whenever I felt like it."

"Lots of work boats for sale. The fishing industry is all shot to hell – the fishermen can't earn enough to pay for their license, fish stocks are so depleted. – They'd take a bit of work to make them livable, though. – You any good with your hands?"

"I used to be a carpenter in a previous incarnation," said Barney, "but I don't know anything much about fishing boats. Would you help me choose one?"

"There's a good one been for sale next to me for two years now. I don't know how much they want but I know they're open to offers. You can have a look at it on Saturday when you come with Maggie and Marlon."

"It was nice of you to offer your boat," said Barney. "For Saturday, I mean. Maggie seemed delighted at the idea. I don't think she gets much change of scenery, somehow. - Can't be much fun being a single parent when you see all your friends going places and having fun while you're stuck at home with a kid."

"I'll need to do a bit of house-cleaning when I finish here. I don't often get women visitors on board the 'Betsy'." He sealed the box of canned tuna and shoved it across to Barney for labeling and piling on the waiting pallets. "I guess maybe we better shift some of this stuff instead of gassing so much."

For the next hour and a half, Clive and Barney methodically worked their way through the jumble of plastic bags and boxes, which had been piled in heaps on the already full pallets. By the time Maggie came back out to announce she was ready to close up, they and the Chinese teenagers had made a definite impression on the food mountain.

"Brilliant," she said. "I can actually see the floor in some places. I thank you, the food bank thanks you, our clients thank you, Eloise thanks you"-

"Who's Eloise?" asked Barney.

"Eloise is in charge of Pest Control," said Maggie.

"The cat," explained Clive, "a mangy old stray."

"See you guys on Saturday, then – unless you've had second thoughts?"

"I'll pick you up about ten-thirty," said Barney. "Tell Marlon to bring a ball to play catch with Ralf."

By Saturday morning, the spell of warm autumn weather remained unbroken and the city's working population poured on to the seawall and the beaches to take full advantage of the Indian summer. Barney parked the little yellow car near the Second Beach open-air pool so Maggie could sit by the snack bar and watch them on the beach. Marlon held Ralf's leash and he and Barney took him for a circular walk around the small park and back along the seawall.

"Seen your dad lately, Marlon?" The boy shook his head.

"He came around once and Mum told him to piss off or she'd call the cops."

"I see."

"She's mad at him 'coz he pushed her downstairs and now she has to walk on crutches."

"Maybe when she doesn't have to use them anymore, she might change her mind."

"Maybe," said Marlon doubtfully. "She hasn't changed her mind about letting me have a dog and I've been asking her for ages." He patted Ralf and ran his fingers backwards up the dog's back the way kids always do.

"But she told me there's no pets allowed in your apartment block."

"We could easy move someplace else. - My dad said he'd get me a dog if I came and lived with him."

"What did you say?"

"I said I'd think about it. – Ralf sure is nice, isn't he?"

"Perhaps we could share him – you and I could take him for walks after school sometimes. Would you like me to ask your mum if it's okay?"

"That would be great - Will you ask her now?"

"Why don't you take Ralf down on the beach to play ball and I'll go and talk to her. Stay in front of the café so we can see you, okay?" Marlon and Ralf tore off across the sand towards the water and Barney strolled back to where Maggie was sitting.

"Marlon asked me if I'd talk to you," he said, "about a dog. - Said it was no use him asking, you always say no."

"He did, did he? What else did he tell you?"

"He mentioned that his dad offered to buy him a dog if he came to live with him."

"That bastard! And what did Marlon say?"

"He's thinking it over." They watched the boy and the little dog racing back and forth at the water's edge. "I said maybe you might let him share Ralf – you know – take him out for walks in the park after school some days."

Maggie looked at her son for a moment and then at Barney. "It sure would take the pressure off me – for someone that small, he can really pile it on."

"I was thinking of the Food Bank day – we could meet him from school and take him and Ralf to the park or down to Sunset Beach – it's closer to your place. You'd be helping me out, too."

"How?"

"Well, Eugene takes Ralf out in the mornings for a long hike but then he's stuck in the apartment for the rest of the day. I feel guilty about leaving him on his own so much."

"I'm convinced, if you're sure you want to."

"Well, kids and dogs go together – look at them." They watched as Marlon rolled on the sand and Ralf pounced on him, licking his face.

"I hope you know what you're letting yourself in for," said Maggie. "Marlon will hold you to it."

"Wait till I get a coffee and we can go over and tell him."

"What a bastard, eh?"

"Marlon?"

"Zeke. – It's so typical of him. He doesn't even like dogs - now do you wonder why I don't trust him? He never said a word to me about this. Poor Marlon – making him choose between me and a dog."

"Seems like a no-brainer to me."

Maggie grinned, "And you're no better – aiding and abetting. – How humiliating, being passed over for a dog."

"Be fair – Marlon said he's still thinking about it." He ducked as Maggie threw her empty paper cup at him. He went over and bought a coffee and they walked slowly down to the beach. Ralf spotted Barney and ran over to him with Marlon chasing behind. He held up a small plastic bag.

"Ralf didn't do anything so I couldn't use the pooper-scooper."

"Better luck next time," said Barney. "I think your mother has something to tell you."

"Can I, Mum? - Look after Ralf sometimes?"

Maggie nodded. "On Wednesdays, after the Food Bank closes. Barney will bring Ralf and you can play with him in the park or down on our beach."

"Terrific," said Marlon, hugging her. "Thanks Barney." – He cuddled the little Yorkie who tried to lick his face and they all began to laugh, glad of an excuse.

Barney flipped open his pocket watch. "I guess we'd better make a move. Clive will be waiting for us. Shall we take the tub ferry or drive, Marlon?"

"Let's go on the little ferry. I'll take Ralf. You can bring the picnic."

Clive was sitting on the dock sunbathing in a deck chair beside his boat when they arrived.

"Welcome aboard the 'Betsy'," he said, indicating the old wooden Dutch sailing boat gently undulating at the dockside. "A poor thing but mine own." He turned to Marlon. "Which one of you is Ralf?"

Marlon grinned. "He is."

"So you must be Marlon. I'm Clive and this is 'Betsy'. Do you want to go inside and see her?" The boy nodded and Clive lifted him over the side onto the deck. He pointed to the hatchway. "Go through that little door and down the steps. Here's Ralf," he said, lifting the little dog on board. "You can show him around, too." The boy and dog disappeared inside and Clive and Barney manoeuvred Maggie onto the boat. "Grab some cushions and make yourself comfortable – we may as well stay topside for now and enjoy the sunshine. How about a beer?"

Barney gathered several faded blue canvas-covered boat cushions and spread them on the raised cabin roof. Maggie sank back on them and laid her crutch on the deck.

"I expect you're as keen to see 'Betsy' as Marlon. –I'll just lie here and soak up the rays – you go ahead."

Below deck, Clive was demonstrating the intricacies of the marine toilet to Marlon.

"Why do you call it the 'head'?" he asked, pumping the handle and turning the stopcock lever the way Clive had showed him.

"'Coz that's its name. – Now look at this – here's where you wash your hands." He pulled down the foldaway stainless steel hand basin and showed the boy how to pump water into it by stepping on the raised rubber dome on the floor.

"It hasn't got a plughole to let the water out," said Marlon.

"Doesn't need one – just tip it up and watch." The boy cautiously raised the hinged basin and the water flowed away down the flared drain on the cabin wall. "You can show your mum how it works later. Let's get a drink first." He opened a small propane-run fridge in the tiny galley. "What do you want – beer or Coke?"

"I'm not allowed Coke."

"Better have a beer then." – He handed Marlon a can of root beer. "Try that. And you can take this one up to your mother. Better give Ralf a bowl of water, too. The tap in the sink works the same way as the 'head' – just pump the dome on the floor." He opened a can of beer and passed it to Barney.

"Well, what do you think? Could you live aboard something like this?"

"I'd love it. There's so much room down here – very deceptive."

"Yeah, she's very beamy – designed to carry maximum cargo. She sails pretty well, too, considering. Built for comfort, not for speed."

"Ideal live-aboard," said Barney. "I don't suppose I'd find another one like this."

"Not unless you want to sail one back from Holland. But the local Japanese fishing boats are pretty spacious as well. Did you notice the one I was telling you about when you came in? I got the keys from the harbourmaster – we can take a look at it later. Have a poke around down here all you want, I'll go up and talk to Maggie." He left Barney to finish the inspection and climbed the narrow steps up to the deck.

"Marlon wants me to do a pee so he can show me how the toilet works," she greeted him. "He says I'd never figure it out on my own, but I guess I'll have to by the time I finish this beer."

"You could always just go over the side – moon at all the yachties."

"No thanks, Clive. I'll take my chances below."

"Better let Marlon teach you, then. Don't want you sinking the boat. Did you remember to bring some pig food?"

"No I didn't. I brought a proper picnic, but you'll just have to wait. I'm not moving from here till I've finished my beer. Pull up a cushion."

Clive propped himself on the foredeck leaning against the furled sail for a seat. "Barney tells me you're being black-mailed."

"What? Oh – Marlon. Yes, I'm in danger of being swapped for something a bit more lively."

"Are you considering shared custody, then?"

"Not a chance. I don't trust him as far as I could boot him with this – she raised her plaster cast leg. And now this business with the dog – it's just so mean – he knows I'm not allowed pets in our building."

"When is the court case coming up?"

"Not for another month. Why?"

"I was wondering whether you'd still have a cast on by then – might help your case – look good in court – sway the jury in your favour, eh?"

"There is no jury – it's family court – you're just in front of a magistrate. Besides, I couldn't bear this thing for another month – I'd go mad with the itch."

Barney reappeared on deck. "Marlon and Ralf are swinging in your hammock down there, Clive. I hope it's okay – I don't know how to break this to you, Maggie, but I think he's seriously considering running away to sea – with Ralf."

"A couple of old seadogs," said Clive. "Keep me company.

Maggie heaved her leg up on some cushions. "Suits me. Solve a lot of my problems. I prefer you to Zeke any day."

"Maggie was just telling me about her custody battle. She's due in court next month."

"Are you worried about it, Maggie?" asked Barney. "Surely it's an open and shut case – especially with that leg injury."

"That's what I told her."

"Clive thinks I should keep the cast on for another month – to influence the judge."

"He might be right – it's pretty damning evidence."

"Well, too bad. It's coming off this week and that's settled. The thought of another month would finish me. I'll probably still be hobbling around on crutches – they'll have to settle for that."

"I could take your picture now while you've still got it on," said Clive.

"Lying on the deck of a sailboat floating around English Bay?" said Maggie. "I doubt if that's going to make anybody feel sorry for me."

"Just a suggestion," said Clive.

"Well, I've got a better one – let's have some lunch. Barney, where did you put my big holdall with the picnic?"

"It's stowed in the cabin below – with Ralf and Marlon. Shall I get it?"

"Wait a minute," said Clive, "I've got an even better idea. We can sail out into the bay and have our picnic there. I promised Marlon he could steer 'Betsy'. He wants to see those big freighters up close. I've borrowed a child's lifejacket for him."

"I'm going to take Marlon up on his offer to show me the toilet," said Maggie. "Then I could lay out the picnic downstairs, if you like. – It's okay; you don't need to help me. I'm good at getting up and down stairs on my backside." She eased herself up and limped to the hatchway as Clive and Barney prepared for sailing.

They motored out under Burrard Bridge and headed for the bay with the sunlight glittering on the water and a small boy clutching a little dog, steering the boat from the top of a pile of cushions.

# CHAPTER 8

When Barney arrived back at his apartment, he found a note taped to his door asking him to contact the neighbour across the hall. Thinking it might be something to do with Rozalin, he rapped on the door. After a few minutes, an elderly woman opened it on the security chain and Barney held up her note.

"You left me a note?"

"You're Rozalin's new tenant, aren't you? I've seen you go in and out."

"That's right. Roper – Barney Roper."

"Well, Mr. Roper, a lady came by today looking for you. She asked me if I would give you a message."

"What is it?"

"She wants you to phone her – she left me her number but wanted me to give it to you in person. Just a minute." She disappeared for a minute and then reappeared with a slip of paper obviously torn from a pocket diary and handed it to him.

"Thank you. – Did she say what it was about?" The old woman shook her head.

"No, just would I hand it to you myself so it wouldn't get lost."

"I see. Well thanks again." He turned and crossed the hall to open his door. He tried to read the note in the subdued hall lighting but without his glasses, he couldn't make it out. Inside the apartment, he began one of his daily hunts to track down a pair of reading glasses. He had several pairs placed strategically about in different rooms but could never lay his hands on any when he needed them. This time he found three pair on the coffee table in the living room. He unfolded the slip of paper and read the phone number written in a rather shaky hand. It meant nothing to Barney, but curious, he dialed the number anyway. A woman's voice answered.

"Oh, hello. My name's Barney Roper. I believe you were trying to reach me?"

"Barney! You got my message. It's me – Trish – remember? – Reykjavik?"

"Trish! How are you? I'd given up hearing from you."

"I'm okay. I only just got your note. It was under the mat all the time. The cleaner found it, put it in her pocket, and forgot about it. She only rediscovered it later but by then I'd moved."

"Yes, I went to your office when you left the hospital but you weren't there so I pushed a note under the door. When I didn't hear from you I assumed I had the wrong place and I didn't know where else to look. So, what happened, anyway?"

"It's a long story – how about meeting for a drink and I can tell you all about it? It would be nice to see a friendly face."

"Sure, anytime. Do you want me to come over to you or would you like to meet over here? Are you still in North Van?"

"Sort of. I'm moving around a bit at the moment, staying with friends. Perhaps I'd better come to you. - Is tomorrow okay?"

"We could meet for lunch on Granville Island," said Barney "– the market food hall? –They do some great seafood chowder."

"Okay, good, I know the place you mean. One o'clock?"

"Fine."

Barney hung up the phone guiltily. – God, he'd forgotten all about her. It had been ages since he had tried to locate her after he arrived. When the trail went cold in North Van and he heard nothing from her, she just sort of slipped to the back of his mind. Occasionally he had considered looking for her again but didn't know where to begin. Now here she was – turning up out of nowhere. Out of the blue, he thought, remembering the harrowing flight to Iceland, which he had put firmly out of his mind. He allowed himself to think of it now – or rather of Trish and how she had locked herself in the plane's toilet. Was she still drinking heavily, he wondered – let's meet for a drink she had said on the phone.

He lay in bed trying to recall what she looked like. He could remember what she was wearing – that fawn-coloured jacket, but her features remained blurred – so many people he had met since he arrived – for some reason the woman with the face mask from the food bank queue floated up before him – had she been in some horrific crash to end up so disfigured?

He drifted off into a disturbed sleep of tilting airplane seats and Trish stroking his hand.

"Hi Barney – am I glad to see you." Trish hugged him and kissed his cheek. "I hope you haven't forgotten me after all this time." She smiled her cool smile at him and he hugged her back, wondering how he could have forgotten her so quickly.

"It's good to see you, too, Trish. You look fine. How are you?"

"I could do with a drink – shall we get one before we eat? We could sit outside at that pub by the ferry dock. It's still warm enough." She threaded her way through the tables and out onto the boardwalk with Barney following. They ordered at the bar and took their glasses out to the tables on the deck.

"Cheers," said Barney, raising his wineglass. "Here's to reunions. So – what have you been up to?"

"Oh, just trying to settle back in. It's been kind of hard adjusting after being in China for two years."

"I bet. How's your work going – the Chinese medicine? You must be popular here in Vancouver – seems like half the population is Asian."

"Well, that's part of the problem. I haven't got any work."

"But your office by Lonsdale Quay? – I thought...."

"It wasn't really my office – I was sort of renting space in that clinic, but I couldn't afford to keep it up - it takes ages to build up a client list – all my old ones seem to have disappeared."

"You mentioned you were staying with friends," said Barney. "Here or on the North Shore?"

"Both. Here, there, anywhere. I've been wearing out my welcome with most of my old acquaintances. Can't afford to get a place on my own – everything's got so expensive since I've been away. Two years is a long time."

"No flat and no work – that's a tough combination – how are you managing?"

"Not very well. I've been borrowing money from my ex-husband but he's cut me off, too. I really need a regular job to get me back on my feet again. I can't afford to set myself up in business here – the start-up costs are too high. Maybe in a year or two"–

"What kind of work are you looking for?"

"Anything. I'm desperate now. I've been job searching for weeks but nobody will take on a woman my age. You got any suggestions?" She had finished her drink and twirled the wineglass stem between her fingers.

"I could do with a top-up – how about you?"

Barney signaled the waiter for another round. "I could ask around for you, if you like. I've met an amazing number of people since I arrived here. - However" –

"What?"

"Most of them are street people – I've been helping out at the local food bank and a mobile soup kitchen on the downtown east side – not exactly prime job-hunting country."

"God, that's what's going to happen to me –I can feel myself sliding downwards." She took a long drink from her replenished glass.

"Let's get some lunch," said Barney. "You'll feel better after you've eaten some chowder."

"I'll feel better after I've finished this drink. All my friends think I've turned into a real boozer since I've been away. But all this business only makes me need a drink even more." She drained her glass. "Enough about my troubles – what else have you been doing since you arrived – you surely didn't come out here just to work in a soup kitchen?"

"Not exactly – but I've met some fascinating people since I started. You'd be amazed at the number of college kids on the streets here in town. Young people just seem to gravitate to the west coast thinking life is easier out here but they find the competition is pretty stiff."

"That makes me feel great – just what I wanted to hear. Thanks, Barney."

"Sorry, Trish – I didn't mean to sound…I wasn't trying to rub your face in it or anything…only explain" –

"I know. I'm just a bit sensitive these days. – Let's have that chowder, shall we?" They left the bar and returned to the market food hall. When they were seated with their food, she questioned him again.

"So what exactly are you doing, Barney?"

"Well, it's hard to explain. I can tell you 'what' I'm doing but the 'why' is a bit more difficult."

"Try me."

"Okay, let's see. – Have you read much Eliot?"

"T.S. Eliot – the poet? – Not much. I liked the 'Lovesong of J. Alfred Prufrock' when I was in college. – Didn't know what he was on about in 'The Waste Land' though."

"Doesn't matter. Anyway, he says that old men ought to be continually questing – 'the wind song, the wave song – in my end is my beginning'- that's what I'm trying to do – explore this stage of my life – see where it leads."

"Sounds like he says it just takes you back to where you started."

"Maybe. Or perhaps it means that the end part of your life is only the beginning. So that's why I'm turning over all these stones – searching for clues."

"Found any yet?"

"A few – just not sure what they mean. I think of my life as a sort of jigsaw puzzle with all these pieces floating around and my job is to put them all together to see what it looks like."

"Am I one of those pieces?"

Barney laughed. "I hadn't thought about it that way – but yeah, maybe you are."

"What about old women – are we supposed to be explorers too, or is this strictly for the boys?"

"I don't know – what do you think? Most women I know don't seem to agonize over the meaning of their lives – they just get on and live it. In my next rebirth I'm definitely coming back as a woman."

"Don't kid yourself – it's not that great, believe me. Although I've done my bit of exploring and enjoyed that. Not sure about my jigsaw puzzle though – so far none of the pieces are matching up."

"When I was a boy my grandfather showed me how to look for the four corner pieces first with two straight sides; then those with one straight side – you put them all together and you've got the frame. After that, you start filling it in. I think that's what I'm doing now."

"I didn't realize jigsaw puzzles were so meaningful," said Trish.

"Oh, very philosophical," said Barney, –"very deep."

"I shall have to go home and try this. What do those corner pieces look like again?"

"Corners are key," said Barney. "You'd think they'd be easy because they've got two straight sides, but there's only four of them and they're hard to find."

"What kind of missing pieces are you looking for, Barney?"

"That's the intriguing part – you don't know till you've found it what you're looking for."

"And how do you know whether it fits?"

"Somebody said it's called an 'aha' moment. Suddenly it slips into place and you say, 'aha!'"

"I certainly haven't had any of those lately," said Trish. –"Have you?"

"One or two, occasionally. - The Buddhist teachers call them 'glimpses of enlightenment.' They say the more you look the more you'll see – glimpse after glimpse. That's all I'm hoping for – a few glimpses."

"At the moment I think I'm looking more for the light at the end of the tunnel. If you hear about anything, give me a call, eh? Anything at all. And thanks for lunch – you never know, you might see me at your soup kitchen next."

"Listen, Trish, if you're stuck I could always – you know – lend you some money."

"Thanks Barney. I'll take a rain-cheque for now."

"I'll call you if I hear of anything."

"Either way – it'll be good to hear from you." She gave him a brief hug and brushed his cheek. At the door to the outside deck she turned and waved and Barney half rose from his seat. Then she was gone.

At his bridge class that afternoon, Barney told the widows at his table about Trish and her predicament. At the mention of herbal medicine, they pricked up their ears. In their hierarchy of interests, health or rather illnesses, ranked right up there beside bridge and scandal. He had been counting on this when he mentioned it and now he pressed home his advantage.

"Trish has spent the last two years in Guangzhou, studying at a Chinese university which specializes in herbal medicine. I don't know about you ladies, but I'll try alternative medicine every time before giving in to the giant pharmaceuticals. Maybe I'm just getting old but natural remedies seem to make more sense to me now, than all this high-tech medicine we get shoved at us in the West."

He glanced at Mildred for support. He had become used to bringing his questions and ideas for the bridge widows to consider and had learned to value their advice. Mildred in particular, took a personal interest in all Barney's ventures and he often phoned her or went round to her huge high-ceilinged apartment on Beach Avenue to sort out a problem over a cup of Earl Grey tea. She finished laying out her dummy hand and looked up.

"My cousin goes to a Chinese herbalist in White Rock. She swears by him. - Says he has remedies for everything from toothache to arthritis and they all seem to work – the only problem is they taste vile, she said."

"Trish mentioned that to me, too," said Barney. "She says that now they're putting them in capsules and tablets so you don't have that awful taste."

"Would she be interested in doing house calls?" asked Lois. "I have two or three friends who might like to try it – but they'd want to hear more about it first."

"I'm sure she would," said Barney. "She's keen to start rebuilding her clientele and she lives in this area."

"If she can do anything about my arthritis, she's got my vote," said Margaret. "Look at my hands – they're getting so twisted I soon won't even be able to play bridge anymore."

"Maybe we can phone a few of our friends and get her some private clients," said Mildred. "At our age most of us need all the help we can get."

"And if she's prepared to do house-calls," said Lois. "I can think of two – no, three people who would be very interested – doctors never want to make house-calls any more. They all want you to go to their fancy new clinics."

"But are you sure it works, Barney? – I wouldn't want to recommend her to my friends if she's some New Age flake," said Margaret.

"All I know is, herbal medicine has been used in China for thousands of years and the last I heard there were over a billion Chinese – so they must be doing something right," he said.

"Leave it with us until next week's session, Barney," said Mildred. "Meantime you can ask her what she feels about doing house-calls. Are you rushing off or can you have lunch with me? We could go to Kam's – they're doing a two-for-one lunchtime special."

Despite their affluence, old habits died hard and the widows still hated to pass up a bargain. "You haven't told me how the art show is coming along yet," she said, as he helped her on with her coat.

At Kam's, Mildred and Barney ordered the special plus an aperitif. Mildred sipped her sherry and listened to him describe the latest twists and turns in the plans for the art show. She was one of Eugene's doggy customers and had been the first person he and Barney had turned to for help and suggestions. Mildred had been one of the movers and shakers of the city's arts world and still sat on one or two prestigious boards and committees. Her contacts were both numerous and impressive and she knew how to call in a favour. It was thanks to her that Barney and Eugene had a venue to stage their launch party.

An empty bank building waiting to undergo refurbishment had been fingered by the tireless Bobbi as the ideal spot. She and the old lady approached the unsuspecting realtor – one of Mildred's contacts who had gained many clients through her.

"You should have seen Bobbi schmooze him," she laughed. "He took us to lunch at the Hotel Vancouver so we put on our slap and dressed to kill – Bobbi looked wonderful - these art students know how to dress for an occasion. I didn't look so bad, myself. Bobbi set him up and I delivered the punchline – like taking candy from a baby, I told her in the ladies afterwards. – Damn good lunch, too. You should try it sometime."

"Out of my league," said Barney. "Kam's two-for-one specials are more my speed. Maybe if the show's a success we can all go there for a celebration lunch on the takings. – It's a good thing Eugene didn't go with you – I don't think he would have enjoyed watching Bobbi 'schmooze' your realtor pal."

"He'd better get used to it – if this thing takes off, she'll be wining and dining all the local glitterati for fund-raising. I can teach her a few tricks but she's halfway there already. – What's the latest from Rozalin – will she come back for the launch or not?"

"We're still working on her. She's not really convinced it's going to happen."

"It'll be a bit of a disappointment if the star of the show doesn't appear."

"That's what I told Eugene but he says we can promote her as the unknown mystery artist – that will bring in the curious – it's all about new unknown painters and artists anyway so it kind of all ties in – at least that's what he and Bobbi think. I'm just along for the ride."

"That's not the way Eugene tells it – he said it was all your idea."

"Maybe. But he and Bobbi are the driving force behind it now – and you."

"I'm happy to do my bit behind the scenes," said Mildred

"Well, said Barney, "I certainly feel a lot happier about the whole thing knowing we've got a seasoned hand on the tiller. I know Bobbi is a miracle worker but she needs somebody like you to curb her wilder schemes."

"Nonsense. I encourage her – wilder the better, I say. There's too many timid souls in this town – we need more Bobbies to stir us up."

"It's no wonder you ran through three husbands, Mildred. No one could keep up to you. Have you got your eye on a fourth?"

"When you get to my age, most of the men are either in wheel chairs or care homes. I don't fancy myself as a nurse. Besides, they'd cramp my style. I pretty much please myself now I'm an old lady. If I had a husband he might not approve of my choice of friends."

"You mean me? – In that case, I'm glad you've decided to remain independent. I think that's how I want to live from now on."

"Once you taste freedom," she said, "it's hard to give it up and go back to the old ways."

"Do you ever get lonely, Mildred?"

"Often. Especially at night. I lie awake and look at the lights on the freighters in English Bay and I get so sad and lonely I start to cry. And the odd thing is I don't know who I'm feeling lonely for. – Not my husbands – they were all too busy to ever have time for real closeness. My mother, maybe – although she's been gone so long I barely remember her, either. Perhaps if I'd had children...."

Barney shook his head. "I don't know. I've had three children and it doesn't stop me from feeling alone. Even when I'm with them sometimes, I feel them receding from me - as if they were drifting away and I'm powerless to stop them. - That's the way I feel and it makes me sad. I know it shouldn't – I mean that's the way life is and I agree – but it doesn't stop me having those feelings."

Mildred took a handkerchief from her handbag and blew her nose loudly. "I took a 'Philosophy for Seniors' course at SFU once and they taught us some Sartre and Wittgenstein. I couldn't make head nor tail of Wittgenstein but I remember Sartre's 'existential angst'. I guess that's what I feel in the middle of the night, watching those freighters out in the bay."

Barney nodded. "My Buddhist teacher back in England liked to mention Suzuki Roshi's remark that life is like a ship that sails out into the middle of the ocean - and sinks."

Mildred held up her hand. "Enough already. I usually save this kind of stuff for the middle of the night. - I don't think I can handle it in the middle of the day as well." She slipped her jacket on and picked up the bill. "My turn to pay. - I'll call you as soon as I have anything to report for your friend Trish."

"Thanks, Mildred. See you soon."

Barney made for the seawall intending to walk off his lunch. He didn't like eating a big meal at midday as it made him sleepy and the urge to succumb to an afternoon nap was too difficult to resist if he was at home. Best to stay outside and keep moving. He headed down False Creek towards Burrard Bridge. As he passed the little tub ferry dock, he suddenly swerved and walked down to the quay and watched while the Aquabus approached.

He would see if Clive was on his boat and they could have another look at the fishing boat for sale next to him. They had only taken a cursory look at it on Saturday when Maggie and Marlon were there but he had liked the high sturdy curve of the wooden hull. The interior was another matter and he wanted to go over it with Clive before he made any decisions. He hopped off the ferry at Granville Island and walked round to the government fishing dock. There was no sign of Clive on the 'Betsy' and he banged on the cabin roof and called out his name. Clive's voice answered from below and he clambered over the side and peered down the hatchway.

"Come on down, Barney. I wasn't expecting to see you so soon – come to have another look at the 'Sea Mist'?" He lay reclining on the cabin settee with an open book on his chest. "Like some coffee? I'll put the kettle on – I could do with a cup to keep me awake."

"Coffee would be good," said Barney. "I've just had a drink and a hot meal – fatal combination for me in the middle of the day. Have you still got the keys for the fishing boat or did you hand them back?"

"No, I've still got them – I told my friend Steve, the harbourmaster, I had a possible buyer and he gave me a spare set to keep. He's keen to see it sold and have someone looking after it – wooden boats need regular attention and this one has been neglected for too long.- We'll take our coffee and have a good look around, okay?"

The two men climbed on deck and studied the hull of the fishing boat moored next to them. Barnacles and mussels completely covered the hull below the waterline but above it, the bow of the 'Sea Mist' looked strong and solid with no flaking paint or spreading seams. They moved to the dock and then walked down to the stern. An ugly painted plywood storage unit had been built on the open rear deck over the hatches, with padlocked sliding doors. The original forward cabin with its traditional curving set of windows had been left untouched.

"What's this thing for? asked Barney. "It doesn't look like a fishing boat to me."

"It belongs to a fishing club. They bought it to use for taking groups up to Desolation Sound for weekend trips and they needed extra storage and bunkroom – ugly isn't it?"

"Sure spoils the look of her. Can we go in the main cabin? I want to see the layout."

Clive unlocked the solid teak door. "Careful, the floorboards are up – Steve's been charging the batteries – there's the lump – six cylinder 'Jimmy' diesel – standard issue in most of the fishing fleet on the west coast."

Barney gazed down at the long muddy green shape filling the hold below the cabin floor. "My god, it's enormous – it must guzzle fuel."

Clive shrugged, "I don't think they're too bad – diesels are economical and these are virtually maintenance-free – built for the military and sold off as surplus to the fishing industry.

The fishermen say they're impossible to kill. That's what you want – total reliability."

Barney shook his head doubtfully. "I don't know – looks daunting to me."

"These are great boats – built by the Japanese fishermen at Steveston for the ocean-going fleet – this one was built in the sixties but it still has the original design from much earlier. They never changed it much."

"If it works don't fix it, eh?"

"The workshops have been preserved as a museum – it was all shut down during the war – the government shipped the Japanese off to internment camps and confiscated most of their land and property – not a pretty story to tell our grandchildren."

"Sounds like it belongs right up there alongside our treatment of the native Indians."

"Yeah, I guess so. Would we have done any differently, though? – Hindsight is a wonderful thing. - Look at this little beauty," said Clive, pointing to a square black and enamel stove in the lower cabin. "Diesel stove – you can cook on it and it heats the whole cabin – too hot for the summer though, that's why they put in this propane two-burner here." He glanced at his watch. "I'm expecting an old friend on 'Betsy' – why don't you have a good poke around and then meet me back on my boat?"

For the next half an hour, Barney went over every inch of the 'Sea Mist' discovering all the cupboards, hidden drawers and lockers and admiring the solid wood construction everywhere. It was built as a working boat and there were no fancy sailboat fittings – everything was heavy-duty instead, which made it appear very safe to his landlubber eye. He fantasized about removing the ugly bunk box on the stern deck and replacing it with a cozy living room cabin like the one on the 'Betsy'.

Back in the main cabin, he skirted respectfully around the huge green marine diesel and replaced the floor panels. He sat in the helmsman's seat and fondled all the controls. Looking out the window forward, he was startled out of his reverie by the sight of a shaven-headed monk in orange robes disappearing down the hatchway on Clive's boat. Intrigued, he finished locking up and went back aboard the 'Betsy'. Down in the cabin, a short stocky man in monk's robes stood and made him a slight bow.

"Barney, this is Bhante Dipa, the friend I was telling you about."

"Clive tells me you are also a Buddhist," said the monk. –"from England. There are many monks there, I believe, but here we are rather an oddity. Still, things are changing." – He laughed suddenly.

"What's so funny?" asked Clive.

"Nothing. I just heard myself. It is strange for a monk to be surprised by change. That is the whole basis of Buddhism – everything is change, nothing stays the same."

"How do you two know each other?" asked Barney.

"We grew up in the same small town on Vancouver Island," said Clive. "Went to school and college together. I was best man at his wedding and him at mine."

"You're married?"

The monk laughed again, shaking his shaven head. "No, that was many, many years ago – long before I became a monk."

"Turns out neither of us was the marrying kind – our wives realized this very soon," said Clive. "They dumped us for more likely prospects."

"You have no children, then?"

The monk nodded vigorously. "I have two very fine children and three grandchildren." He grinned at Barney's puzzled expression. "My wife remarried and she and her husband asked me to be the godfather of their children – I am a very fortunate man, eh?"

"Good karma," said Clive. "My ex won't have anything to do with me."

"Yes," said the monk, somberly. "It is very sad – His wife doesn't understand him." He glanced at Clive and then at Barney. A grin spread across his smooth round face and all three men burst out laughing.

"How did you become a monk?" said Barney. –"On the rebound?"

"In a way, yes. After my marriage broke up, I couldn't settle to anything and neither could Clive. He had bought an old sailboat and we decided to sail to Tahiti."

"In the 'Betsy'?"

"Oh no, this is a palace compared to that first boat, eh Clive?"

"Yeah, she was not the safest thing on the water – we had a couple of close shaves and decided to abandon the idea of Tahiti and ended up in Honolulu. I sold her there and we got jobs on a freighter going to Ceylon. I wanted to travel round India but Larry – Bhante Dipa, decided to stay in Ceylon."

"Is that where you became a monk?"

Bhante Dipa nodded. "Yes, eventually. My mother told me we had distant relatives who used to be tea planters in Sri Lanka, so I looked them up. They were very old by this time and no longer in the business, but they were very kind to me, took me all over the country in their old car. We visited several monasteries and they introduced me to lots of monks who would invite me to stay. Gradually, I found I was spending more and more time at the one monastery and the chief monk asked me if I would like to train there. I would teach them English and they would teach me about Buddhism. So I did. I stayed there for twenty-two years."

"What happened?"

"My old teacher – the abbot, said I should go back home and teach. He said they had plenty of teaching monks in Ceylon and didn't need me. So I came back to BC and moved to Salt Spring Island."

"Couldn't have been much call for Buddhist monks there," said Barney, remembering his camping trips around the popular tourist island.

"No, it was pretty quiet at first, so I just got on with building my cabin. My mother had left me some money when she died and I bought the piece of land with it. I grew most of my own food – being a vegetarian helps; I did some tutoring, and slowly people began to come to my meditation classes. You don't need much if you're a monk."

"And now he teaches all over BC," said Clive. "You must have seen posters for his classes in the libraries and community centres."

"Whenever I come over to Vancouver, Clive lets me stay on the 'Betsy'. It's very handy for downtown here. And Clive is used to my odd habits."

"Yeah, sometimes I sail over to Salt Spring and stay at his place. -You could come with me if you fancy it – me and Bhante have built some bunk houses for his meditation guests to stay in."

"They're very basic but comfortable," said Bhante Dipa. "We all take our meals together – you would be very welcome to come – just send me an email to make sure I'm there and that there's spare room."

"Sounds great," said Barney. "I'd like that – things have been moving pretty fast for me since I arrived – a weekend retreat would be good. I didn't know you were a Buddhist, Clive."

"I'm not – at least not a committed one like Bhante here, but I love the philosophy – makes complete sense for me – but when it comes to meditation, I don't have the discipline to practise every day. When I'm at sea, though, I think about it a lot – staring at the empty ocean."

"Me, too," said Bhante. "I have a fine view of Georgia Straight from my cabin and the sea is perfect for calming the mind for meditation."

"When someone gets to my age, said Barney – I'm sixty eight – do you think it's better to be involved with the world or simply observe it? – for a layman, I mean."

"Why not do both?" said Bhante. "I do. People think that Buddhism means quietism – it's just the opposite – in order to practise the teachings properly, you must get involved – that's what they were designed for – it's a way of living and compassion for others is what it's all about."

"My problem," said Barney, "is that when I get involved in anything my Buddhist practice disappears out the window."

The monk laughed. "You must be more like a Volkswagen – that's what I tell my students," said Bhante. "Do you remember that ad they used for a long time? – It just showed a plain picture of the standard Volkswagen beetle car – the shape everybody recognizes – and underneath at the bottom of the page, a single line – 'We all know what practice makes.'"

"Great ad," said Clive. "I remember it. I bet it sold a lot of cars."

"Well," said Bhante, "there's no mystery about it – you learn the teachings and you practise them – and if you 'practise diligently' as the Buddha said, you get better and better and eventually - you get enlightened."

"You make it all sound so easy," said Barney. "That's not my experience."

"No, not easy – but possible. Everyone can become enlightened, according to the Buddha – it may take a few lifetimes," the monk grinned, "but eventually you get there. Have you been practising meditation long, Barney?"

"Off and on – nearly ten years – but you'd never guess it – I still make a hash of most things I do."

"I doubt that," said Bhante. "You mustn't be too hard on yourself – we westerners carry an extra burden that the Buddha never had" –

"What's that, then?"

"'The protestant work ethic,'" said Bhante. "Once you shift that weight off your shoulders, it makes life a lot easier – look at Clive," he smiled.

"Yep," said Clive, "I never fell into its clutches – escaped unscathed – well, nearly."

"You're a happy man, Clive?"

"Contented, anyway. – Whether that makes me a good Buddhist or not, I'm not sure. You'll have to ask Bhante."

"He's on the way," said Bhante, "- on the way."

"Wish I felt the same," said Barney. "I feel more like Shelley – 'I fall upon the thorns of life – I bleed.'"

The three men laughed and Bhante rose to his feet. "Will you excuse me, I have some notes I must prepare for tonight's lecture. I hope to see you on Salt Spring, Barney, and hear some more of your exploits. Clive says you help run a soup kitchen – I've been trying for a long time to set up a night shelter – maybe we can compare notes." They shook hands and the monk retired into the rear cabin. Barney and Clive returned to the 'Sea Mist' for a final look.

"If I bought her, would you help me do her up, Clive? – Make sure I didn't make any ghastly mistakes – like this," he said, pointing to the plywood bunkhouse.

"Be glad to," said Clive. "I love telling other people what to do. First thing, you need to do is get her surveyed and then put in an offer. If she's sound – and I think she is, you could have yourself a very cheap boat."

"I just wish that old engine didn't frighten me so much," said Barney. "It's like an enormous green dragon lurking in the bilges."

"You'll learn to love it," said Clive, "- or at least respect it."

"I'd better be getting back home," said Barney. "This art show is starting to hot up –Bobbi and Eugene want me to go over the arrangements with them this evening. Do you think Bhante Dipa would be interested in coming to it?"

"I'll ask him. I know he loves calligraphy – he's done some beautiful pieces. If you come over to Salt Spring with me you can see some of his work."

"I'll tell Bobbi – maybe she'll want to include them in the show. – Let me know when the surveyor finishes his report, Clive and we can decide on an offer."

Barney left the fishing dock and walked back to catch the little ferry back to the West End. He would have liked to quiz the monk more closely – he liked his practical approach to life. Perhaps he could talk through some of his difficulties with him and try to get a clearer idea of how he should proceed. Things were getting a bit hectic and although he enjoyed all the excitement and stimulation of his new life here on the west coast, Barney felt he wasn't always seeing the larger picture. He thought of the Russian peasant proverb –'to live your life is not as simple as to cross a field'.

Back at the apartment, he was greeted by first Ralf, then Bobbi and Eugene, who had let themselves in with Eugene's key. They were becoming regular visitors now that the art show was becoming a reality and they liked to come over and drink beer and eat Barney's chili while they pored endlessly over the details for the show. True to her word, Bobbi had found half a dozen other students whose work they all agreed was up to the exacting standards they had set.

The apartment was now a changing kaleidoscope of colourful pieces that they rearranged continually with much heated discussion. Rozalin's collages from the basement store were moved up and downstairs as they tried them out around the walls of the apartment. Barney left the choice of work up to Eugene, who knew her work intimately and remembered when many of them were painted.

Often, the apartment was full of students from the art college, bringing their portfolios and pieces to be scrutinized by Bobbi's critical eye for inclusion or rejection from the show. Barney doled out consoling portions of chili to the unsuccessful and celebratory beers for the chosen few. The art show had galvanized many of the students into completing half-finished pieces, which had been lying about their rooms all year. Often they arrived with paint still wet on the canvas and had to prop the piece up on the kitchen counter to keep Ralf from smearing them with his nose. The smell of fresh linseed oil seemed to hold a great attraction for him.

This evening the discussion amongst the three of them centered on how to make the show unique amongst all the competing demands for people's attention in a city grown used to expecting the unusual.

"I've been thinking of making it like a fashion show with a catwalk," said Bobbi, "with the artists being the models and holding their own pictures in a continuous moving circuit and with an announcer introducing each piece. – Eugene thinks an art auction would be better."

"Only instead of a regular auction this would be for the option to be the first to get the picture on loan. The highest bidder pays for the first choice," explained Eugene.

"What if nobody bids?" said Barney, "then what?"

"Have you ever been to an art auction?" asked Eugene. "Somebody always bids something – they can't resist – and it's not as if they're buying it – it's only an option to borrow."

"I've already thought of that," said Bobbi. "We plant students in the crowd, to start the bidding and if no one else bids we don't charge them."

"I thought you wanted a fashion show?" said Barney.

"I do, but Eugene's auction is a good idea – get a bit of competition going."

"Maybe you can combine the two, somehow," said Barney.

Eugene frowned. "How?"

"I don't know – you and Bobbi work it out. –I'm tired. I'm going to bed. Turn out the lights when you leave." Barney shooed Ralf into his basket in the kitchen and went off to bed.

An hour later, he was woken from a deep sleep by the intercom buzzer. He stumbled out into the darkened hall, half-asleep.

"Hello?"

"Barney? – It's Trish – I know it's late, but please can I come up?"

"Huh? - Oh, yeah – okay." He pressed the door button and stood for a moment in the dark, then turned on the hall light and looked at his bleary eyes in the mirror. – What the hell was she doing here at this time of night? – He went into the bedroom to find his pocket watch and snapped it open – one-thirty-five. He pulled on his dressing gown and ran his fingers through his hair. A knock came on the door and he went out to open it.

"Trish – what's the matter? – It's half past one – are you okay?" A whiff of alcohol preceded her entry.

"Sorry, Barney, I was hoping you were still up. I've got to talk to you."

"Okay, sure – what about? – You want some coffee?"

She shook her head. "No thanks – it keeps me awake. – You know what you were saying, this afternoon – about helping me out?"

Barney nodded, "You need some money?"

"No – I need somewhere to stay – I've been walking around all evening trying to get up my nerve to ask you – I had a drink or two for Dutch courage. I'm afraid I didn't tell you the whole truth today. - I said I was staying with a friend.-"

"What happened – you have a row?"

"Not with her – her husband – he told her I'd have to leave or he would – he was tired of me sleeping in their living room. I can't go back – I promised her a week ago I'd leave."

"Look," said Barney, "you can stay here tonight and we can talk about it in the morning, okay? – You can use the spare room. It's a bit full of paintings at the moment – I'll go and clear you a space."

She followed him into the small bedroom and sank onto the bed.

"I'll get you a towel – the shower is across the hall.-You need anything else? Here – lift your feet up." He pulled off her shoes and swung her legs onto the bed. "See you in the morning."

She nodded. "Goodnight – and thanks, Barney."

He waved it aside and returned to his bedroom, only vaguely hearing her as she ran the shower. He was sound asleep by the time she came out and only dimly aware that she had crawled into bed with him and curved herself against his back. He slept on.

# CHAPTER 9

Rozalin LeClair had been staying in Giverny on the outskirts of Paris when Cassie finally tracked her down. She had been sketching the house where Monet painted his famous lily pond series, trying to avoid copying any of his paintings and instead only showing the lily ponds obliquely as an adjunct to the old house. Every day for a week now, she left her little *pension* in the village and walked to the gardens to sketch a different view.

She had pretty much decided it was time to move on when Cassie appeared. Rozalin didn't recognize her at first from Barney's description but after she had introduced herself, she began to see the likeness to her father. He had told her that his youngest child was studying French literature at the Sorbonne but despite his urging they had not met until now.

"You were lucky to catch me," said Rozalin. "I was about to pack up and leave tomorrow morning. What brings you way out here – not bad news, I hope?"

Cassie flopped down on the lawn beside Rozalin's portable easel and stool. "No, not at all. –I'm here on an errand of mercy."

"For me or to me?"

"For Barney – my dad, and someone called Eugene – a friend of yours, Dad says."

Rozalin abandoned her sketch and turned to face Cassie. She noticed her strong features and high forehead and thought what a good artist's model the girl would make. "That's right. Eugene is my greatest admirer and a true patron – he owns a collection of my work."

"Is he rich?" asked Cassie, leaning over to study the sketch on the easel.

"Oh, he doesn't have any of these – this is just my bread and butter painting – to earn a living. – No, he's not rich – he's my dog-walker. Eugene is an art student – a very good one as it happens – he walks dogs to pay his tuition." She studied Cassie's face. "He's about your age - twenty?"

"Twenty-one. - So what kind of your paintings does he collect, then?"

"More collages than paintings – they're what I do for myself – I've never sold any – except to Eugene. None of the galleries at home are interested – too bizarre, one dealer told me –"

"Too off the wall, eh?"

"They're certainly that," laughed Rozalin. "I've been storing them in my basement 'gallery'" – she made quote marks with her fingers "– for years."

"How come Eugene can afford them if he's so broke?"

"We have an arrangement – I pay him with my work and he walks my little dog. – You still haven't told me why you're here."

"Dad – Barney, asked me to find you. He and Eugene want me to persuade you to go back to Vancouver for the opening of your retrospective. He says you don't believe it will happen and I'm supposed to try to convince you."

"Eugene has been trying to persuade me for nearly three years without success," said Rozalin, folding up her easel and packing away her sketches. "You can try if you want – what about over lunch in the village? – there's a lovely little café I found on my first day with a few tables in the garden."

The two women walked back down the quiet lane towards the village, Cassie carrying the folding stool.

"How much longer do you have in Paris, Cassie?"

"Only a couple more months – but I may stay on – it depends."

"On who? – I assume there is a who?"

-Yes. Zinadine – he's asked me to go back to Africa with him – the Sudan– used to be a French colony."

"And will you?"

"I was thinking of trying to get a job with the UN as a translator and go out to work in the third world for awhile. But Zinadine says they need aid workers in his country who can speak the language too."

"He sounds pretty keen for you to go – what's the hitch? Your parents?"

"Oh, Dad's all for it – says he'll come out and join me – but Mum wants me to take a nice safe job with the UN in Paris – close to home and she can visit me regularly – and go shopping. –I think she thinks UN jobs are there for the taking – I told her there's about a hundred applicants for every position and they only take the 'crème de la crème.'"

In the little café, the aged *patron* fussed over his two charges, pampering them with an assortment of hors d'oeuvres made by his wife in the kitchen. The old woman came out to see who her late customers were and stood beaming at them with her arms folded across her ample stomach. She greeted Rozalin like a daughter and expressed her admiration for Cassie's immaculate French.

The *patron* shooed his wife back out to the kitchen with their order and plied them with more wine. Rozalin complimented him on his choice of house wine and he retreated behind the bar smiling broadly – A few moments later he returned with an opened bottle and clean glasses " Pour la Blanquette de veau," he explained. "Spécialité de la maison," he poured the wine with a modest flourish. He stood stroking the ends of his drooping mustache, waiting for them to try it.

"Buvez, - buvez," he urged. The two women saluted him and sipped the wine, making appropriate noises of approval.

Cassie tipped her glass at the old man, "`a vous, monsieur – santé". He nodded again and shuffled back to the kitchen to help his wife.

"This is what I miss in Vancouver," said Rozalin, sipping her wine. "Places like this just don't exist in North America."

"- Or England," said Cassie, "- they're all poncey high class restaurants charging crazy prices. – Another reason not to go home," she smiled at Rozalin. "– Is that why you won't go back for your show?"

Rozalin laughed, "It's a good excuse. - No, I'm only half-finished what I came here to do. I can't afford to simply abandon my work and go back for something that will probably turn out to be a non-event."

"Not the way Dad tells it," said Cassie. She speared a piece of veal on her fork and waved it expansively in the air. "It's going to be huge – the talk of the town, he says– and you're the star of the show," she said, pointing her fork at Rozalin.

"Maybe," said Rozalin. "– We'll see. I'm still not convinced. – I know Eugene means well but I've tried having a show before – no one's interested."

"Well, they are now, according to Dad. It's gathering momentum every week. I'd go like a shot if it was me – you can always come back after it's over."

"Expensive trip for nothing, though, if it bombs," said Rozalin.

"Aren't you flattered that all these people are going to so much trouble for you?"

"I didn't ask them to, remember?"

"Even so. It could be your big break-through. No more painting by numbers –"

"Is that what your father called my work? He told me he liked them."

"No, but you know what I mean," said Cassie.

"I'll think about it."

"Good," said Cassie, "I can go back to Paris with a clear conscience." She attacked her food happily and the two women finished their meal under the indulgent gaze of the old *patron* and his beaming wife.

On the slow SNCF train back to Paris, Cassie had plenty of time to mull over her next move. Rozalin had picked up on her relationship with Zinadine straight away – what she hadn't guessed was how deeply Cassie had become embroiled with him. If her mother knew, she would immediately assume her worst fears were realized – that her prediction that Cassie would be fair game for the first Frenchman to turn her head and she would get up the stump and then be unceremoniously dumped.

Cassie had indeed followed her mother's scenario unerringly and become pregnant a bare four months into her stay. She had been horribly homesick for her family but refused to say anything as she knew they were scattered and far from home – each busy with their own changing lives.

She was fair game for the first sympathetic boy she met in her class on seventeenth century French drama. Louis had taken her to see Racine's 'Phèdre' in a student production and later in his room whispered seductive lines from the old play in her ear –*'c'est trop peut dire aimer, cherie, je t'adore'*– while he slipped his hand under her blouse and expertly undid her bra. Cassie had stopped taking the pill out of a misplaced loyalty to her old boyfriend Will, back in England and her temporary lapse was seized on by her healthy young woman's body.

Louis told her he would pay for the abortion and wanted to continue seeing her but she was too traumatized by the whole messy business to speak to anyone for days after. When she did, it was not Louis she turned to but Lottie. They had met when Lottie had come over to sit beside her as she sat in one of the student cafés miserably staring into her coffee.

Lottie had long straw-coloured hair in a French plait over her shoulder and even longer legs, which she was not averse to using to her advantage. Her father was a Czech diplomat based in Paris and Lottie had her own small apartment near the Sorbonne.

"I cannot bear to see anyone looking so miserable," she announced in her heavily accented English, "- so I have come over to cheer you up. At first I thought you must be from Scandinavia, you looked so sad, but then I saw your copy of 'Pride and Prejudice' and I knew straight away – some man has done this to her – some French student has broken her heart – am I right?"

"Sort of – not exactly," Cassie ventured a weak smile. "– But you were right – I'm English."

"Do not let them get to you – they are like horses; when they throw you off, you must get up straight away and climb on another one. Believe me, I know. I have much experience of men – remember, they are only physically stronger, like the horses – but you are the rider – you hold the reins, okay?"

"I guess so – maybe."

"But it hurts when you get thrown off, yes? You are badly bruised, I think– but no broken bones?"

"Internal injuries, more like. – It could have been worse."

"Ahh, you see – already you are feeling a little better. Soon you will be ready for another ride – only this time you have learned a trick or two and you will keep the whip hand."

"I don't know about that," said Cassie. "– I think I'll stick to walking for the time being."

"But that is a big mistake – you must not admit defeat – you are English! You come from a race of strong women – you

172

have taught us all how to ride – look at Boadicea – Elizabeth the First - Queen Victoria – Maggie Thatcher! - Where would you be if they had all meekly given up at the first fence?"

"Maggie Thatcher is not my choice for a role model," said Cassie. "– I prefer Jane Austin."

"-And I prefer Simone de Beauvoir – she could write and think and act – even Sartre was no match for her. - And she could drink him under the table." – Lottie signaled the waiter and ordered two Armagnacs.

"– First, we must drink to our heroes and then to ourselves and then you must come and meet some new people and test your new skills." The waiter set down the two glasses and Lottie raised hers "– To Boadicea, who taught us to ride – and to us!"

"Cheers," said Cassie "– To Madame de Beauvoir." She drank the Armagnac down in one swallow. Lottie smiled her wide-mouthed smile.

"You see? – Your English blood is up. – Les Anglais!" She drained her glass in one gulp. "– And now we must go back into the fray." She linked her arm through Cassie's and strode on her long sleek legs out of the café followed by the gaze of a dozen young men.

The weeks and months that followed her encounter with Lottie swept Cassie into a whirl of left-wing politics - crowds of young men and women for whom university was only a base for their passionate political recruiting; where classes are relentlessly cut in favour of all-night café debates and heroic drinking followed by free-for-all sexual encounters with a continual changing of partners.

Her Czech friend Lottie was constantly dumping her conquests, who rebounded onto Cassie, placed as she was in the penumbra of her mentor. She enjoyed the excitement; the almost continual adrenalin rush and cherry-picked her way through the endless line of Lottie's castoffs.

Meanwhile, she kept up a long-distance relationship with her old boyfriend Will, back at North London Poly. He provided the stability she needed to prevent her from being overwhelmed by the onrushing Parisian whirligig. Somehow, Cassie managed to attend enough classes to scrape through her year and gain her degree.

In the midst of all this, stood Zinadine Touray and she stepped off Lottie's spinning carousel into the sober light of her future, reflected in his shining black face. He brought her up short and confronted her with a different reality from the impassioned rhetoric roiling about her in the cafés of the Sorbonne. Zinadine was studying law, which was anathema to most of Lottie's coterie who saw the law as the embodiment of the establishment they were determined to oust. He quickly disabused Cassie of these naïve assumptions.

The lawyers were the lawmakers and shaped the country for good or ill, he told her. If there was to be any real change in his country, he had to get his hands on the levers of power and the lawyers controlled the levers. Cassie urged her own case for social change through education – nothing would change until people learned how to deal with their oppressors.

"But we are both in agreement about one thing at least," said Zinadine. "We need change. Which comes first is another argument – a rather old one, I think."

"Chicken and egg arguments are a specialty of this place - I'm fed up with them," said Cassie. "I just want to get on with the job – not discuss how to do it endlessly."

"If you come to Sudan with me, we will be a powerful force for change. Stay here in Paris and you will end up shuffling papers at the UN all day and in the evening having chicken and egg arguments with Lottie's crowd."

"I could go back to England."

"You could," said Zinadine, "- but why? England's important battles are already won – they are only just beginning in my country. Come and see for yourself the real face of Africa."

"Aren't I already looking at it?" asked Cassie, smiling up at her shining black challenger.

"Yes, you are," he grinned widely, "-Do you like it?"

She did. And now she moved into another orbit – a black one of serious young men and women with single-minded aims – they would play the colonialists at their own game – exploitation. They took their skills and their guilt money with smiling faces, living for the day when they could return home and throw the usurpers out. They welcomed Cassie to their cause, at the same time letting her know she could never be more than a fellow-traveller; her skills were needed but her white face marked her out as ultimately untrustworthy.

Zinadine was her passport to the inner circle and she met confident, bold young men and women, whom he assured her were the next generation of leaders from countries whose names she barely recognized, so newly minted were they.

She reported all this to her parents and they reacted pretty much as she had expected. Barney emailed her long self-deprecating tales of his explorations of the soft underbelly of Vancouver – with people living on the streets the same as in the Third World but with a peculiar West Coast twist – they had their cell phones, their Nike trainers and their Starbucks coffee too. He applauded her intention to become an aid worker in Africa – her instincts were good, she had only to follow them. He was confident she would make a good fist of it wherever they led.

Alice was another matter. Her mother told her to meet her at the Gare du Nord Eurostar terminal the following weekend. The pretext was an archaeology conference she had been invited to as a student delegate, but her evenings would be free to spend with Cassie – they could compare notes on their student experiences, Alice had said, but Cassie was not taken in and she began rehearsing her arguments.

When her mother had first told her of her intention to return to university and do post-graduate work, she had been loyally supportive. Her support wavered slightly at the news that her parents had sold the family home. Cassie had not lived at home for nearly three years except for brief periods during the holidays but the thought of her old childhood home no longer being there, at least not for her – came as a surprising shock. She received an even bigger shock when her mother stepped off the Eurostar express on the arm of a large, shaggy bear of a man who was obviously more than a fellow passenger. Alice greeted her effusively to cover her nervousness.

"Darling, this is Hector Savage, my thesis tutor at Oxford – he wangled me the invite to the conference when I told him you were here."

"Heck," said Hector, enveloping Cassie's proffered hand in his large one. "Nice to meet you, at last. Your mother has been bragging about you practically the whole trip." He smiled at Cassie and picked up both their cases. "– Lead on,

Cassie. We're starving and we've been saving ourselves for a good blowout at one of your student haunts. Alice – your mother – says how much she envies you the food here – Oxford students have to survive on junk food – personally I think she exaggerates; I don't find it that bad."

"He wouldn't," Alice said to Cassie, "- not on a professor's salary - We poor students survive lower down the food chain." Heck made a wry face at Cassie and smiled.

"Well, you can make up for it here. I'm sure Cassie knows lots of good cheap places."

Cassie confined herself to smiling and observing the banter between her mother and Heck. Her initial surprise had made her a bit stiff and formal but she warmed to his avuncular manner and set aside her reservations at this unexpected turn of events.

"Where are you staying?" she asked. "– I hope Mum hasn't suggested my place – it would be standing room only."

"Oh no, sweetheart. Heck – we - booked a little one-star hotel near the university – it will be handy for the conference and to you."

"Yes," said Heck smoothly, "- we managed to get the last two rooms they had – the conference has filled up all the local hotels."

It was Cassie's turn to smile. "– Lucky you," she said. Alice blushed and took her daughter's arm.

"Now where did you say this restaurant was – not too far, I hope – I'm famished – but first I need a drink." Cassie steered them to a sidewalk café and they ordered drinks. Heck and Alice drank wine and she had a beer. They watched the early evening crowds hurrying past and enjoyed the spring sunshine.

"April in Paris," said Heck, "Cheers."

"April in Paris," echoed Alice and Cassie darted a quick glance at her mother, half-expecting her to start singing. Alice smiled and patted her hand "– It's alright, darling – I won't embarrass you." Heck looked quizzically at her but decided it was a family joke and said nothing. He sipped his wine.

"Not bad, for a house red. What do you think, Alice – should I put it on the list for the Common Room cellar?"

"You're the expert, Heck. You know me, - I'll drink anything."

"So, Doctor Savage," said Cassie, "- what are your patient's chances – will she survive at Oxford?"

Heck appeared to ponder this for a moment or two, drumming the table with his large fingers. "– Difficult to say at this stage – your mother suffers from quite a common malady among my students and a lot of them do succumb to the disease."

"I see," said Cassie, playing the straight man "– and what might that be?"

"Technically it's called 'hubris' but more commonly known as swollen head." He looked gravely at Cassie and they both turned to look at Alice.

"Just because I challenge him in his seminars and don't sit there meekly swallowing everything he says like the rest of his students; worshipping the great god Savage," said Alice airily.

"You see what I mean, Cassie," said Heck "– it's quite far advanced."

"Anyway," continued Alice, "– he's a fine one to talk – he writes a pot-boiler and gets lionized in the popular press and starts to pontificate on everything. - Talk about swollen heads!"

Heck appealed to Cassie. "I had the temerity to criticize certain rather shaky assumptions she had made in her thesis and she came down on me like a shelf of books – After all, I am meant to be her thesis advisor."

"Are you sure you two are going to be safe to leave wandering around Paris together?" said Cassie, "- I suppose I could offer my services as a referee."

"We'll be fine, sweetheart," said Alice. "– And anyway, we won't be wandering around loose that much - Heck is delivering a paper at the conference in a couple of days so he's a bit touchy," she smiled at him sweetly. "- He's afraid I might challenge him in front of all his august colleagues. – I shan't, of course. I know my place and I shall sit in it meekly – it's a small price to pay for a whole week in Paris."

"Mother sent me your new book, 'The Enemy Within' - she raved about it. –I'm sorry I haven't had a chance to read it yet – usual student excuses – too busy studying."

"She's right, of course," said Heck. "– It is a sort of 'pot boiler'- it was fun, though –"

Heck had a meeting with his French publisher the following afternoon and Alice and Cassie arranged to meet in the Galeries LaFayette to do some shopping. Alice had promised to help her replenish her wardrobe. Cassie helped them locate their hotel tucked in the back streets of the fifth arrondissement behind the Sorbonne and returned to her own room to wait for Zinadine. He was at a Pan African students meeting and might be hours yet.

She lay back on her bed with a textbook across her stomach and thought about her mother. Going back to university certainly agreed with her – she hadn't seen her so animated for a long time. Usually she came home to find her mother stressed out from her job and too tired to do anything more than listen to Cassie's latest exploits. Today she had hardly had a chance to tell her mother anything of her plans. She had expected Alice to tackle her straight away about turning down the chance to work at the UN and had her arguments ready but she would save them for tomorrow.

She abandoned her book and got into bed – she was too tired to wait up for Zinadine – he would have to tell her about the meeting tomorrow. She thought of Heck and her mother and smiled to herself in the dark. Could her mother possibly be having an affair with her professor at her age? He was certainly attractive if not exactly good-looking and she could see how her mother might well be drawn to him, even if he did seem younger than her.

Cassie felt a sudden pang of disloyalty to her father for feeling so well disposed towards this new man in her mother's life. Still, who knew what Barney was up to in Canada – they must have talked over this eventuality before they decided to separate for a year. She made a mental note to check it out with her mother tomorrow and dropped off to sleep.

In the afternoon, she spent a half hour tracking Alice down in the balconied depths of the Galeries. She found her in the perfumerie department trying free samples from the testers on display.

"Mother, for god's sake – you'll smell like a tart's boudoir."

"I know, but I can't resist –try this one, it's gorgeous," - she sprayed a cool mist on Cassie's arm before she could pull it away.

"Come on, - you promised to buy me some clothes and I'm going to hold you to it," said Cassie, pulling Alice by the arm and heading for the stairs. "– There's a sale on I want to see on the third floor. –"

They plundered the rails together, with Alice adding more items to Cassie's armload of clothes to try on. She sat outside the changing room as her daughter popped in and out, appearing in a different outfit each time. Cassie did not have her mother's flamboyant tastes and rejected most of the items Alice had selected, choosing instead a handful of simple, almost plain combinations of skirts, tops and trousers.

"Anyone would think you were going to be a nun," complained Alice. "Couldn't you choose something a bit more cheerful?"

"These are fine, mother. – They'll be perfect in Africa," she said, deliberately eyeing Alice.

"So you're really going through with this, are you? - Throwing up an opportunity to live in Paris and have a career in the UN. – I know some people who would kill for a chance like that."

"I already live in Paris – and I've told you a dozen times that it's not a foregone conclusion I will get the UN job – I've only been offered an interview –"

"All the same, it seems like you're throwing away a once-in-a-lifetime chance. And you know how dangerous and unstable most of these new African countries are – you see it practically every week on the news."

"Zinadine says the Sudan's not like that – it's fairly safe," said Cassie from behind the changing room curtain. Emboldened by the physical barrier, she added, "He says they need people like me out there to help rebuild the country – he says it's a chance to do something meaningful with my life instead of shuffling papers around at the UN."

The curtain swished aside and Alice stood there. "– And who exactly is this Zinadine? – he seems to have a lot to say for himself."

"I told you, he's one of my friends from Africa."

"You've told me about lots of people. – Is he someone special?"

"Yes."

"And he's the real reason you're going to Africa?"

"No. Partly – we've been kind of living together for the last few months."

Alice's eyes suddenly brimmed with tears and she gathered her daughter into her arms. "Oh sweetheart - If anything happened to you, I'd die – I know it –"

"Nothing will happen, mother, I promise." She stroked her mother's back. "I know you think I'm still a baby, but I'm twenty-two – nearly."

Alice released her and wiped her eyes with a tissue, shaking her head. "– You're wrong - I know you're not a baby and that you've slept with Will, but it's still hard to let you go – and Africa is so dangerous – I want to meet this young man. Why didn't you tell me you were living with him all this time?"

"Maybe the same reason you didn't tell me about Heck –I thought you wouldn't approve."

Alice sat down heavily on the bench in the changing room. "Listen, Cassie. Heck and I are not living together – we're just - good friends. – Besides, I'm still married to your father."

"I wanted to ask you about that," said Cassie, "- What kind of arrangement have you and Dad made anyway?"

"We didn't discuss it a great deal as we didn't think it would be much of an issue – we just agreed that if either of us met someone – we were – I don't know – released from our vow, I guess. It was his idea – I just sort of went along with it, and now –"

"You've met someone."

Alice nodded, smiling ruefully.

"Have you slept with him?"

Alice nodded again, "I expect you think I'm a terrible old hypocrite, but–"

"I liked him," said Cassie.

"So do I, God help me – he's fifty-three– seven years younger than me."

"You're not exactly cradle-snatching, mother. I expect he knows what he's doing."

"He says it doesn't make any difference to him – That's what I said to your father – he was eight years older than me."

"So – your turn now. What's the problem?"

"I have a sixty-year-old body, that's what's the problem – Anyway, enough about me; I really want to talk to you about Hunter."

"What about him?"

"He's disappeared. At least from my sight – have you heard from him?"

Cassie shook her head. "Not for ages – he doesn't reply to his old email address – I've been waiting for him to send me a new one – doesn't Netta know where he is?"

"No. She's the one who made me worried about him in the first place. She wrote to ask me where he was because she'd lost touch with him too.

"That doesn't sound like Hunter – he and Netta would never lose contact."

"That's why she was worried – she asked me to try to find him – she says he's been acting very strange and thinks he might do something foolish –"

"Like what?"

"She didn't say – did he seem okay the last time you spoke to him, Cassie?"

"I haven't spoken to him since I left England but we were emailing for a while. I don't know what's come over Hunter – he was such a high flyer at university and then – nothing – just travelling and drifting, doing dead-end jobs. – The last he wrote me he was working as a gardener for some wealthy couple in Hampstead."

"That was ages ago. He told me that, too when he visited me just after I moved to Oxford."

"Did he tell you he'd met some woman?" asked Cassie.

"No – who?"

"He didn't say – only that he'd just met her and that she was older than him."

"Maybe that's why we haven't heard from him – he's too busy with her – and learning how to garden."

"He was a biologist, mother."

"Maybe so, but he never showed any interest in our garden – I had to bribe him to cut the grass. And yet when he came to my tiny little flat in Oxford, he said it was a shame we'd sold the house – he would miss the garden."

"I miss it, too."

"The garden?"

"No – yes – the house, the street, the garden – everything. – Do you remember how we used to sleep in the tent in the garden and Dad would bring us gypsy toast for breakfast?"

"I had to promise not to lock the back door in case you heard a strange noise and wanted to come back inside," said Alice.

"Hunter read us stories using a torch till the batteries ran out, then he'd make up the rest and tell us in the dark. – We knew the endings anyway – I practically knew them all by heart – I just liked looking at the illustrations."

"I still have them all – safely stored away in a box – for your children." Alice began gathering up the unwanted clothes "– We'd better get out of here before they throw us out - Let's go and have some tea outside. Heck should be finished his meeting by now – I told him we'd be in the same café you took us to last night – the Two Parrots?"

"That's right near Zinadine's room," said Cassie.

"What a coincidence."

"No, it's not. That's why I took you there – he and I always meet at Les Deux Macau – he should be along shortly."

The two women strolled through the late afternoon shoppers, carrying their purchases and enjoying the warm spring weather and each other's company in equal measure. At the café, they sat contentedly basking in the sunshine, drinking tea from heavy white cups and waiting for their men.

# CHAPTER 10

When Heck had first proposed that Alice accompany him to Paris for the archaeology conference, she had hesitated; worried she might jeopardize his position if they should meet colleagues from the university. Heck had assured her there would be no one else from Oxford as far as he knew, and anyway, she had a perfectly legitimate reason to be there as a student delegate. Alice didn't need much persuading. The chance to spend time together as a normal couple without constantly worrying whether people would notice had made their relationship seem furtive and undercover.

At first, the need to keep it secret from the university authorities had been a challenge – a game they enjoyed playing but with serious consequences if they were caught. The university took a dim view of faculty who had affairs with students and Heck stood to lose his job if they found out.

It was Alice who appointed herself the watchdog role, always being scrupulously careful not to be seen anywhere with him which might be deemed compromising. It was she who kept him at arm's length when they were in public, remaining polite but aloof in all their chance encounters at the university and around town.

As her tutor, she was legitimately entitled to visit him in his capacious top-floor study and seminar room, with its comfortable old padded armchairs and couches. Heck would lock the door and carry her bodily to one of the couches where they would embrace fiercely for many minutes before every tutorial.

These were conducted from the settee with his head on her lap, his reading glasses perched on the end of his nose and piles of books and sheafs of notes heaped on the floor beside them. He was an excellent tutor and Alice a willing student and their allotted two hours flew past with disappointing speed.

At the end of the sessions, Alice studiously placed everything back on the seminar table and reapplied her makeup. If another student was waiting, they made their farewells before he unlocked the door. There had been no question that they allow their embraces to lead to anything further in Heck's study – Alice had been very firm about that and he acquiesced reluctantly, knowing it would be only a matter of time before they were discovered. And in truth, they both enjoyed these relaxed encounters when they could just be together like any ordinary couple sharing an evening at home.

In Alice's tiny flat above the bookstore, the roles were reversed and Heck became the willing student on the infrequent nights she allowed him to visit – ever mindful of his reputation. She refused point-blank to go to his big rambling house except to occasional parties he held for his post-grad students. Far too dangerous, she told him.

Heck would arrive always after dark and she let him in the back door where she kept her bike. Her iron-clad rule was that he had to leave before dawn and she always set the alarm. Usually he arrived with an armful of groceries – he liked to cook and Alice freely admitted she was only an indifferent cook but an excellent trencher-woman. Heck began by opening a bottle of wine from the Faculty Common Room selection and they shared a glass while he prepared the food.

In the safety of her own place, Alice relaxed and swanned in and out of the kitchen, nibbling at bits he prepared and feeding him others, cuddling him from behind and pulling him away from the kitchen to dance between the furniture in her cluttered living room. They would stand swaying in the middle of the room until the music from her portable CD player stopped and then she would push him back towards the kitchen. They ate by the oriel window where Alice set the table and finished off the bottle sprawled on the window seat gazing out at the tree-lined avenue.

After dinner, Alice went into the bedroom while Heck cleared the table. By the time he joined her she was already in bed, waiting for him. For the first few times, she lay firmly on her back, resisting any attempts Heck made to pull her on top of him until he had turned the light out. Then she willingly straddled him and rode up and down in the dark, waiting. When he began to moan, she stopped his mouth with kisses until he broke free with a roar. Then she clamped her hand firmly over his mouth.

"Agghh- ! mmphff-. unnghh!" roared Heck, writhing beneath her. Alice continued her rhythmic motion until he subsided and she felt it safe to remove her hand. She lay forward on his chest, her face in the hollow of his neck and eased out her aching legs. His sterterous breathing became more regular.

"Alice, you're going to smother me one of these times doing that," he said, stroking her back.

She smiled and felt for his mouth with her fingers, kissing him in the dark. "It's either that or have the police round because the neighbours think I'm being murdered."

"I'm not that loud," protested Heck into her hair. "– Am I?"

"Ho! You sound like a bull – roaring."

"Well, whose fault is that?" he said, running his hands down her flanks and over her bottom.

"I'm not complaining," said Alice. "– You are."

"Alice?"

"Mmm?"

"I've been thinking of leaving St Swithens – giving in my notice this year."

Alice propped her head up on her elbow on his chest. She stared into his face in the dark "– Are you insane? – What for, for god's sake?"

Heck pulled her back down and continued stroking her back. "– All this –" he waved his arm in the darkness "– sneaking about at night, lurking in alleyways –frightened to make a noise. If I went to London, say – there'd be no more student/teacher ethical conflict – we could live together normally."

"You hate London."

"I could get used to it – with you." He nuzzled her cheek but she pulled away.

"Just because I cover your mouth with my hand during sex, you want to throw over your whole career here? No – no way – I would never agree to that – in a year's time you'd be blaming me for it all – no thank you."

"Okay, okay, it was only an idea-"

"You'll just have to get used to me in my dominatrix role, that's all."

"Maybe I could buy you some leather gear – I know a shop in town that sells that stuff."

"I'll bet you do," said Alice, rolling off him and heading for the bathroom "–Get some handcuffs while you're at it. – I may need them."

After Heck had gone home, Alice was unable to get back to sleep. She took her duvet, curled up in her favourite place on the oriel window seat, and watched the dawn break over the leafy avenue. She listened to the astonishing crescendo of the dawn chorus as it swelled louder and louder. It mystified her how she had previously been able to sleep through such a cacophony of bird song. She often sat here waiting for the light on nights when Heck came around.

It was agony for her each time she evicted him from her bed when what she wanted was the exact opposite – to cling to him in those delicious moments of floating up to wakefulness and revelling in their unfolding intimacy. It was at moments like these when sleep deserted her that she retreated to her post at the window seat with her notebook, hoping for inspiration for her thesis.

Alice had compiled a formidable amount of research on her chosen topic and Heck urged her to keep reviewing it to see where the gaps lay. She had been on several field trips gathering material and even went as far as Scotland once to a newly uncovered dig on the Antonine Wall. Heck had led the excavation and invited her ostensibly because of the promising villa site, which might prove fruitful for her thesis.

Alice smiled to herself as she recalled that early encounter. She and Heck had not yet begun any physical relationship although they had been out together socially a few times. It was late October and the dig was winding down for the season. Most of the students had left and there were only a scattering of tents remaining on the remote site. Alice had pitched in with the general drudgery of site work and was rewarded by a grateful student.

Auberon, the lanky scarecrow youth she had met at the post-grad 'do' had helped her interpret his baffling 'geo-phiz' findings on the villa in return for several evenings' help she gave him with organizing his chaotic notes.

She had gained a reputation amongst the post-grad community for her efficiency and ability to pull seemingly disparate material together into a logical and coherent whole – the result of long years of assessing case notes and compiling dossiers. Alice had been the recipient of more than one student's gratitude and Auberon was by no means the first. The result of all this had been a willing sharing of material and hard-won insights with Alice and she had made enormous strides in her own thesis because of it.

Eventually even Auberon had left and Heck and Alice volunteered to stay and close down the site and store away all the remaining materials until the spring. Their two alpine tents stood separated by the mountain of neatly stacked gear waiting to be stored in the Land Rover for the trip back to Oxford.

Alice spent a last chilly day carefully labelling and photographing her finds from the villa while Heck continued the endless packing up. Food stocks were low and they cobbled together a makeshift last meal over the camp stove. They sat side by side drinking the dregs of two bottles of Heck's red wine and watching the changing colours of the Grampian Mountains forming the backdrop.

A sudden squall followed by a sharp dip in the temperature sent them scuttling for the nearest tent. They lay in their damp clothes, listening to the rain drumming on the canvas and trying not to cause leaks by touching the sides. Alice had made the first move by shedding her wet pullover and sliding into a sleeping bag to remove her jeans and socks. Heck watched her performance as she struggled with the wet denim. Finally, she produced the jeans from beneath the covers like a magician and handed them to him.

"Your turn," said Alice, burrowing down inside the bag.

"That happens to be my sleeping bag," said Heck. "– Hand it over."

"Not a chance," said Alice "–I'm freezing. – You could run over and get mine," she offered graciously.

"I'm not budging till this downpour is over," said Heck, lying back on the air mattress. "I'll just use my coat."

"You can't sleep in those wet clothes – you'll get pneumonia. Take them off."

Heck dutifully shucked his outer layers and lay back down in his boxer shorts under his dank coat waggling his stockinged feet. Alice shifted over beside him inside her sleeping bag. It was the first time they had been in such close confines since they met. Heck placed a tentative arm around her shoulders. They lay listening to the rain, which showed no signs of letting up.

"Alice?"

"Mmm?"

"Do you want me to sleep in the other tent?"

Alice burrowed closer – "No."

"Neither do I. – We could unzip the bag and use it for a blanket and put our coats on top."

"Okay - but you'd have to take your socks off."

"Deal," said Heck, expertly unzipping the bag and sliding it out from under Alice. She lay firmly on her back clad only in her underwear. He threw the opened bag over her and left his arm resting across her. She put her arms round his neck and drew him down on top of her. For a long time they lay without moving, listening to the rain.

"Are you waiting for me?" asked Alice. "–Or am I waiting for you?"

"Just give me the nod," grinned Heck.

"I thought I already had."

"Right–" He slid his hand down her side, but she stopped him briefly while she arched her back to unfasten her bra and slip it off. She raised her buttocks while he slid off her knickers and she helped him out of his underpants.

"You've still got your socks on –"

"I forgot – I got distracted," said Heck.

"Only prostitutes sleep with men with their socks on."

"Is that a fact?" said Heck, removing the offending garments. They jockeyed for position briefly but Alice won out, remaining on her back and they glided up and down to the rhythm of the rain.

"It was very decent of you to offer to close down the site," said Alice, running her fingers up and down his back. "– Do you think Auberon suspected anything?"

"Auberon only thinks of one thing," said Heck. "– Archaeology. He eats, sleeps and breathes it."

"And you don't?"

"Not anymore – not now. This beats geo-phiz hands down."

"You planned this all along, didn't you," said Alice. "– Admit it."

Heck nodded "–I didn't reckon on the rain though – that was a bonus."

"Or me being so brazen," said Alice, nibbling at his earlobe.

"I need all the help I can get," admitted Heck. "– I'm no Don Juan."

For a while, they undulated companionably in the now darkened tent, barely able to make out each other's faces. Eventually Alice spoke.

"Shall I go first?"

He nodded assent and she pressed his head down on her breast, guided his hands with hers while she moved and tensed, and gave herself up to the urgings of her body in long shuddering climaxes.

"Mmmmm – that was nice – it's been a long time." She stroked his back and they lay still for several moments, kissing occasionally. Alice traced the outline of his ear with her finger.

"– I don't suppose you'd be interested in finishing what you started?"

"Try me," said Heck, and she rolled him onto his back, swung her leg over him and rose to sit astride him in the dark.

It was only when his moans led to roars, that Alice first began to perfect her technique of clamping her hand over his mouth to stifle them.

"-What are you doing?" gasped Heck when he had regained his breath.

"You were making a terrible racket, and anybody might hear."

"We're in the middle of nowhere, Alice."

"We're in a tent – sound carries right through the walls."

"There's nobody out there except sheep."

"All the same, someone might have come along. – Did I put you off your stroke?"

"No, not quite."

"Well, then," she leaned down in the dark and kissed him, then suddenly stiffened and screamed in pain.

"What – what's wrong?" said Heck, lunging up to a sitting position.

"My leg – owwhhh!"

"What – did you get bitten?" Heck scrabbled around in his rucksack for a torch.

"Cramp!" said Alice, clutching her thigh, "- Ohh shit!"

"Lie down," ordered Heck, pushing her face-down. "– Where?" He still hadn't found his torch and Alice steered his hand to her left thigh.

"Here – aaghh!"

Heck found the knotted muscle and started to knead it vigorously with his long fingers. Alice shrieked again. "– Christ! I'm not a bloody horse – go easy!"

"Sorry –" Heck prodded it more gently and massaged it with long deep strokes.

"Ahh, that's better – lower," she instructed. "- There, right there – ahh – God, I thought I'd been stabbed."

"Now who's making the racket? I didn't notice you worrying about the neighbours just then."

"You said they were only sheep."

"It's like a scene from the moors murders," said Heck, continuing to massage with one hand while he fished about for the missing torch– "right - here we are – let's have a look –" He shone the light on Alice's bare rump, and then slid his hand appreciatively up over it. Alice turned her head to look over her shoulder at him.

"Alright Doctor, just keep your mind on your work."

Heck grinned and returned to massaging her leg. "That better?"

"Mmm, - much. – Thanks."

"Anything else I can help you with?"

"I'm thinking," said Alice.

"In that case," said Heck, leaning down to kiss her bare bottom, "– Where was I when you so rudely interrupted?"

"You were going to go to sleep," she said, rolling over and reaching for his straying hand. Heck kissed his way slowly up her body to her mouth.

"Are you sure you're feeling sleepy?"

"Very," said Alice, switching off the torch and turning to curl her back to him. She pulled his arm over her like a blanket. "– And so are you."

On the return trip to Oxford, Heck detoured to show Alice the long curving line of Roman forts that stretched all the way back through Eastern Scotland to Hadrian's Wall. All of the sites were closed for the season but they managed to wander around most of the unfenced ones and Heck gave her potted histories of each. His knowledge of Romano-British history was encyclopedic and Alice picked his brains ruthlessly, garnering material for her thesis.

Back in Oxford, she plunged into her research and seminars with delight. Whole days vanished in the Bodleian Library while she scoured the stacks under the great rotunda. She continued doing her editorial work with her fellow students and cooked mountains of pasta in a vain attempt to sate their raging appetites.

"Auberon," she said to him once, after she swore he had eaten his own body weight in spaghetti bolognaise "– didn't your mother ever feed you as a child?"

"Not like you, Alice," he grinned, wiping his mouth. "– Not like you. –I'm stuffed." He pushed back his chair.

"Well, that's a relief – maybe we can do a bit of archaeology now – unless you want to go and sleep it off." Alice pushed a neat stack of re-organised notes in front of him, while removing his plate. "Here's the latest version of your last lot of notes – I hope they make more sense to you than they did to me – honestly, Auberon, I don't know how they ever let you into Oxford – these were a complete dog's breakfast."

He grinned again, "Oh, they're letting anyone in these days – hadn't you noticed?" Alice threw a tea towel at him.

"Don't press your luck, sonny – just because you can make sense out of that 'geo-phiz' contraption – where's the results you promised me, by the way?"

"I forgot to bring them with me," said Auberon, flipping admiringly through the sheaf of notes. "–This is great, Alice – I love you –" He hugged her and kissed her cheek.

"Don't think you're getting any more meals out of me until I see those results. I'm onto your little game."

"I promise," said Auberon, pulling on his old leather jacket. He towered over her, his long, lanky young man's frame seeming even taller beside Alice. "–You know, I'd marry you like a shot - if you weren't already spoken for –" He paused in the doorway and smiled at her.

"What's that supposed to mean?" said Alice, suddenly rattled. But Auberon only smiled again as he closed the door.

When Heck arrived later that evening, he found a badly shaken Alice. She turned on him before he could get his coat off.

"What have you been saying to Auberon?" she demanded. "– Or anyone else, for that matter –"

"Auberon? – about what?" He tried to kiss her but she held him off.

"About us – you haven't been bragging down at the Mitre, have you?"

"Why, what did he say?"

"He seemed to imply that I was your property."

"What? – Where did he get that idea from?"

"From you, presumably," said Alice. "– Where else? – I certainly didn't say anything."

"Alice – you don't think I …? – This is ridiculous – tell me what he said exactly. Come over here and sit down –" They sat in the window seat and Alice reconstructed the conversation for him. He frowned and digested the implication of Auberon's remark. "– Did he actually mention my name?"

Alice shook her head dumbly.

"– Maybe he was just teasing – you know Auberon – he probably was referring to your husband."

"It didn't sound like that to me." She got up and went over to look out the oriel window. "– I think you should leave, Heck, and not see me any more –"

"Alice – you're over-reacting – Auberon knows nothing."

"Maybe he's seen you come here at night – or leave in the morning."

Heck snorted, "Are you kidding? – He never goes to a morning class – can't get up before noon –"

"I still think we should break it off, Heck – you could lose your job – your reputation – it's not worth risking your career."

"You're not seriously suggesting we stop seeing each other, Alice? – Because of a chance remark – what would we do? – I'm still your tutor and your thesis advisor. – We have to continue – just be more careful."

"I don't want you to come here anymore, Heck – I'd feel horrible if you lost your job because of me – it would spoil everything. I'd sooner leave myself – maybe I should anyway."

"Alice – please – don't talk like this – we'll think of something – we could arrange to meet somewhere else – out of town, maybe."

"I don't know, Heck – but not here – Now go, please – I'm frightened just having you here – we must have been crazy thinking we could carry on this way in a place like Oxford without somebody finding out about it."

"Promise me you'll meet me somewhere else – We can at least discuss it over the phone."

"Maybe – alright – where though? – And how?"

"God – I don't know – let me think about it and call you later – Jesus, that bloody Auberon!"

"Be careful when you leave, Heck. – And whatever you do, don't say anything to Auberon – or anyone else, either."

"Jesus – what a mess – I'll call you tomorrow, I promise."

Alice spent a sleepless night and missed her seminar class the next morning. Heck phoned as soon as it was over. "Alice? – What happened – where were you? – I could hardly think straight when you didn't show up –"

"I overslept – I was awake all night and then I fell asleep about dawn."

"I thought you'd gone away – promise me you won't leave town, Alice."

"I won't – just don't come over right now, okay? – I'm too nervous."

"Alice, I was thinking what we should do – I didn't sleep much, either. – If you took the bus to Datchet this evening, I'd meet you there and we could spend the weekend some place in the country – find a quiet B&B somewhere - how does that sound?"

"Okay, I guess – as long as we're far away from Oxford."

"Don't worry, I'll choose somewhere safe –"

The days and weeks that followed were a blur of activity for Alice as she buried herself in her studies in an attempt to fill the void left by her abruptly ended relationship with Heck. They had made several unsuccessful forays into the beautiful countryside of Oxfordshire and neighbouring

Warwickshire, but she could not relax and was forever looking over her shoulder, fearful of recognition.

Their earlier carefree times had vanished and left only an uneasiness and furtiveness, which both of them had to admit to. Heck had reiterated his intention to give in his notice and move to another university and although Alice objected strenuously, he remained firm. It was time for a change anyway, he told her. He was becoming stale and too comfortable at St. Swithens and needed a new challenge.

"It needed you to come along and tell me I was reduced to writing pot-boilers, Alice."

"Please, Heck, don't make me feel any guiltier than I already am. Let's just break things off until this year is over and I've finished my classes here. I can work on writing my thesis in London next year and we can decide then if we want to go on – it's only a few more months."

"You mean not meet at all?"

"These weekends aren't working, Heck. They're only making us more unhappy, worrying about being caught like a couple of guilty teenagers."

"What about our tutorials? – we'll have to continue those at least."

"No more sessions on your seminar couch, Heck. I'll bet that's where this whole rumour got started – with us being together behind a locked door. – We can meet in the Bodleian Library - in public."

And that was how they had left it. Alice even stopped going to Heck's informal post-grad parties in his big rambling house, or attending only briefly and occasionally to avoid arousing suspicion; begging off early, pleading pressure of work.

She filled the gaps left in her evenings with helping her fellow grad students when they asked for her editorial assistance, even continuing to sort through Auberon's chaotic research. He was nearing his thesis submission and had grown increasingly dependent on Alice to help him marshal his material. He made no further mention of his earlier remark and she wisely decided not to allude to it again. Maybe Heck had been right and it was only a joking remark. At any rate, she would give him no further cause to comment.

Gradually as the weeks passed and the panic that had spooked her began to subside, Alice relaxed her guard. Although she adamantly refused to return to their old habits of intimacy, she was able to resume some sort of normal behaviour with Heck. She began to challenge him again in the safety of the seminar classes and the feeling of misery, which had settled on her, slowly lifted. She was naturally ebullient and she bounced back with renewed enjoyment into her role as a mature student.

She started having weekly Friday evening parties in her flat and inviting cross-sections of the student community to drop in for food or a drink. Her training in feeding hordes of teenagers resurfaced and she covered the countertops of her tiny kitchen with buffet-style food and a carton each of red and white wine to start things off. She kept it deliberately informal by collecting heaps of cushions from charity shops and scattering them about on the floor. She herself took the lead by always sitting on one and leaning back against the wall, leaving people to help themselves.

The little flat above the bookshop filled rapidly on Friday nights with people dropping in and out over the course of the evening and using it as a meeting place either before or after going out. Alice herself would occasionally de-camp with a group of students for a couple of hours to see a film or hear a visiting speaker, leaving the others to carry on until she returned.

Because her hospitality was so freely offered, it was seldom abused and students who would not normally lift a finger in their own parents' homes, would take it upon themselves to clear up the debris and aftermath of these Friday night get-togethers.

Alice would often leave them talking and arguing long into the night while she brewed a small pot of tea and retired to her bedroom to read. The background hum of conversation lulled her to sleep. A lifetime of rising early for children and work meant that she was often padding about in the morning, quietly restoring order out of chaos and brewing pots of coffee for the inevitable handful of students who had opted to spend the remainder of the night on cushions on the floor, rather than trekking back to some distant room.

It was on one of these Friday nights that her old friend Stevie had arrived to spend a weekend. While she and Heck had been seeing each other she had stalled inviting her friend to stay, but now that she was once again holding open house, she had urged Stevie to come.

Her Friday evenings had become so much a fixture that there was no question of cancelling one – the students would have just showed up anyway, so she simply press-ganged Stevie into helping her prepare. Her friend had arrived just after lunch and they used her car to collect food and drink from the supermarket. Stevie parked her car in the alleyway behind the bookshop and they carted the supplies up to the little kitchen.

Stevie, whose own house was a spacious Georgian farmhouse, laughed aloud with pleasure when she saw the size of Alice's student quarters.

"Alice, it's wonderful – I love it – and you've made it so cosy."

She plonked her large frame down on the oriel window seat. "– I can just see you sitting here with a book."

Alice smiled, "My favourite place – whenever it all gets too much and I think I've made a terrible mistake coming to Oxford, I just curl up there in the foetal position and gaze out the window."

"I would kill for a little place like this," said Stevie. "– And in Oxford! – Trust you to come up trumps – I'd have wound up in some dreary bed-sitter in a basement in the suburbs."

Alice smiled at her friend. The thought of Stevie, whose lifestyle could best be described as four-star, living in a basement, was laughable. "Well, you've got the whole weekend to play at being a student," she said. "You can start by helping me get some of this food ready."

"You've got enough pasta here to feed the five thousand, Alice."

"Pasta's cheap and students are hollow inside – or have you forgotten so soon?"

The two women worked methodically and happily preparing the food for the evening; covering each dish and storing it in the old walk-in pantry off the kitchen. Unlike Alice, Stevie was an excellent cook and at home she had an enviable 'batterie de cuisine' at her disposal. Here in Alice's cramped little kitchen, she was obviously enjoying the challenge of making do with only the basic equipment her friend had accumulated from charity shops.

As she whisked a cheese sauce with only a fork, she informed Alice that she would bring her one of her collection of whisks next time she came to Oxford.

"If you have parties this size, I guess I can stop worrying about you being lonely here, Alice."

"I was a bit at first, but everybody sort of adopted me as a surrogate mother. Most of them are still babies and just want looking after – and feeding," she said, putting a mound of carrot and celery sticks in a plastic tub. "– I didn't particularly want to become Mother Teresa but – you do what you have to –"

"Any time you get tired of the role, I'll take over," said Stevie. "I haven't had a houseful of young people since Caroline's wedding – do you really do this every Friday?"

"Yes, I've become an Oxford institution in only seven months."

"And is it only graduate students or do you ask any faculty members?"

"I don't really invite anybody anymore – they just show up for awhile to see who's here and then move on or come back later."

"What time does it all end?"

"I don't know, exactly – I usually leave them to it and go to bed around one. I'll chase them out tonight as you'll be sleeping right there," she pointed to the squashy old overstuffed sofa. "– Do you think you can last till one?"

"Don't worry about me, I'll be fine. This is all a bonus – I thought we'd be just sitting around talking all weekend."

"I sometimes go to one of the student pubs for an hour or so later in the evening with a few of the regulars – would you like to do that? – we don't have to, if you don't fancy it."

"Why not? – I'm game – things can get very dull around home – it's not the same since you and Barney left. – What do you hear from him? He never sends us anything other than a postcard –"

"Oh, you know Barney – he's ploughing his own furrow – we keep in touch by email – from the sounds of things, I don't think we'll see him back here any time soon."

"Why, where's he off to now, for god's sake?"

"Africa; China – Tibet."

"He's really taking this Third Age business seriously, then?"

"Seems like – says he wants to work in a third world country next – as an aid worker volunteer – He told Cassie if she went to Africa, he'd come and join her."

"I thought you said she was getting a job in Paris with the UN?"

"Not anymore – she met a boy from the Sudan and he's persuaded her to go out there with him."

"Sudan- that's not that place where all the fighting was going on recently, is it?"

"I don't think so. Cassie says it's supposed to be very stable and calm there. I did my best to talk her out of it, but she won't change her mind."

"Paris *and* the UN – if I had a job offer like that, wild horses wouldn't drag me away  - he must be very persuasive, this boyfriend of hers."

"I was supposed to meet him when Heck and I were in Paris for the archaeology conference, but he never made an appearance. I think Cassie warned him I'd be gunning for him."

"So when do I get to meet Heck? – You *are* planning to produce him this weekend, Alice? - Tell me about your Paris trip - Did you stay with Cassie or with him?"

"With him. We had a funny little hotel near the Sorbonne where he was giving his paper on the Romans in Scotland – en Ecosse – he was nervous as a cat because he was giving it in French."

"Does Cassie know you're sleeping with him?"

Alice nodded, "I had to tell her, in the end – even though Heck had booked separate rooms. - She just asked me, straight out and I couldn't lie to her."

"You astound me, Alice," said Stevie. "–How you have the nerve to take all your clothes off in front of a complete stranger – If I did that, they'd run a mile."

"He's not exactly a stranger, Stevie. I met him on the first day I arrived in Oxford – and he is my thesis advisor."

"You know what I mean. – I don't even like Charles seeing me in the noddy anymore – too many raddles. Not that he can see anything once he takes his glasses off – I'm just a blur. He says I look like one of those nude paintings by Renoir – you know, those big fat women who look like melting strawberry ice-cream."

"I make sure I'm in bed first," said Alice "– and lying on my back. That way gravity takes over and smoothes out all my wrinkles."

"You let him have sex with the light on? My god – a man six years younger than you. – Isn't that a bit risky?"

"Oh, I stick to the missionary position – I don't look too bad that way – except for my breasts – they roll into my armpits unless I keep my arms at my sides. If he wants to try anything fancy, it's strictly lights out."

"He must have thought you were a virgin the first time he saw you lying rigid like that," laughed Stevie. "– Or else you were planning something kinky."

"He might have – especially when I nearly smothered him when he started roaring. He makes so much noise I have to put my hand over his mouth – it's quite funny – his face goes red and his eyes bulge," she started giggling too and the two women stood in the kitchen clutching each other and shrieking with laughter.

"God, I would love to be a fly on the wall," said Stevie, wiping her eyes on her apron. "– I'm not going to be able to keep a straight face when I meet this man."

"You'd better, or you can forget about seeing him – if you make the slightest hint, Stevie –" she brandished the butcher's knife at her.

"Okay, okay –" Stevie pursed her lips and made a zipping motion with her hand. "– I promise."

They finished putting the last of the food away and carried mugs of tea over to the sofa and sat in companionable silence for a while.

"Is it how you'd expected it would be, Alice?" asked Stevie, waving her hand in a wide encompassing circle. "–All this?"

"In some ways, yes. – I love all the academic stuff, - the research - and the field trips and digs – it's hard work sometimes, but I still enjoy it all," said Alice. "– I hadn't reckoned on the other bit, though –"

"Heck?"

"Yes. It's been a kind of roller-coaster time."

"Are you sorry you got involved, Alice?"

"Don't be daft – that's been the best part – it just –took me by surprise, is all. I hadn't foreseen that particular eventuality. – I guess I kind of saw myself alone here, -like a nun, studying in my little monastic cell –"

"Some nun you'd make," said Stevie. "–You'd end up with all the monks queuing outside your cell."

"Probably – I was never much good at resisting forbidden fruit. I don't have your capacity for self-discipline, Stevie."

"Me? – It's timidity that's my strong point – stick in the middle of the crowd – keep your head down – that's been my philosophy. I envy what you've done, Alice. – I could only dream about it. You take risks – I just take care."

"I wish I'd taken a bit more care, sometimes – you've still got a home and a husband."

"You had all that – and it wasn't enough. It's not enough for me either, but I haven't got your nerve to throw it all in and do what you've done."

"What's stopping you? – Charles?"

"Charles wouldn't even notice I was gone – he's so embroiled in his business, I've just become part of the fixtures and fittings."

"Nonsense – he dotes on you, Stevie."

"Maybe. – Charles isn't the problem, it's me. He's perfectly happy doing what he likes and I'm just along for the ride. I guess I didn't realize how bored I was getting with the scenery until you and Barney decided to up sticks and go – I really miss you, Alice –" She leaned across the sofa and the two women hugged each other awkwardly. "–I've heard some women really do go crazy in the menopause – do you think that's what's happening to me?"

"I hope so," grinned Alice. "–I could use some company. –It gets scary out here by myself sometimes – that's when I miss you."

"Not Barney? – Don't you miss him, Alice?"

"Sure, but not the same way – he was good company but we could never talk the way you and I do."

"Charles and I hardly talk at all – except about the house or the kids – or the garden."

"If I had a garden like yours, I'd never leave it. That is my dream home – a Georgian house with a walled garden – and you've got it. I try not to envy you, Stevie, but it's hard."

"It's the only thing that keeps me sane, I think. – Pottering about in my garden. – I thought when I had grandchildren I would feel less restless, but I don't. I love to see them but I'm always relieved when they go. And Charles is no better – he pretends to want them to stay but he's just as relieved as me to see them leave. – What's wrong with our generation, Alice? I don't remember my grandparents bitching and moaning like we do all the time. They always seemed so contented to me as a kid."

"Mine too. I adored my grandparents – probably because they spoiled me rotten – tough act to follow – I expect I'll make a hash of it when my turn comes. Some role-models we'll be – Barney in Tibet in some monastery and me in a hole in the ground in Scotland." Alice looked at her watch. "– We'd better make a move if you want to meet Heck. He's offered to buy us afternoon tea in town at four."

The teashop was crowded with students dutifully entertaining visiting parents and they found a table in the corner.

"Neutral territory," explained Alice. "–We can afford to be seen here together with you as chaperone."

"You make me feel like someone's granny," protested Stevie.

"You are someone's granny. – Now remember what you promised – not a word about what I told you –"

"Not a dickie-bird," promised Stevie, looking towards the cake counter. "– Is that him, Alice?"

Alice turned to look and Heck spotted her. He threaded his way through the tables to them, and Alice introduced him. While they waited for the tea, Stevie pulled a book from her handbag.

"Alice told me so much about your book; I bought a copy for you to sign."

"This will become very rare, Stevie," said Heck, writing on the flyleaf. "– My first and last attempt at fiction – Alice has shown me the error of my ways."

"Don't listen to him, Stevie. He got a mild ticking-off from the Dean and he's tried to blame me for stopping writing - just because I offered some innocuous comment about it."

"She called it a potboiler," Heck told Stevie "– Very hurtful thing to say, wouldn't you agree?"

Stevie nodded sympathetically, "I've felt the side of her tongue on many occasions, Heck. I wouldn't take it too personally, I'm sure it's a fine book."

"I've already told him that, he's only fishing for compliments. – Are you two going to have one of these cakes or not?"

"I'll share one with you, Alice – they go straight on my hips but I can't help myself. - Will you be coming to Alice's gathering tonight, Heck?"

"Banned," said Heck, "–Alice says I put too much of a damper on the works – always 'pontificating' I believe is the word she used."

"The students just clam up whenever he's around," said Alice defensively, "-It turns into a lecture instead of a party. – I've been to his parties, I know what happens – all that adulation gets very tedious."

"Alice runs the anarchist branch of the archaeology department," explained Heck, "much more fun for the students – you'll enjoy yourself, Stevie. – I have a tutorial in a few minutes - I'm afraid you'll have to excuse me. Next time, you'll have to come to one of my parties, – they're not as dull as Alice makes out."

"The wine is definitely better," Alice conceded. "– Bye, Heck, thanks for tea."

They watched him until he left the teashop and Stevie turned to look at her friend. "Well, well – aren't you the dark horse?"

Alice smiled happily, "-Yes, he is kind of nice, isn't he?"

"Nice! – And to think I've been worrying about you all this time. –So. Where do you go from here, Alice? – Have you told Barney about him?"

"Not yet. – He doesn't tell me what he gets up to and I don't ask – it cuts both ways."

"But you must have thought about it – what does Heck say?"

"He wants me to move to London with him so we can live together – he's talking about handing in his notice at St. Swithens."

"That sounds pretty serious to me – what did you say?"

"I told him he was crazy to even think about it, but he's dead set on going anyway, even if I don't go with him – says he's become stale here and wants a fresh start."

"Now where have I heard that before?" said Stevie. "– Let me see, could it possibly have been Barney?"

"Yes, I know – people of a certain age – men particularly, seem to catch some sort of virus – addles their brain and they go berserk."

"Is that what happened to Barney?"

"Can you think of any other explanation for throwing up everything and going off half-way round the world to live in a rented room?"

"Growing old, maybe?"

"The dreaded Third Age – God preserve us, Stevie."

"Oh, I don't know – I used to like listening to Barney rabbit on about it – sounded nice and freeing – a good excuse to pack it all in and do something completely different. – I don't see Charles ever succumbing, though. – He's welded to his computer."

Alice shook her head. "Not me. I'm in denial - like Woody Allen – he said, 'recently I turned sixty – practically a third of my life is over.'"

"Sixty – god, it sounds ancient – I have to believe it though when I look in the mirror. – What's your secret, Alice?"

"I already told you– assume the missionary position and let gravity take over."

Back in Alice's flat, they began laying out the food and scattering the heaps of cushions amongst the furniture. Stevie opened one of the classy bottles of red wine she had brought and they shared it while they waited for the first students to arrive.

Just after seven, Amrit and Deva arrived with their new baby. Amrit was doing his doctorate and they were here on a fellowship from New Delhi. Alice had been helping him to polish his written prose, which was riddled with all the odd turns of phrase Indians used when they adopted the English language.

"Please to not worry, Mrs. Roper. We shall not be staying – only we came to show you our new baby. – Here she is –" he pulled Deva forward with the tiny baby in her arms.

"Oh, she's gorgeous," said Alice. "– What will you call her, Deva?"

"I was thinking Rita – do you think it fits?"

"Perfect – look Stevie – look at these beautiful little fingers."

"Please may I hold her?" said Stevie. "– I have two grandchildren – I promise to be very careful." – She sat on the sofa and Deva put the baby in her lap.

Alice handed Amrit and Deva glasses of wine and then raised her own. "– To Rita." They all drank a toast. "– You must be very proud, Amrit."

Amrit beamed "– Oh we are pleased as punch."

Alice smiled at them. "–I should think you would be – congratulations!" She set her glass down. "– My turn now, Stevie. You can get them something to eat while I hold her."

"No, really, Mrs. Roper," said Deva. "– I made Amrit promise we wouldn't stay – nobody wants babies spoiling a party."

"Just for awhile, Deva. She'll be the star of the evening – everyone will want to hold her. – Please – have some food. Stevie and I will be hurt if you don't –we've been slaving away all afternoon. Look – here's Auberon and Sally –"

The room began to fill up with people – mostly the married couples at first, the men thumping Amrit on the back and the women crowding round Deva to admire the baby. Alice had been playing some classical piano CDs but as the younger single students arrived, the music changed to a louder insistent beat and the level of conversation noise rose.

Amrit and Deva made their goodbyes and left with the baby, after promising to return during the daytime later in the week. Stevie sat on the floor with a group of graduate students Alice had introduced her to, listening to them recite the litany of the persecuted life of students, wherever two or three are gathered together. Auberon was explaining to Sally and Alice his latest theory on the future of 'geo-phiz' and how his thesis was going to revolutionise archaeology.

"Digs will become a thing of the past, Alice. – You can put away your spade and trowel – no more navvying and scrabbling about in the mud."

"But that's what I like best," protested Alice. "– And besides, I've got a brand new state of the art spade – don't make me redundant yet, Auberon."

"Relax Alice," said Sally. "–You of all people should know you have nothing to fear from Auberon's thesis – nobody can make head or tail of it – least of all him."

Auberon paused with his fork in mid-air from shovelling down one of Stevie's casseroles. "– Don't be so sure – Alice is whipping it into shape for me."

"Well, I'm going to start dragging my heels, if you're planning to make me obsolete, Auberon. It's for sure I'll never learn to get my head around all your geo-physics bells and whistles."

"Doc Savage told me he would recommend me to his publisher, if I could get it into a readable state. He suggested that I ask you to co-edit it, Alice."

"He did? But he knows I'm hopeless at geo-physics–"

"That doesn't matter – he says you're a brilliant editor and that's what I need – what do you say, Alice?"

"You really want me to edit it?–with my shaky technical knowledge?"

"It'll never get off the ground without you," said Sally. "–I've seen some of your efforts on the early chapters – amazing transformation – from gobbledygook to lucid prose. I don't know how you did it."

"It's just good old plain English," said Alice, "- it's the only thing I know."

Stevie crossed the room to Alice. "A bunch of them are going to the King's Head to celebrate Ian's birthday – they want us to come, too."

"Brilliant," said Auberon. "– We're celebrating too. Me and Alice are going to be partners."

"God help you, Alice," said Sally "– You'll need it."

"Partners?" said Stevie.

Alice rose from her cushion. "– I'll tell you on the way to the pub." She spoke to one or two of the students on her way out and a clutch of them left the flat.

Stevie and Alice were swept along with the group to the noisy interior of the King's Head where Stevie insisted on buying the first round.

"–To Ian and Auberon and Alice – Cheers!"

For the next hour or two, Stevie and Alice drank manfully with the students but they were no match for them, especially Sally and a skinny girl with spiky orange hair drinking vodka alco-pops.

"My god," said Stevie "– did our kids really drink like this, Alice? Their poor livers –" She took a wine spritzer from a young man and followed him over to join a group in a heated debate in the corner.

Alice and Auberon joined a cluster round the skinny orange-haired girl who was acting out a love scene with Sally from some foreign film. The two of them spoke in cod-Bulgarian, staring mournfully at each other and waving their arms in extravagant gestures while the others tried to guess which film it was. Alice and Stevie were persuaded to do a turn and they did a creditable send-up of a scene from Bergman's 'Virgin Spring' with Alice scourging the shivering Stevie with birch twigs and the two of them mimed rolling naked in the snow.

Alice was persuaded to do an encore speech in her magnificent Swedish accent, which she matched with an equally doleful expression. She and Stevie accepted one final parting drink and the two of them linked arms and did a soft-shoe vaudeville exit waving imaginary top hats and canes and singing 'Good-bye – ee, goodbye –ee, wipe a tear, tiny tear from your eye –ee.' They made a last false gag-exit, snatching at their lapels and disappeared to loud cheers.

The two of them stood leaning against the outside of the pub, breathing in the soft night air, then headed unsteadily up the street singing sixties golden oldies and bickering over the lyrics. Stevie leaned heavily on Alice's arm and spoke conspiratorially in her ear.

"I swear to God, Alice, that tall boy was trying to chat me up. – Geoffrey, that was his name. I'm old enough to be his mother."

"That's why he did it, probably. I'm always being propositioned by earnest young men looking for a mother-figure."

"Did you ever take them up on it?" said Stevie.

"Once or twice, when I first arrived – before I met Heck."

"What was it like? – I mean they're so young!"

"It's okay – it's kind of exciting – they go off like fire-crackers practically before you get started."

"Damn!" said Stevie, "- I wish I'd had the nerve to say yes."

"Too late now," said Alice, taking her friend's arm. "– Never mind, I'll make you a nice cup of tea, instead."

They arrived back in the flat to find only a handful of stragglers sprawled about the living room. One of the girls detached herself from a boy on the sofa and came over to speak to Alice.

"Someone rang for you earlier. He said it was important. I wrote the number down on the pad by the phone – it looks funny – I think it was long-distance."

"Thanks Charlene. Did he say who it was?"

Charlene went over to the small table in the corner with the phone on it. "– I wrote it down for you, Alice. – Here it is. –

Barney – that's all he said –and to ask you to call back." She handed Alice the notepad.

"Something wrong?" asked Stevie, who was starting to clear up.

"I'm not sure. I got a call from Barney – he wants me to ring him back."

"You'd better wait a while – it's the middle of the night there, isn't it?"

"I'm not sure – I always get muddled up whether they're ahead or behind us – I'll call him first thing in the morning. Let's have some tea and I'll shoo this lot out so I can make your bed up."

She and Stevie drank tea on the oriel window seat while Charlene and her boyfriend cleared the debris around them and stacked all the dishes by the sink. Charlene offered to wash up but Alice told her to leave them for the morning and the two women were left to mull over the evening.

"You know, Alice, seeing all those kids just starting out – didn't half make me feel old. I've got to get off my backside and do something before it's too late – I'll be sixty next September."

"'Gather ye roses while ye may.'"

"Right – absolutely. – I'm going to tell Charles when I get home."

"Tell him what?"

"I don't know – I'll think of something – tell him I'm sick of our boring life and our boring house and our boring friends.

"Thanks a lot," said Alice.

"Oh, not you – you know who I mean."

"But you love your house, Stevie – and your garden – how could you bear to leave that?"

"I don't know – some days I think I could just walk away from it all – walk out and close the door behind me and disappear."

"Like Lord Lucan."

"Yes. Not a trace. Start all over again – completely different life – never a backward glance."

"You're a hopeless romantic, Stevie – you know you'd miss us all dreadfully after ten minutes."

"I know," sighed Stevie, climbing under the covers on the sofa. "– But I can dream." She smiled at Alice, "-tonight I shall dream of firecrackers."

Alice turned out the lights and hugged her old friend "– Goodnight, Stevie." She went into her bedroom, and once in bed, fell instantly into a dreamless sleep.

When she awoke, she heard Stevie in the kitchen, washing up from the night before. She looked at the clock and remembered the phone call. She padded out into the living room and dialed the number by the phone. Barney's voice answered. "–Hello? Is that you, Barney? – It's Alice."

"Alice! You got my message – that girl who answered seemed pretty vague – How are you Alice?"

"Coping – it's been quite a change."

"And Oxford – was that a good move?"

"Definitely. Best thing I ever did."

"Aren't you going to ask me how I'm doing?"

"How are you doing, Barney? – How is Vancouver? Was that a good move, too?"

"Yes, I think so. I'm pretty busy with a lot of different things."

"Is that what you want – just to keep busy?"

"It's more exploring different avenues – but it gets kind of hectic at times."

"What was it you wanted, Barney? – You said it was urgent."

"Have you heard from Netta?"

"Why, is something wrong?"

"Not with Netta, no – it's Hunter – she's worried about him."

"Why – what's happened? Is he in trouble?"

"I don't know. Netta says he's disappeared – she can't locate him, anywhere. His email address is defunct and none of their friends has seen him. – Have you been in touch with him lately, Alice?"

"No, not for ages. He came to visit me when I first arrived here in Oxford but I haven't spoken to him for months."

"What did he say – was he planning to go away?"

"He was pretty vague – you know what Hunter's like – he pretty much kept me at arm's length – although he did mention some woman he'd met. – Have you been in contact with him recently, Barney?"

"I had a couple of emails when I first arrived – but my latest ones have been undelivered – I've been relying on Netta for news of him – you know how close they've always been – so when she said she'd lost contact with him it got me worried too. Will you see what you can find out your end, Alice and let me know? Hunter and I haven't been exactly close this last couple of years – he tells you and Netta a lot more than he tells me. – You don't think he's in any trouble, do you? Netta seems convinced there's something wrong."

"He seemed okay the last time we spoke, Barney. Maybe he's just preoccupied with this woman-friend."

"Let me know if you hear anything or if you think I should come back, Alice. - I hope this is just Netta over-reacting."

"Barney? - Did Hunter ever say anything to you about Netta?"

"Hunter? No - only that he wished she hadn't gone to America to live with her father."

"I see - nothing else?"

"No - why? - do you think he's just cross with her and not answering?"

"Maybe - but why cut off from the rest of us, though?"

"God alone knows - Hunter was always in his own little dream world - Netta was the only one who really understood him."

"Yes. Well, I'll call you if I find out anything."

"- Thanks Alice."

She hung up the phone and stood staring at it for a moment. Stevie came into the living room with a cup of tea for her. "- Alice?"

"It's Hunter," she said. "-He's disappeared."

# CHAPTER 11

It was the first time Barney had spoken to Alice since leaving London and it left him feeling vaguely unsettled. They had agreed to keep in touch by email rather than by phone during this year apart so they wouldn't be caught up in each other's life. Hearing her voice again after all these months, with that cool aloofness in it, made him realize how far apart they had grown and how quickly.

He had wanted to ask her more about what she was doing in Oxford but her tone of voice had not encouraged any return to the old easy intimacy they had once shared. At least she hadn't sounded too alarmed about Hunter, he thought. That was a good sign – he had always gauged his own level of emotional response based on Alice's reactions to events. When it came to his son, he was even more reliant on her reading of a situation. Hunter confided in Alice far more readily than his own mother, who was usually too preoccupied with her new family.

He had grown away from Barney in the last couple of years so that now they corresponded on a superficial level of basic contact and exchange of news. He supposed this was how it was with most sons and fathers as they grew older and was relieved that it had never broken out into open hostility. Give him enough slack and he'll eventually come back, was Barney's policy with Hunter. Alice, as usual, disagreed. She said Hunter would read this as indifference and she wouldn't blame him – it was Barney's own fault if they had become estranged.

It was odd how the reverse seemed to apply to Netta. She and Barney had kept up a weekly exchange of phone calls and emails and they had long conversations on subjects far removed from a simple exchange of news. He loved to hear of her exploits in the world of film criticism and relied heavily on her recommendations in his forays into the cinema – especially foreign films. Although he always endorsed her choice, they had heated debates over the relative merits of some of them.

He knew long before Alice that Netta was living with her boyfriend, Philip and had made up her mind to go back to England to live with him. Barney had helped her make up her mind by letting her air her objections. He was puzzled that for no apparent reason, she still seemed reluctant to return to the UK. Unless it was because of Hunter. He knew how upset Hunter had been at her leaving and how possessive he was of her – none of his girlfriends had ever measured up to Netta. Barney had witnessed a string of young women take him on in turn, only to give up when they realized they could never match Netta's appeal to Hunter.

Barney had taken Hunter to task about his infatuation with his stepsister, telling him that he was making it difficult for her to develop friendships with other men when he monopolized so much of her time. His son had not taken kindly to this bit of fatherly advice and their estrangement grew even wider. When Netta announced she was moving to the States to live with her father's new family, Barney was secretly pleased. Maybe now she and Hunter would both get on with their own separate lives instead of living in each other's pockets.

For more than a month now, Trish had been living with him in Rozalin's apartment. He had thought if he could help her get back on her feet; help her find a job and her own place, she might get control of her drinking. He made a point of not keeping any stocks of alcohol about the apartment and took to drinking juice and water with their meals. Mildred had lined up a half dozen of her bridge friends as potential clients and Trish began her home visits. But these were women who wanted attention as much as medical help. They would prolong Trish's formal house calls with offers of drinks and invitations to stay for a meal. After Trish had come rolling home on several occasions, Barney took his problem to the widows at the Monday bridge club.

"I know you've all been acting in her best interests, but it's not working out – she's slipping back into her old habits," he said.

"Maybe the house calls weren't such a good idea, after all," said Mildred. "Some of my friends are pretty hardened drinkers and they don't need much excuse to have an extra gin or two."

"When I heard she was going to see Delia, I knew straight away what would happen," nodded Irene. "That woman can't go two hours without a stiffener."

"Perhaps we can tell people she has a drink problem and not to offer her anything when she comes," suggested Doris.

"I was hoping we could avoid mentioning it," said Barney, "afraid it might put people off – but now, I'm not so sure."

"Well," said Mildred, "We can ask them to keep it formal – after all, they don't ask their doctors to join them for a drink when they're doing house calls. – But she'll have to do her part – act the professional and they'll treat her like one. Do you think you can convince her, Barney?"

"I'll lay it on the line – tell her if she steps over – no more referrals. – Thanks, Mildred."

The old woman gave him a beady look. "Are you having any luck finding her a place of her own, yet? -That might help her keep her eye on the ball."

Barney flushed. "I've tried, but she says everything is too expensive and she's not ready to be on her own yet. She always seems to have an excuse when I suggest it."

"I'll bet she does," said Irene. "I would too, if I was sharing your bed, Barney."

The other women laughed. "Too right," said Doris, "I'll change places with her any time she wants."

"I'm sure it's not like that at all," smiled Mildred. "I expect Barney is only acting in her best interests – you did say she was using your spare room, didn't you?" The women laughed again, enjoying his discomfort.

"It wasn't my intention," admitted Barney, "but somehow it ended up that way. – I guess you're right, Mildred – I'm not helping matters, am I?"

"What about your boat?" asked Irene. "Couldn't she use that in the meantime till she can afford an apartment?"

"I suppose so, yeah," said Barney. "It's getting quite comfortable. Clive and I are nearly finished the main cabin. – Would you like to come and see it?"

"I'd love to," said Doris.

"He was asking me, weren't you Barney?" said Irene. "I'll check it out and see if it's suitable for Trish."

"We'll all come," said Mildred. "I want to see it too."

It was agreed the bridge widows would all visit the following day and Barney took the tub ferry across False Creek to tidy up and warn Clive of their arrival.

"What do you think, Clive? Would you mind having Trish for a neighbour for a little while? – It'll only be until she can find somewhere permanent she can afford. Maybe you can help steer her off the booze."

"I don't know, Barney. I'm not keen on wet-nursing anyone. – When's she coming? I'm due to go over to Bhante Dipa's on Salt Spring in a few days. – You haven't forgotten, have you? You were going to come with me?"

"Do you think Trish could come too? - When she was in China, she told me she really got stuck into meditation."

"She'd have to sleep on the boat – he's only got two guest cabins left unbooked and we'd be using those. – It's not really a big retreat centre."

"Sounds fine to me – and it will help her get used to the idea of staying on a boat. Maybe Bhante Dipa could get her back meditating – it might help her sort herself out."

"We'd better clean up the cabin on 'Sea Mist' if you're having all these visitors," said Clive. "We've left it in an unholy mess."

"I'm really looking forward to going out for her maiden voyage, Clive. – How soon do you think she'll be ready?"

"We still need to get the 'green dragon' serviced. – Once that's done, we can head up to Howe Sound for a couple of days' trial run."

"Good. I'll sort out the cabin and then go home and break the news to Trish."

"You mean you haven't mentioned this to her yet?"

"No. I wanted to check it out with you first."

"This should be interesting," said Clive. "What if she hates boats?"

"I'm counting on you to convince her," said Barney. "An old sea dog shouldn't have any trouble persuading her it's a good idea. Women are suckers for crusty old salts like you."

"Hey, it's your boat she'll be living on, not mine. – I'm only going to be her neighbour, remember?"

"Yeah, whatever," said Barney. "Between me, you and Bhante Dipa she'll be like putty in our hands – not to mention the bridge widows."

"Hmm," said Clive. "We'll see."

They spent the rest of the afternoon tidying up the 'Sea Mist' in preparation for her visitors and then Barney went back to the apartment to wait for Trish. It would be nice to have the place to himself again – it was becoming clogged with all the work for the art show and with Trish there as well, they were constantly shifting stuff about to make room.

Bobbi was working on one of her endless lists at the kitchen table when he arrived, with Ralf curled up on her lap.

"Where's Eugene?" asked Barney. "I thought he was supposed to be starting to shift some of this stuff back downstairs?"

"He's gone to find Kasim to give him a hand. – Do you want some tea? I just made a pot."

"What are you working on now?" he asked, pouring himself a mug of tea.

"I'm revising the sponsor list – you should see some of the names we've got – Mildred is a magician – she just keeps coming up with them and I gather them in."

"Yeah, she told me you two were a pretty formidable team. – Had any more lunches at the Hotel Vancouver lately?"

"No, but I've been to the Royal Yacht Club twice and Monsoon once. –Eugene says I'm getting fat." She patted her non-existent stomach.

"All in a worthy cause. – Has Trish called yet?"

"Not since I've been here, but she left a note saying she'd be back soon."

"Listen, Bobbi – would you mind finishing that off over at Eugene's? – I've got something I need to discuss with Trish when she comes in – okay?"

"Sure," she said, collecting up her notes. "– Can I take Ralf with me?"

"I guess so. Between you and Marlon, I hardly see him anymore. Poor old Ralf will be getting totally confused about his main carer. - By the time Roz gets back from France, he'll have forgotten who she is."

"Thanks, Barney." She kissed the top of his head, tucked Ralf under her arm and headed for the door. "Everything okay with you and Trish?"

"Yeah – it's just some things I need to talk over with her privately. – Tell Eugene he and Kasim can shift this stuff tomorrow."

She left and Barney wandered aimlessly around the apartment from room to room. He went out on the balcony and stared at the bay. Mildred was right, this involvement with Trish was just muddying the water – it wasn't helping her sort her problems out and he had never intended to get mixed up with her  - but when she had crawled into bed with him that first night she stayed over, it had felt so good to have someone's arms around him again.

In fact, nothing had happened between them that night; they just took turns being held – it was only the following morning when he came back from the bathroom and the sunlight shone on her curving thigh that Barney's resolve collapsed and he had crept back into bed and prodded her awake. Trish had been celibate even longer than he had and she needed little persuading.

For two long weeks they seemed to spend more time in bed than out, only leaping up when Eugene came to collect Ralf in the morning and Trish would scramble back into the spare bedroom. It was only after Bobbi had let herself in with Eugene's key and found them in bed together that they gave up any pretence of just sharing the apartment.

The shock of being discovered had sent a wave of guilt washing over Barney as if his own daughter had caught him. After that morning, they still slept in the same bed, but Barney had no heart for sex. Occasionally Trish had roused him to perform but he did so only perfunctorily to satisfy her and then drifted off to sleep. He knew he should call a halt but each time he gave in when Trish slipped in beside him.

This evening as he sat on the balcony watching the lights on the ferry as it headed for the big red neon Q across the inlet, he determined to sort things out with Trish and stop being so self-indulgent. He stayed up another half-hour and then went to bed to read and wait. He found a pair of pajama bottoms still folded up in the pocket of his rucksack and put them on before he got into bed.

He started re-reading 'Buddhism Without Belief' for the second time, pleased with how much of it he was in complete agreement. It was all so fine and clear the way it was laid out. Barney nodded, smiled, and closed his eyes for a moment to savour a particularly well-turned phrase.

Once again, the thought of becoming a monk drifted into his mind – he could go to Thailand, maybe, or back to England or even stay here in BC. He padded quietly up and down a woodland path through dappled sunlight, averting his gaze from passing village women; sat alone in deep meditation under a spreading bodhi tree, listening to the murmuring sounds and inhaling the pungent aromas – he felt the warm touch of skin and opened his eyes as Trish kissed his cheek. He drew her down beside him and she snuggled under his arm. Her warm breath smelled faintly of alcohol when they embraced.

"Trish? – "

She removed his reading glasses and set his book on the side table, deliberately leaning across him so her breast covered his mouth.

"Trish –"

She lay back down beside him and slid her hand down his side until it reached his pajamas. Her fingers found the cord and released it, and her hand continued down.

"Trish, I –"

She rolled on top of him and put her mouth to his ear. "Yes?"

"Nothing," said Barney and he allowed his hands to grasp her bottom.

Over breakfast, he outlined his proposal to Trish as she sat drinking black coffee and watched him eat scrambled eggs and toast.

"It was Mildred's idea, really. She said if you had your own place you'd get back on your feet quicker –"

Trish smiled, "You giving me the bum's rush, Barney?"

"No – not exactly – you don't have to decide right now. – Wait till you see it and then you can make up your mind."

"Sounds like it's been made up for me. – What else did Mildred and the bridge widows have to say?"

"Well, they think the house calls were a mistake – all those old birds pouring out gin and sob stories about their dead husbands."

"It's not all like that, Barney."

"No? Where were you last night until midnight? – working?"

"Okay, so I had a few drinks with a client – what's wrong with that?"

"It's unprofessional – you don't really expect people to take you seriously if you sit around half the night with them getting pissed, do you?"

"You make it sound worse than it is – I don't 'get pissed', for a start."

"It's no use, Trish. I see you every night. –How long have you been here now – a month?"

"Not very long."

"A month – and how much have you saved from all those client referrals?"

"I had bills to pay – I owed money, Barney."

"How much, Trish?"

"Nothing."

"Okay, here's the deal. You go and live on the 'Sea Mist' – rent-free. It's nice and central, right by Granville Island. Clive is on the next boat – if you need anything just ask him. The widows will keep sending you referrals on one condition – you keep it professional – no more booze or no more clients – it's your choice."

"What about us?"

"It was a mistake, Trish. – I made a mistake, I'm sorry. It's a dead end - it's not going anywhere."

"Because I like a drink?"

"Because I'm twelve years older than you."

"I don't care, Barney."

"I do.–I've just extricated myself from a long relationship, Trish. It's not what I want – what I want now I need to do alone. Anyway, I'd rather be your friend. How about it, will you come and have a look at the 'Sea Mist'?"

"Right now?"

"Right now."

"Okay, if you insist –"

"I do," said Barney, putting on his jacket. Trish stood up.

"Do I need to take everything with me now?"

Barney shook his head. "I told you, we're just having a look."

At the fishermen's dock, Barney found Clive talking to Steve the harbourmaster and he introduced Trish, explaining she might be staying on the 'Sea Mist' for a while. They did a conducted tour of the boat, introducing her to the mysteries of marine plumbing and Clive invited them back to the 'Betsy' for coffee. It was Barney's day for the soup kitchen run and he left Trish with Clive to discuss the details of living aboard.

He drove across the city to the food bank warehouse to collect his supplies for the evening round. Maggie was not in the office so he went out back onto the loading dock. He found her driving the forklift with her crutch balanced across her knee.

"How's it feel having that cast off, Maggie?"

"Bliss," she said, hauling up the leg of her jeans to show him. "Only my leg looks like alligator hide – no skirts for me for awhile."

"Still think it's a shame you had it removed before the court hearing – all that lovely sympathy wasted."

"My alligator hide looks even worse and I've still got my crutch – that'll have to do. - I've got another favour to ask you, Barney."

"You want me to bribe the judge."

"Not quite. I wondered if you would look after Marlon that day. Only my mum wants to be there with me and I don't like the idea of Marlon listening to all the stuff that's going to come up about me and his dad."

"Sure. Ralf and I will keep him busy. We can have supper on the 'Sea Mist' with Trish and Clive."

"Clive will be in court with me. –He's one of my character witnesses."

"Okay – no problem. I'll show Marlon how to make 'gypsy toast' on the diesel stove and Trish can teach him how to swear in Mandarin."

"Very useful life skills, I'm sure," said Maggie. "Especially the Mandarin. Thanks, Barney. I was kinda hoping you could be in court, too, but maybe it's just as well. You might not want to be my friend after you'd heard what a mean bitch I am."

"I doubt it," said Barney. "What's the latest on Zeke, anyway?"

"Oh, he tells me he's a reformed character – says he's been seeing this 'anger management' counselor and she's really helping him understand himself."

"Sounds promising," said Barney.

"Maybe – and maybe he's only doing it so it will sound good in court – improve his chances of custody."

"Like your plaster cast, eh?"

"That was your idea, Barney. Besides, it's gone now. – Whose side are you on, anyway?"

"I'm on Marlon's side."

"Yeah, I know. I'm kinda touchy these days. – I'll be glad when it's all over," said Maggie. "I've got your stuff ready by the dock if you want to back your car in."

"What's on the menu tonight – soup and pasta?"

"Soup and chili, - exciting, huh?"

"It's a soup kitchen, Maggie – don't want to raise their expectations too high."

"Right. – Give my regards to Hastings Street," said Maggie.

Barney loaded the last of the boxes into the yellow compact and waved goodbye. He drove back downtown through the late afternoon traffic to the storage locker unit that served as the base for 'Pop's Mobile Night Kitchen.' It had begun as a chance encounter shortly after Barney started working at the food bank – someone in the warehouse had mentioned a mobile free hot food run called 'Mom's Kitchen' which had been going for years in the area around Robson, Davie and Granville. Barney had joined them a few times, helping out on the circuit – they were always short of volunteers to drive the electric buggies they used, to pull the wagons of food along the sidewalks. After a while, he asked why they never served the downtown east-side area and had been told it was too dangerous – none of the volunteers would risk going there.

In a rash moment, Barney had offered to do a run down Hastings as far as Main and back through Chinatown. He knew police cruisers patrolled the area almost continuously but it was still plenty scary at night. As Thursday night approached each week, he felt the old fear tightening his chest, constricting his breathing and he always slept badly the night before his run. It had soon become nicknamed 'Pop's Kitchen' by the volunteers who loaded the buggies with soup, sandwiches and hot drinks -donated courtesy of Mom's supply lines which stretched into North Vancouver and south into Richmond and Surrey.

Barney was secretly relieved whenever he saw a second buggy being prepared as it meant some new volunteer had been press-ganged into accompanying him. They seldom lasted more than once or twice though, before he was back on his own. Tonight when he backed the little yellow car down the drive there was only his buggy standing waiting with its trailer loaded with thermos jugs, cool-boxes and hampers full of sandwiches. Behind it stood a gleaming black classic Harley-Davidson motorcycle. Ramon appeared in the doorway when he heard the car pull in.

"Got you a special escort tonight, Barney," he said, flashing his gap-toothed smile. "Meet Duke and Marlene." Two large bulky figures in black leathers loomed behind him in the dim light of the hallway. The tallest one stepped forward and held out her hand.

"Hey, Barney," said Marlene, "-been hearing good things about you."

"Yeah, old Ramon here says you could use some help," said Duke, as he crushed Barney's hand in his. "Me an' Marlene been feelin' it was pay-back time again – looks like you're it – if you want us."

Barney waggled his fingers painfully. "Great. You got a buggy ready for them, Ramon?"

"I already offered but they has declined," said Ramon.

"Yeah," said Marlene. "Duke says it would be bad for our image if any of his buddies saw us drivin' one of these little sidewalk scooters."

"I reckon for tonight we'll just ride shotgun on this," said Duke, fondling the handlebars of the Harley.

"I don't know whether you'll be able to keep up on that thing or not," said Barney. "I shift right along on the old red rocket here." He climbed onto the buggy and switched it on.

"I'll let you know if we run into difficulties," said Duke above the blatter of the Harley's engine. – "Lead on."

Barney swung out onto the sidewalk and Duke followed behind in the inside lane with Marlene smiling over his head. They worked their way down Granville Street, handing out cups of chili and sandwiches; Marlene bantering with the men and Duke watching benignly from the street where he lounged back on the bike, his little black soup-bowl helmet perched like a cardinal's skullcap on the back of his head to cover up the bald spot above his ponytail.

After the crush of pedestrians and street people working the crowds around the Orpheum theatre and Robson Street, Barney wheeled his buggy downhill towards Hastings Street. It was almost better when the groups of people clustered around the cart than on this half-empty street, he thought – safety in numbers. He glanced over his shoulder at the reassuring sight of Marlene smiling over the head of Duke behind him. He pulled up beside a knot of people under the canopy of the old Woodward building. Two of the men ceased haggling over a padded jacket and came over to him.

"What you got tonight, man?" said one of them.

"Chili, sandwiches, coffee." Barney recited the litany of tuna, peanut butter, ham and cheese. Marlene scooped chili for them from the thermos packs while he filled plastic cups with sweet coffee. More people crowded round and they worked busily for several minutes.

A young man pushed his way into the group, his shirt unbuttoned to the waist, his thin arms and chest covered with a swirl of new age dragon tattoos. He peered wildly into Barney's face.

"Where's Mom?" he demanded. "She should be here. I need to see her."

"Mom doesn't do this round," said Barney. "She's up on Davie Street. – You want something to eat? A coffee?"

"Gimme a coffee – I have to see Mom – got to tell her somethin'." His body twisted and jerked, nearly bending him double and he spilled half the cup of coffee as he lurched and swayed in front of Barney. Marlene moved up to him.

"Take it easy, pal. – You want me to give her a message?"

The young man stared up at Marlene in her glistening black leathers. "You a cop?"

"No way, pal. Your secret's safe with me. – I'm Marlene – a friend of Mom's."

"Hey, Marlene. You tell her, okay?"

"Tell her what, pal?"

The young man reeled away to steady himself against a newspaper stand. He balanced his coffee cup carefully on top of it and stared at it intently. "Tell her Simon says –"

"Simon says – yeah okay, - what?"

"Marlene – look –" he pulled up his sleeve revealing bruises and punctures on his inside arm. "You tell her- Simon says, okay?" He took a brief sip from his coffee and lurched over to Duke sitting sideways on the Harley. "Hey, you sure you're not cops?"

"Do I look like a cop?" demanded Duke, crossing his large arms over his larger paunch.

"Naw," the young man conceded, swinging back to Marlene. "You ain't cops. – Hey Marlene, - you tell Mom okay?"

"Okay pal, I'll tell her. –You want something to eat?"

"Gimme a peanut butter sandwich, Marlene. – Don't forget, eh?"

Marlene handed him the sandwich and he stared at it for a moment, then stuffed it in the pocket of his filthy jeans.

"I won't forget – Simon says," she said. "How about some chili?"

He shook his head and waved his hand in front of his face, as if brushing aside a distracting thought. "No chili,

Marlene. – You with that guy over there?" He gestured vaguely in the direction of Duke, spilling the rest of his coffee. She nodded and smiled.

"He treat you right, Marlene?"

"He's okay," she said. "Have some more coffee, Simon."

"No more coffee – bad for you."  He grinned at Marlene, plucking at his sleeve again and pointing to his perforated arm. "Almost clean again, Marlene - Clean. Tell Mom, okay? - Tell her Simon says –" He swayed back and forth searching her face.

"I'll tell her, pal."

"I like you, Marlene."

"I like you too, Simon."  He stroked the shining leather sleeve of her jacket and whirled off down the street. Barney and Duke sat on their machines waiting for her.

"Another conquest, Marlene," said Barney, switching on his buggy. Marlene swung her leg over the Harley and put her arms round Duke's ample girth.

"Yeah, I guess so."  The Harley blatted into life and the little cavalcade continued down Hastings Street to the next knot of street people – the drunks leaning motionless at odd angles and the druggies whirling, dancing, gesticulating wildly, continuously on the move.

"Don't these people have anywhere to go?" asked Marlene. "I thought there was night hostels?"

"There are," said Barney, "but they fill up fast – especially when it's wet or cold. –I've been working on the minister at St Stephens where the food bank is, to open the church hall at night. But he won't do it."

"Why not? I know St Stephens – it's a perfect location."

"Security," said Barney, "He's afraid they'd wreck the place. He says if I supply security, he'll consider it."

"Sounds fair enough," said Duke. – Go for it."

"I already tried – too expensive – these security companies charge a fortune – insurance fees, they say."

"How many guys you need?" asked Duke.

"Four minimum – two on the doors and two inside to keep order."

"I know some guys in the bike club might do it," said Duke. "You want me to ask them?"

"It's only one night a week," said Barney, "that's all he'd agree to."

"Let me ask around," said Duke. "If we made it the same night as the soup kitchen run, me and Marlene could do a shift, eh honey?"

Marlene nodded. "We could ask Dale and Larry – I bet they'd do it."

"Are they bikers, too?" asked Barney.

"Yeah, sort of – they're dentists – on Davie Street. Two big gay guys -"

"You should see their bikes," said Duke. "Beautiful classic Electroglides – worth a fortune. They got leathers worth more than some bikes –"

"Dentists!" said Barney, "are you serious?"

"Oh we got all sorts in the classic club," said Marlene. "Dentists, doctors, lawyers, truckers – mostly truckers."

"We even got a bishop," said Duke. "He don't come out much – but he's got a nice old bike – had it from new," he told me.

"Now I know you're having me on," said Barney. "A bishop–"

"No, it's true," said Marlene. "He wears his leathers and a dog collar – claims he can't take it off in public."

"He only rides in the good weather," said Duke. "He's gettin' pretty old – and he has to ride alone – his old lady won't come with him."

"I think she's just worried about him," explained Marlene, "afraid he might have a fall. She's not a snob or anything. – We met her, didn't we Duke – remember?"

Barney grinned. "Better not ask him, then – stick with the dentists."

They finished the circuit and Duke and Marlene escorted Barney back to the storage unit before roaring off on the gleaming Harley. Barney helped Ramon lock up and then drove across Burrard Bridge to Fisherman's Dock and parked on the darkened quay. He walked down the steep ramp and out along the wooden dock to the 'Sea Mist'. A light shone through the curtain on the cabin window and he rapped lightly on the roof of the deck.

"Clive – is that you?"

"No – it's me, Barney." A moment later Trish's face appeared at the porthole and then he heard a bolt sliding back and the cabin door opened.

"Barney – I wasn't expecting to see you tonight – I thought you were doing the soup kitchen run?"

"I know – I had some unexpected help so I finished early. – Are you settling in okay?"

"I love it," said Trish, beckoning him in and taking his jacket. "It's so cosy and snug. – I'm a bit nervous, though. I've locked every door and window."

"There's no need to, Trish. –Someone's on duty from the harbourmaster's office round the clock and there are plenty of people on different boats keeping an eye on things."

"Clive's been great - showing me how everything operates and he insisted on cooking a meal for me this evening on the 'Betsy'."

"Did he mention going over to Salt Spring this weekend?"

"Yes - he said you and he were sailing over and he asked if I'd like to join you. I think he was just being polite so I told him I wasn't much of a sailor."

"You'd really like Bhante Dipa, Trish – why don't you come? His retreat centre is supposed to be very secluded and peaceful."

"You sure I wouldn't be cramping your style? – I thought maybe it was a kind of men's thing."

"No, lots of women go as well – even Mildred and some of the bridge widows have been there."

"Okay, I'll think about it. You like some coffee? – That's all I can offer you until I go shopping. It's great having Granville Island market on my doorstep and Clive says I can buy fish straight off the boats at the dock here." She went into the uncompleted galley and put the kettle on. Barney followed her to the doorway.

"I know it's not finished yet," he said, "but everything works and Clive and I will soon have it done. We can work on it while you're out with your clients, Trish."

"I don't mind – it's kind of fun – sort of like camping. Come and see the bedroom."

She led him back through the boat and opened the sliding door into the rear cabin. The bed was made up properly with sheets, duvet, and pillows instead of the bare mattress and sleeping bag Barney had used. The concealed lighting gave the old polished wood a warm glow and a bunch of yellow mums stood in a jar on the shelf by the bed.

"Clive gave me those when I arrived – he's very sweet under that crusty shell."

"Sounds like you made a hit with him, Trish – cooking you dinner and buying you flowers –"

"Fish and chips – very appropriate, don't you think?"

"My favourite. Well, I'd better go – I just felt like seeing someone normal after my soup run – it always leaves me a bit strung out."

"Barney? – Would you do me a favour?" She took his empty coffee mug and put it on the galley counter. She returned to stand in front of him. "Please would you stay tonight?"

"Look, Trish –"

"I know – I know what you're going to say – but just till I get used to it here – please?"

"Trish, the whole point of this thing –"

"We don't have to do anything, Barney. – I just need you to be with me– please don't make me beg."

"Jesus, Trish –"

"Thanks, Barney – just for tonight – here, sit down – I'll take your shoes off –" She pushed him down on the bed and began pulling off his shoes and socks.

"I'm not sure this is a very good idea," he protested weakly. Trish put her finger over his lips and then continued removing his clothes. He sat passively on the edge of the bed and allowed her to finish undressing him; then watched as she quickly slipped out of her clothes and came to put her arms around him. He stood up while she pulled back the duvet and slipped under it, holding it up for him.

"Mmm, this is nice," she said, snuggling into his shoulder and putting her arm across his chest. "– Hold me tighter, Barney." He put his other arm around her and pulled her closer.

"Good, - that's good," she said. "I wish I could just stay right here and never leave." She reached over and switched off the light, then snuggled back down again. In the dark, she kissed his cheek and slipped her hand down between his legs, touching him lightly. He lay inert.

"Barney – would you like me to..." She made a slight move downward, but he gripped her shoulder, stopping her.

After a moment he said, "My wife said she read somewhere, in one of her self-help books probably, that women have sex in order to be intimate - and men are intimate in order to have sex."

Trish continued stroking him lightly with her fingertips.

"Seems like a good fit to me – yin and yang – I like that. – Don't you?"

"I never thought about it in that way," said Barney. "You mean each gets what they want?"

"That's right," she said. "Now 'lie back and think of England.'" – And she slipped slowly down his body.

The 'Sea Mist' tugged gently at her moorings and Barney could just make out the curve of Trish's back in the pale light from the cabin porthole. He remembered something Bhante Dipa had told him about how people thought it must be difficult to be a monk, - but how he always told them it was much more difficult to be a layperson. He gripped Trish's back tightly and followed her advice.

At three a.m., a persistent buzzing roused Barney from a deep slumber. He lay for a minute trying to identify the sound before realizing it was his new mobile phone, which Bobbi had persuaded him to buy. He reached across Trish's sleeping form and picked it up. "Hello?"

"Dad? – It's me, Cassie."

"Cassie! – Hello, sweetheart–"

"Netta gave me your number – what time is it there, anyway?"

"I don't know – middle of the night – what's up?"

"Sorry. – Dad, it's Hunter – I found him – well, not me exactly – Will found him – you remember my old boyfriend, Will – from Kentish Town?"

"Yeah, sure – where is he? – Hunter, I mean –"

"He's in south London – in a Salvation Army hostel in Brixton."

"Jesus – Brixton! – how did you find him there?"

"Pure chance – Will sent me an email saying he met one of Hunter's old mates in a pub – this guy said Hunter had dropped out of sight and he went looking for him – turns out he's been in south London all along but nobody thought to look for him in a hostel."

"Did he say whether he's okay?"

"Says he's okay, but he looks a bit rough –"

"What – drunk? – drugs?"

"Will said he looks like shit –"

"Has Will seen him?"

"No – that's just what this guy said. – I didn't like to tell Mum so I thought I'd better phone you. – It's semester break next week and I'm coming back to London – I'm going to look him up."

"God – Listen sweetheart – send me an email as soon as you locate him, okay? Do you think I should come home too?"

"Wait till I get back to London, Dad. - As soon as I find him I'll let you know. – You can decide then – he might be fine."

"Living in a Salvation Army hostel? - Why not George and Martha's – they rattle around in that huge empty barn of a place in Highgate –"

"Yeah, I know. – Still, you know what Hunter's like – he's too proud to ask –"

"He's too proud for his own good – call me as soon as you can, Cassie. – How's Paris? – You and Zinadine still planning to go to the Sudan or has your mother persuaded you to take up that UN offer?"

"I've pretty much decided to go – Zinadine is trying to arrange a volunteer placement for me in an orphanage he knows – I'll tell you all about it, later, Dad. My phone card's nearly run out."

"Okay, sweetheart – I'll wait for your email – thanks for letting me know."

"Bye Dad."

# CHAPTER 12

Hunter slipped between the hedges of the darkened alley and made his way carefully through the familiar rear garden of the large house that backed onto Wimbledon Common. Carefully he entered the garden shed and removed the light aluminum ladder from its hooks on the wall. He carried it over to lean against the garage side facing the rear. Before climbing up it, he made one last tour round the back to make sure there were no lights on in any of the rooms. A dim glow from the upper hallway was all that was visible and he returned to ascend the ladder onto the flat roof of the garage. He crossed to a small window leading into the hallway.

He had used this route on several occasions now, having first learned it in the other direction, to escape when they heard Mona's husband's big Mercedes pull into the drive. Now he carefully slid open the window and lowered himself onto the carpeted floor. He made his way silently down the corridor to the nursery, paused to listen for a moment and then slipped into the bedroom. He waited for a minute or two for his eyes to become accustomed to the dark, reluctant to switch on the tiny torch he had brought with him.

The familiar surroundings began to take shape in the gloom and he recognized the mobile dangling above the cot – the only thing he had been able to persuade Mona to accept from him for the baby. He stood staring down at the sleeping infant, then crouched down and with one hand shielding the torch, switched it on. The reflected light allowed him to see the baby's face and he marveled again at the tiny perfect features, the pouting rosebud mouth. He studied the face intently for several minutes, then switched off the torch and carefully squatted on the floor.

He looked at his wristwatch and saw that he had a full hour's safety margin before he needed to leave. He listened for the child's breathing and tried to settle his own to the same rhythm. It was so calm and peaceful here, he had trouble not drifting off to sleep.

For a while, he stared at the sleeping baby content just to be in the same room, even if only for an hour. It seemed so unfair that he was forced to sneak around like this in order to see his own son, but Mona was adamant. When she told him she was pregnant, she had also said they must break it off. She did not want to risk her husband finding out about them, she said. She wanted him to believe the baby was his. Hunter was confused by this sudden change in her behavior towards him. Up until this time, she had acted as if she could not get enough of him and now she was spurning him completely.

He even received a letter from her husband, thanking him for his work as gardener but saying his services were no longer required and enclosing a cheque for a month's payment in advance. When he went round to the house, Mona refused to open the door.

On the few occasions when she went out for a walk, her long black coat stretched tightly over her bulging abdomen, he tried to follow her and get her to talk. But she only rebuffed him, telling him he was simply infatuated and tormenting him further, by asking what made him so sure it was his child she was carrying. She warned him finally, when he persisted in following her, that she would call the police if he didn't stop bothering her. He continued stalking her, but now keeping out of sight, his anguish deepening as her belly swelled ever larger.

Back in his dingy room at the hostel, he relived their whole relationship in his mind over and over, trying to make sense of this unforeseen turn of events. When she had first told him she was pregnant, Hunter's first reaction was dismay, but the more he thought about it the more he came round to the idea that this could be the very thing to help him turn his life around. He had been drifting for so long before he met Mona he had lost track of when it had all begun. Academically he was brighter than Netta but he lacked her dogged determination to see things through. His bursts of high energy might result in some excellent essays or perhaps high marks in an exam but a rapid sinking back inevitably followed, and he made only desultory efforts to complete his studies.

Eventually, Hunter gave up any pretence of interest in university life. He left college and travelled the backpacker trail through Southeast Asia, keeping only tenuous contact via sporadic emails and cryptic postcards to his family but mostly to Netta.

Back in England after eighteen months of aimless drifting, Hunter took up a series of jobs, always being careful to leave whenever they threatened to become interesting or involving. His relationships with young women followed a similar pattern. He would occasionally visit Alice in Oxford and she attempted to re-awaken his academic interests by taking him to public lectures and introducing him to other students.

Once he had even accompanied her on a weekend dig and one of the girls invited him to a party back in Oxford. Hunter spent the night with her and she gave him a lift back to London. He promised to return but somehow never did. Back at Alice's tiny flat the following month, she finally tackled him head-on.

"What happened to that girl you met on the dig, Hunter? I thought the two of you hit it off rather well."

"Yeah, she was nice," said Hunter. "– we went to an old black and white showing at the NFT that I saw with Netta years ago. She gave me a lift back to London. "

"Are you still seeing her?"

"No. We sort of lost touch – my fault I guess. I was supposed to look her up."

"Why didn't you?"

"I dunno. – I'm kinda seeing a woman in London. – She's older than me –"

"And? – Come on, Hunter – it's me, Alice, remember? All those nights you used to sit on the edge of my bed telling me the crazy things you and your friends got up to –"

"It's kinda messy, Alice. – She's married, - but her husband is away most of the time."

"What's her name?"

"Mona – she's thirty-four – ten years older than me –"

"Is she living with you?"

"No, she won't come near my place. – I don't blame her, really – it's only a bed-sit."

"Where does she live, then?"

"Wimbledon –by the Common – they have a big old Victorian place with a huge garden – that's how I met her."

"On Wimbledon Common?"

"No. By an ad in '*The Lady*'."

"'*The Lady*'!" laughed Alice. "Since when did you start reading '*The Lady*'?"

"Someone told me it was where the live-in jobs were advertised – Mona was looking for a gardener – 'suit college student' it said, so I applied and she hired me."

"How long have you been working there, Hunter?"

"All last winter –"

"Strange time to hire a gardener," said Alice. "– So how did you and she – Mona is it? – become involved?"

"Her husband is away a lot – abroad mostly – he's a perfume buyer and he markets these really expensive perfumes in the Middle East – the Arabs love that kind of stuff, she says. I started doing odd jobs around the house when there was nothing to do in the garden and Mona used to make me lunch – and sometimes dinner, too."

"I see – doesn't she have any children?"

"No – she can't – well, - he can't, she says – they've had tests and everything. – She's okay, but he's just shooting blanks."

"Hunter – what an expression!"

"Well, you asked –"

"So, how long have you and Mona been having an affair?"

"Practically from the beginning – It wasn't my idea – she just sort of egged me on."

"Why, what did she do?"

"Well, she was explaining how the perfume business worked and how they make up the different scents – that's what they call them – and she would test them on me – not on me, on her – and let me smell them. They smell completely different on your skin. She said her husband told her how the Arab women use perfume on different parts of their bodies – like the backs of their knees and their insteps, on their earlobes –"

"Oh, I've been doing that – behind my ears -since I was a teen-ager," said Alice, intrigued. "Where else, did she say?"

"All the 'erogenous zones' Mona called them. She puts some on herself somewhere, then asks me to find where it is exactly, by smelling. - At first, I couldn't even tell whether she was wearing any or not unless it was really strong – but then after a bit I got quite good at it—I had to guess which perfume it was – it was sort of a game."

"And Mona was the prize," smiled Alice.

Hunter grinned foolishly, "Yeah. – She's quite a woman –"

"She certainly sounds it," said Alice. "Have you thought where any of this is leading, Hunter? I mean, are either of you serious or…"

"I'm getting pretty serious, but I don't think Mona is – she certainly doesn't want to leave her husband anyway –"

"But she wants to have a baby – your baby, Hunter?"

"I dunno, Alice. – Maybe."

"Promise me you'll be careful, darling. – Are you – you know – taking any precautions?"

"Mona says she is. – I offered but she said it's not necessary –"

"I see," said Alice.

The dial on Hunter's watch that Mona had given him glowed luminous in the darkened nursery. He calculated he could safely stay for another twenty minutes. The child stirred restlessly. Hunter crept closer to the cot and watched the smooth round face. The baby opened his eyes and looked at him unblinkingly. Hunter smiled back into the tiny face. Without warning, the baby's face crumpled and the mouth opened into a cry.

Frightened, Hunter made shushing noises but the child only howled louder. He glanced round at the door, then got to his feet awkwardly. His foot had gone to sleep under him and he stumbled as he headed for the door. It opened before he could reach it and Mona stood there in her dressing gown in the light of the hall. She screamed when she saw him, then brushed past him to the cot and snatched up the baby.

"Hunter! What? – How did you get in here? – What are you doing? – are you crazy, breaking into my house?"

"Mona, please, listen – I can explain –"

"Get out!" she screamed, "- get out! Mario – Mario!"

Hunter headed for the door again and started down the hall towards his escape route. He opened the window and swung one leg out when the bedroom door burst open and a dishevelled man in pajamas propelled himself onto Hunter and sent him sprawling on the floor. They grappled for a few minutes but the man was heavy-set and powerful and he pinned Hunter to the floor, twisting one arm behind his back. Mona appeared, with the baby still crying loudly.

"Police - call the police, Mona. – I've got him – he won't get away –"

"It's Hunter, Mario – he was in the baby's room – I think he was trying to kidnap him."

"Fucking bastard!" shouted Mario, punching Hunter's head and pounding him on the back "– I'll kill you, you sonofabitch!"

"No, no – Mona – please – it wasn't anything like that – I promise! – I only wanted to see him is all –"

"Get the police, Mona – go on!" She hurried into the bedroom and juggled the baby while she dialed. Hunter heard her excited voice speaking incoherently above the child's screaming. He lay perfectly still with the big man astride his back, breathing heavily.

They were still in the same position when the police arrived barely five minutes later. The words 'kidnap' and 'baby' must have spread rapidly, as two more cruisers wailed up at the big house a few minutes later. Hunter was handcuffed and bundled into the first police car. It seemed only a matter of minutes before he was sitting in a bare cell beneath the police station. He sat dumbly on the thin mattress with its sour smell of sweat permeating the narrow room.

The rest of the night passed in a blur of faces as different police officers took him to the interview room and asked him interminable incomprehensible questions. He was allowed to return to his cell at last and he lay curled up miserably on the sour mattress. At length someone brought him a paper cup of bitter coffee and said he could make one phone call. He called Netta.

"Hunter? – Is that you? – Where have you been? – I've been going frantic looking for you – why haven't you called me?"

"I'm sorry, Netta. – I've been trying to get myself sorted out –"

"For eighteen months? – How long have you been back in England? Cassie said somebody told her you were staying in some Salvation Army hostel in south London – what's going on, Hunter? Are you alright?"

"Yeah, I'm okay, Netta – only something's happened and I need your help."

"What is it? – are you sick? – Where are you? I phoned all the hostels in south London but they wouldn't tell me anything – they said they weren't allowed to give out personal information."

"No, it's nothing like that – I'm in jail, Netta."

"Jail! – Why? – Did you have an accident?"

"No. – It's hard to explain – I was caught in someone's house and they called the police."

"Stealing! – Hunter, are you doing drugs?"

"Netta, please – just listen, will you? – It was all a mistake, but they said I'm going to be charged with breaking and entering and maybe something much more serious –"

"What? – tell me, Hunter."

"Attempted kidnapping."

"Oh God, Hunter – where are you?"

"I'm in London – Wimbledon – in the police station jail. – I think I need a solicitor, Netta – do you know anyone?"

"I'll find someone, Hunter, don't worry – I'm coming down there right away."

"No, Netta. I don't think they'll let you see me – just my solicitor," they said.

"Okay – okay – I'll find someone – Philip will know one – can I call you back, Hunter?"

"No. – No calls, they said – only this one."

"Oh, okay. – Hunter? - Can I ask you something?"

"What?"

"Did you really try to kidnap someone?"

"No, Netta, I told you – it was all a mistake, but the police don't believe me and neither does Mona –"

"Mona? – Who's Mona? – is she the one they thought you were going to kidnap?"

"No, not Mona – her baby –"

"A baby! Oh God, Hunter, what have you done? – God, a baby!"

"Netta – Netta – please – just find a solicitor? Please?"

"I will, Hunter, I promise – right now."

"Netta? – I didn't do anything wrong, I swear to God. – I know it sounds bad, but –"

"It's okay, Hunter. – I believe you – only it's such a shock, hearing you suddenly like this – and then all this stuff – don't worry – we'll be there soon – Philip is right here. Bye, Hunter – bye."

Back in his cell, Hunter found a tray with congealing fried eggs and cold toast. He pushed it aside and sipped at the tepid mug of over-sweetened tea. Netta's frightened voice had jolted him out of his numbness – could they really charge him with kidnapping his own son? He slumped down the wall to sit on the floor, unable to bear the smell of the mattress.

He thought of all the Sunday tabloid newspapers he had seen with their lurid headlines about desperate mothers and fathers who had tried to kidnap their children and he knew he was in very deep trouble. He felt his bladder weakening, stood up shakily, and crossed to the bare toilet bowl. Not trusting his legs, he lowered his jeans and sat on the cold china rim. It triggered a flood of urine followed by a wave of nausea. He flushed the cistern and returned to sit crouched in the corner of the small cell, his arms clasped around his bent legs and his head resting on his knees. He stared at a loose tile on the floor and tried to make his mind as empty as possible.

A thick-set man in a baggy sports jacket entered the cell with a clipboard of notes. Hunter wondered idly if this could be his solicitor so soon.

"I'm Detective-Sergeant Hertz," he said. "I've been put in charge of your case, Roper." He perched on the side of the cot, then thought better of it and came to squat down near Hunter. "I've been reading this report, and it doesn't look good. – You're in a lot of trouble, Roper – you wanna tell me about it?"

Hunter shook his head. "I've been telling them all night long and they still don't believe me."

"Yeah, I read what you said – but it doesn't add up – why would you go to all the trouble of breaking into their house if you were only going to turn around and leave again?"

"I already said a hundred times - I just wanted to see my baby son, is all."

The detective-sergeant riffed through the papers again. "We got reports here go back several months, Roper - says you were stalking the mother all the time she was pregnant – she even had a court restraining order banning you from coming anywhere near the house. – This ain't gonna look good in court, son. You were caught right in the baby's nursery."

"I don't want to say anything more until I have a solicitor here, okay?"

"Suit yourself, son. I'm only trying to help. You're due to appear in court this morning and I have to decide what to charge you with. Attempted kidnapping is a very serious offence – you need to know that. – You sure you don't want to tell me your side of it? - I already spoke to Mr. and Mrs. Lupatti."

Hunter shook his head and the detective nodded and rose to his feet.

"Okay son, I'll see you in court later." He motioned to the guard and left the cell.

Hunter continued to stare at the loose tile on the floor. The guard removed the tray of uneaten food and asked Hunter if he wanted another cup of tea or coffee. Hunter chose tea and the guard brought him one. He waited what seemed like hours before the solicitor finally arrived and he was led into an interrogation room. She was a tall Indian woman in western clothes with large expressive hands. She opened her laptop computer on the desk and smiled encouragingly at Hunter.

"Philip phoned me and asked me to come," she said. "I've known him since we were students, but I've only just recently met Netta. My name is Nadia – Nadia Kumar." She held out her hand, clasping Hunter's firmly with her long fingers. "We haven't got much time before you're due in court, Hunter. We'd better get started."

Hunter related once again all the incidents of the previous night and answered Nadia's probing questions while she typed rapidly on the laptop. As she was leaving, she asked him one last question. "You said you'd been visiting the baby regularly in the night, after the   banning order?"

He nodded. "For nearly two months, now."

"I need to make some phone calls, Hunter. – But I'll see you in the court, okay?"

On the way back to the cell, Hunter asked the guard if he could have another blanket and he spread it over the mattress. It didn't entirely blot out the sour reek but at least he could lie down and try to think what to do. Nadia had told him he would be allowed visitors after his court appearance and that she would make an application for bail. That meant he would have to ask Alice or his father or even George and Martha to put up bail. He hated the thought of involving his grandparents – Netta's actually, but they had taken him on since he was a small child and he thought of them as his own.

A short time later, he was driven to the local magistrates' court and formally charged with breaking and entering. Nadia's request for bail was turned down as further charges were pending. It was all over in a matter of minutes and Hunter barely had time to speak to Nadia afterwards before he was driven back to jail. She tried to assure him that it was only routine and she would appeal against the bail refusal but it might take a few days. He asked her to phone Netta to come and visit him.

Clarence, the guard who had given him the blanket, had left his copy of 'The Sun' on Hunter's cot and he methodically read and re-read the tabloid from front to back and then all the adverts as well, until Clarence unlocked the door and told him he had a visitor. Netta sat very still and straight at the table in the interview room. He was seated opposite her and Clarence sat in one corner behind his newspaper. Hunter reached across and took her hands.

"Hello, Netta."

"Oh, Hunter, this is so awful." Tears quickly brimmed in her eyes and ran down her cheeks. "– I haven't seen you for so long and now this – what are we going to do? Shall I call Barney? I nearly did before I left and then I thought I'd better wait – have you spoken to him recently?"

Hunter shook his head. "No. We don't really speak – just the odd email. Did you speak to Nadia?"

"Yes, she phoned me and told me about the bail and maybe more charges –she said they were considering an attempted kidnapping charge but she was going to speak to the prosecuting barrister – she said it might be several days before she knew anything more."

"I'm sorry to get you mixed up in all this, Netta – only I didn't know who else to ask. Please try not to worry – Nadia is great – thanks for finding her for me –"

"I don't really know her but Philip does – they're old school chums – he suggested her straight away. She sounded nice on the telephone. – Hunter?"

"What?"

"The baby – the one they say you were going to kidnap – is it really yours?"

"I'm pretty sure – how can you tell though? – Mona said it was at first, but then she said she didn't know for sure."

"What's its name?"

"I don't know – she wouldn't tell me –"

Netta's eyes filled with tears again. "Oh god, Hunter –"

"I call him George; he reminds me of Granddad – same bald head–" he smiled at Netta and took both her hands again.

"I don't care if no one else believes me, Netta, as long as you do."

"I want to, Hunter, but I don't understand – you've changed so much-"

"It's the baby, I guess. I've felt different ever since I knew I was going to be a father. I swore I would stop drifting – get a proper job at last – make Dad and Alice proud of me – and George and Martha, too. Then, when Mona just cut off like that – wouldn't talk to me – wouldn't let me see the baby, - I just sort of fell apart – I couldn't concentrate on anything else – all I wanted was to be able to look at him – touch him – hold him. But she wouldn't let me anywhere near. She hired a nanny to take him out in the park in his pram and I used to follow her and try to talk to her."

"What happened?"

"She told Mona about me, I guess – that's when she got the court order – banning me from coming anywhere near the area."

"She sounds horrible – I hate her."

"I don't – I just want her to be reasonable – but how can I make her understand if she won't even talk to me?"

"Why didn't you ask someone for help – social services or Legal Aid or something?"

"I don't know, Netta. I never thought of it – my mind doesn't work that way, I guess."

"You could have asked me, Hunter –"

"You weren't here, you were in America."

Netta blew her nose and rubbed her eyes. "God – it makes me so angry. –You had every right – there was no need to sneak around like some thief – and now this mess. I'm going to do something –" she rose from the table.

"What?"

"I'm not sure yet. I believe you now, Hunter – and I think I understand."

"Do you think you could speak to Mona? – Make her understand? – I swear I never intended to take the baby – I never touched him even – in case he woke up."

"I'll try, Hunter. I'll try." She gripped his hands tightly, then nodded to Clarence and left the room.

Clarence led him back to his cell. "You want some food now, son? You haven't eaten all day." Hunter realized suddenly he was famished.

"Yes, please, Clarence. I feel a little better – something to eat would be good."

"If you want anything – a book or such-like, you can ask your sister to bring it in to you – the sergeant won't mind."

"Thanks Clarence, I will." He sat on the edge of his bunk reviewing what Netta and Nadia had said, waiting for his food. When it arrived after about twenty minutes, he devoured it hungrily while Clarence went off to make some tea.

Lying on the narrow bunk with the sour-smelling mattress, Hunter had plenty of time to think about where he had gone wrong. He tried to unpick the strands of his life over the past three years and found there were whole sections he could not account for. He wondered if he began with the events of the last few days and then worked back systematically, day by day, if he would be able to remember every single day.

For the next few hours, he struggled with his self-imposed task. It was hard work trying to keep chronological order straight and he kept forgetting what he had already recalled and muddling the sequence of events. If he could write it all down, then he might be able to go faster. He got up off the bunk and rapped on the door to get the guard's attention.

"Clarence, do you think I could borrow a pen and some paper to write on?"

"You wanna write a letter, son?"

"No – yes – I want to write to my father," said Hunter, the words springing unbidden into his mouth.

"Okay, I'll see what I can do." Clarence disappeared and returned about five minutes later with a ruled pad and a ballpoint pen. "Couldn't find any envelopes - you'll have to wait till the secretary comes in later."

"Thanks Clarence, these are fine – thanks a lot."

"You can give the letter to your solicitor to post when she comes in."

The cell door closed and Hunter sat back down on the cot with the pad balanced on his hunched-up knees. He had not even been thinking of his father when he asked for the paper – why had the idea suddenly popped into his mind? He supposed he might try writing to him – he gauged the thickness of the notepad – there was plenty of paper. He tried briefly to remember where he had got to in his recollections and realized he would have to start all over again if he was going to write it down. He abandoned the idea and started to write to Barney instead.

'Dear Dad,

Not sure whether to give you the good news or the bad news first – I guess the good news – I've become a father – a baby boy. The bad news is I'm in jail. It's because I'm a father that I'm in jail. It's because I'm a father that I'm writing to you – because I'm in jail, I may lose my son.

My solicitor and Netta are trying to get me out of jail but I don't really care about that – I only want to be able to see my own son and now it looks as though the court will ban me from ever having anything to do with him and I'm desperate – I don't know what to do and that's why I'm writing to you – we're both fathers and we both have sons – I thought maybe if I got back together with you, somehow you could show me how to get back with my son.

You were always pretty good at helping me get my head straight and I've been thinking about how it's only since you and I sort of drifted apart that my life has got into a muddle. These last three years I don't really know where they've gone. Ever since you told me I should leave Netta alone to get on with her own life, I've been searching for something to do with mine.

I know you told me to go travelling – do you remember that little Zen saying you sent me? – 'If you love your child – send him on a journey.' Well, I spent a year and a half wandering over Southeast Asia and had lots of adventures but it didn't seem to get me any closer to knowing what to do with my life, so I came back to London.

I didn't tell anyone at first, because I was just bumming around – no proper job or anything – but then I met this woman and it seemed like I might finally get my act together with her, especially when she told me she was pregnant – only she was married. She had the baby and refused to let me see him – I got desperate and started sneaking into her house to visit my son in the middle of the night and after a while I got caught and now I'm in jail.

They say I might be charged with attempted kidnapping and I don't even care about that either – only that I might never be able to see my son. And that's why I need your help, Dad. What do you think I should do? I need you to tell me how to act like a real father because looking back now, I see I was only behaving like a kid, not a man. Maybe that is what my journey was supposed to be about, finding out how to become a man. You've done it, Dad, so you can tell me how. I'm ready to learn now.

Love from your son, Hunter.

P.S. I call my son, George.

P.P.S. – Alice knows all about Mona, that's her name – but she doesn't know about the baby. Only Netta – I had to tell her.'

Hunter lay back on the bunk and re-read the letter to Barney. He closed his eyes and tried to call up an image of his father but nothing came. Puzzled, he tried to picture an occasion from his childhood that might let him see his face. He ran through several birthdays, Christmases, and camping holidays, which he remembered clearly but none of the images were of his father – only of himself and Netta and objects like a new bike and a lighted Christmas pudding.

He could visualize his own mother with her worried, preoccupied air and her strands of hair pulling out from her ponytail. And Alice, - he could see her face easily, her wide smile and deep brown eyes. Vaguely disturbed by his inability to see his father's face, only this shadowy figure somewhere in the background, he opened his eyes and sat up again. Turning over a page on the ruled notepad, he decided to write to Alice.

'Dear Alice,

I'm sorry you have to hear this at all, but it's best if you hear it from me and not from Netta or Dad. They can tell you what has happened but not how or why. Netta is pretty upset and I'm sorry now I involved her – but I guess I just turned to her instinctively like I always did whenever I got into trouble, knowing she would know how to sort it out – and in a way she has – she's found me a good solicitor, who's working on my case and I hope she'll be able to get me out of here soon.

I'm in Wimbledon jail and probably will be here for at least a week while Nadia – that's my solicitor's name, tries to arrange bail. She will be in touch with you or you could get her number from Netta. Do you think you could come and visit me here so I can explain what has happened in person? It's a bit complicated and I'd feel better telling you face to face.

Try not to let Netta upset you – it's not quite as bad as she makes out. Please don't say anything to George and Martha yet. There's a detective called Hertz who will probably want to speak to you, too.

Love, Hunter.'

He lay back on the cot and stared up at the cracked ceiling. For the first time since this whole thing had blown up in his face, he felt calm and at peace with himself. He closed his eyes and tried once more to picture his father but managed only to see his own son's tiny face looking at him from his cot, through the bars.

# CHAPTER 13

On Wednesday morning, Barney went down to the 'Sea Mist' early to catch Trish before she went off to work. He walked down the quiet dockside and rapped on the cabin roof – there was no reply and he peered in the porthole window but there was no sign of anyone present. Puzzled, he looked at his pocket watch and saw it was still only seven-thirty. He wondered if he should disturb Clive so early and decided to wait for half an hour first.

Back up at the fishermen's seafood shack he bought a coffee and returned to sit on the deck of his boat. The hum of the waking city and a few fishermen moving about their boats made a pleasant backdrop. It would be nice to be able to live aboard his own boat for the coming summer. But not with Trish – he would have to help her find a proper place of her own first.

He finished his coffee and went to knock on the 'Betsy's cabin roof. After a few moments, Clive's unshaven face appeared at a porthole. He seemed startled to see Barney standing there and signalled five minutes with his raised hand. Barney waited on the rear deck. When Clive opened the cabin door, he had dressed but not brushed his hair and it stood out in stray white tufts at the back of his head.

"Barney - What are you doing up and about so early?"

"I was looking for Trish before she went to work but she doesn't seem to be here. Do you know where she is, Clive?"

A sheepish grin spread over Clive's face. "Yeah, as a matter of fact, I do," he said. "She's below, in the shower."

"Oh," said Barney. "– I see. – She spent the night here, then?" –Clive nodded. Barney struggled on. "– Is this – uh - a new arrangement or just a one-off?"

Clive shook his head. "No, it's been going on for a week or so. – You did say you and Trish were finished, Barney."

"Oh. Yeah – just a bit surprised, that's all."

"Propinquity," said Clive.

"Right. Sure – look, I can come back later – this is obviously not a good time," said Barney, backing towards the deck edge. "I'm sorry I disturbed you" – his rear foot tripped over a coil of rope and he fell backwards, striking his head against a bronze deck winch. He watched a seagull perched on the top of the 'Betsy's mast and then nothing.

He came to, still staring up at the tops of masts but this time they were moving past him, as he was being stretchered up the dock ramp to the waiting ambulance. Trish's worried face peered between the two paramedics. He smiled at her and tried to speak but something was covering his mouth – he closed his eyes again.

In the Emergency Department at St Paul's, Barney was x-rayed and diagnosed as a severe concussion. He was sent up to the head injuries ward to be kept under close observation. The deadline for the night shelter opening was only eight hours away. Barney drifted in and out of consciousness. On one occasion, he was aware of Clive and Trish's faces peering at him and on another, he recognized Maggie's. They seemed to be saying something to him but he couldn't make it out – the effort was too much and he closed his eyes again.

He woke at last to someone gently shaking his arm. A young Indian interne with deep bags under his eyes was speaking to him. "Mr. Roper? – Mr. Roper – can you hear me?"

"Yes," said Barney. "What is it?"

"There are some people here who want to see you, Mr. Roper. – Do you want to see them? – How do you feel?"

"Okay, I think," said Barney, struggling to sit up.

"Take it easy, Mr. Roper. I'll crank your bed up and you'll be able to see better."

A nurse lowered the side of his bed and propped more pillows behind him. The door opened and Maggie, Trish and Mildred filed in.

"My three guardian angels around my bed," he smiled as they took turns kissing his cheek.

"More like three galley slaves," said Mildred, plunking herself down in a chair by the bed. "We've been working our backsides to the bone while you've been lying here sleeping."

"Why – what happened?" said Barney.

"The Night Shelter opening, of course," said Mildred. "You didn't think we were going to call it off after all the work we've put in, did you?"

"How did it go?" asked Barney.

Maggie took his hand and squeezed it. "Like a military operation, Barney. Nobody put a foot wrong – you'd have loved it. – You'd think we'd been doing it for years."

"But who...?"

"Bobbi, of course," said Mildred. "I called her and told her you were out for the count and she took over – organized the whole thing. I swear that girl will be Prime Minister one day."

"Trish and I did all the food at night and Mildred's crowd came in to do the breakfast detail in the morning," said Maggie.

Trish took Barney's other hand. "Poor Clive is shattered – he's back on the 'Betsy', sleeping it off. - He and Eugene set up all the camp beds and ferried all the stuff from the Food Bank. Then they had to dismantle them all in the morning and store them for next week."

"Did many street people show up, then?" asked Barney.

"Packed to the rafters," said Mildred. "Marlene and her motorcycle friends did your soup kitchen run and gave out the notices Bobbi made up, to everyone along the route."

"And six of Duke's buddies turned up in all their gear to handle the security," said Maggie. "Two of the biggest were on the doors, like bouncers – both in flame-red leather."

"Dentists!" said Mildred from her chair. "Did you know that, Barney?"

He smiled and nodded. "Larry and Dale – they said they'd be there."

"And Bhante Dipa, too," said Trish. "He said he was on latrine duty – every time I looked up from the kitchen, he was standing guard by the washroom doors in his orange robes and yellow rubber gloves, brandishing a toilet brush and grinning like a maniac."

"He must have spoken to every single person who showed up," said Maggie, "- male and female. He told me it was the perfect location for meeting people and he invited them all to stay for a group meditation in the morning after we cleared the hall."

Barney laughed. "Did anyone take him up on it?"

"Oh yes," said Mildred. "Lots – including me and all the kitchen crew. Do you know he stayed awake all night? He said monks often meditate all night long. He was fresh as a daisy in the morning."

"Doesn't sound like I was even missed," said Barney.

Trish patted his hand. "Of course, you were – lots of people asked where you were – anyway, we did it for you, Barney – that's why it happened."

"Bhante Dipa is coming in to see you this evening," said Maggie, "before he goes back to Salt Spring."

Mildred rose from her chair and stood by the bed. "Don't think you can pull this caper with the Art Show opening, Barney. I want you up and on the job before then."

"I'll be there," promised Barney.

Mildred turned to leave. "Oh, by the way. Bobbi invited the entire motorcycle club to provide a guard of honor for the opening night and the dentists said yes. That should make quite a splash, eh?" She and Maggie left but Barney hung onto Trish's hand.

"Trish, I wanted to speak to you before, but –"

"Me, too, Barney. I'm sorry about what happened the other morning –it was my fault – I should have told you sooner –"

"It doesn't matter – I'm glad, if it's what you want – and Clive."

"I think so – it's a little early yet, but – he's a nice man, Barney," she smiled. "Nearly as nice as you."

"The reason I came down to see you was because Roz is coming back and I'll need somewhere to live. I was going to ask you what you thought about getting yourself an apartment – I could maybe help you till you felt ready to take over."

"It may not be necessary, Barney. Clive wants me to move on to the 'Betsy'. We could be neighbours, instead," said Trish.

"Sure," said Barney, "Why not?" – He released Trish's hand and she kissed his forehead and left.

On Saturday morning, Barney was released from hospital and he decided to walk back from St Paul's to the apartment. It was a balmy sunny morning and he strolled slowly down through Heritage Square past Barclay Manor on his way home. Two street kids were lounging on the park benches in the sunshine. The girl spotted Barney and came towards him.

"Hey man, how about a tooney for me 'n my friend?" She thrust a grimy hand out at Barney. He stared at her for a minute, then smiled.

"What you lookin' at, man?"

"How's your knee?" asked Barney. "You still doing 'snatch and grab'?"

The girl peered at him. "What you talkin' about, man? – Do I know you?"

"We met a few months ago – on the seawall – you had an accident, remember? – hurt your knee."

"Yeah – that's right." A smile of recognition spread across her face, revealing her blackened teeth. "Yeah, man – you gave me twenty bucks –"

"Loaned you twenty bucks," corrected Barney. "Remember?"

"I ain't got it now, man –"

"That's okay," said Barney. "I wasn't expecting it back. – Just wondered what happened to it."

"Yeah – you said to pass it on – I remember –"

"And did you?"

"Are you kidding?"

"Just wondering, that's all," said Barney. He took some change from his pocket and handed her a two-dollar coin. The girl took it with a nod and he smiled at her again. "What's your name?"

"Why – you gonna report me?"

"What for? Breaking your promise?"

"Sky," said the girl.

"Pardon?"

"Sky – my name's Sky."

"Sky – unusual name," said Barney.

"You got a problem with it, man?"

"No, I like it. – Sky."

"I chose it – it's not my real name – I hate my real name, Edith – what's yours, man?"

"Barney."

"Barney – that's not such a great name either."

"Maybe I should change mine too," said Barney.

"Change your name - change your life," said Sky.

"Maybe I will," said Barney. "Maybe I will. Goodbye, Sky."

The girl started back towards her companion. "See you – Barney," she smiled her blackened smile. She stopped and turned. "Hey, man – your daughter –she still in France?"

Barney nodded. "Paris."

"Paris," repeated Sky as she turned to re-join her friend on the park bench.

No one was at the apartment when Barney arrived home. He wandered through the empty rooms, which seemed spacious now that most of the piles of pictures and art pieces for the show had been removed. He assumed Eugene and Bobbi had taken everything down to the empty venue where the show was due to take place the following week. He thought of going down to see if he could help but changed his mind and went out to sit on the balcony in the morning sun. The ferry ploughing across the harbour to the big red Q at Lonsdale Quay reminded him of his first morning in Vancouver.

He let his mind wander over all that had happened in the last few months. Was this what he hoped would happen when he had left the UK and Alice? Did he want to do more of the same? Or were all his projects just like Bhante Dipa had said –'displacement activity' – pencil sharpening? He recalled the monk's offer of a long retreat at his Salt Spring center – should he take him up on it now or stick with his original plan to go and travel in China?

Even amidst all the frantic busyness of the last few weeks, he had managed to keep attending his Mandarin classes at Kitsilano night school. That much seemed clear – for good or ill, he would probably go to Chengdu – the demand for English teachers far exceeded supply and he could probably find enough work to subsidize his travels. The retreat would have to be put on hold until he came back.

In the living room, the phone rang softly. Probably someone for Bobbi, he thought and went to answer it.

"Hello, is that Mr. Roper?"

"Yes," said Barney. "Who's this?"

"David Kelso – the bishop – We met at the motorcycle club?"

"Bishop – yes, of course –"

"Something's come up, Mr. Roper, with regard to the night shelter, and I wanted to ask your advice."

"Is there a problem, then?"

"As a matter of fact, there is," said the bishop. "It seems that some of the parishioners at St Stephen's are upset they were not consulted about the night shelter – apparently Reverend O'Neill only asked a few committee members first – then they heard that a Buddhist monk was leading meditation groups which the minister was attending – and things got a bit heated – they're threatening to call the whole thing off and ask for Reverend O'Neill's resignation."

"I see," said Barney. "Sounds a bit of a knee-jerk reaction."

"Well, it all blew up because the first trial evening was so successful and some bright spark had the idea to invite the local TV station to cover it. That was the first most of the St Stephens parishioners knew of it, when they saw it on TV."

"So how can I help, bishop? – Did you have something in mind?"

"I do, actually. It struck me if I could persuade this Buddhist monk to come and speak to the St Stephens people he might be able to smooth some ruffled feathers. Do you know where I can find him?"

"Yes," said Barney. "His retreat center is on Salt Spring Island – but he's not on the telephone – you can e-mail him, though."

"I think it might be better if I spoke to him in person," said the bishop. "Do you think he's there at present?"

"Yes, he went back home yesterday. – You could take the ferry direct but he's a bit remote from the port."

"I was thinking of going on my bike," said the bishop. "I haven't been out on it for quite a while and this weather is perfect – do you know how to get there?"

"Only by boat, but I'm sure anyone on Salt Spring will know where it is," said Barney.

"I was wondering if you'd consider coming with me?" said the bishop. "Help smooth the way, so to speak. My Harley has a sidecar. - My wife, Madeleine says it's very comfortable when I can persuade her to join me. We could catch the afternoon ferry, if you're free. –"

"I'd love to go," said Barney.

"Good," said the bishop. "I'll meet you at the Horseshoe Bay ferry terminal."

Barney changed into some jeans and a sweater and jacket. He phoned Eugene to tell him where he was going and then called Mildred.

"You're not going to believe who I was just speaking to," he said.

"The bishop," said Mildred.

"How did you know?"

"I put him onto you, of course."

"You mean this whole thing was your idea?" asked Barney.

"It's only a handful of old reactionaries at St Stephens who've got their backs up because they weren't consulted. I'm sure Bhante Dipa will win them over once they meet him."

"It would be a shame for all that work to be wasted," said Barney. "From what you and Maggie and Trish were telling me, it could be really successful."

"There's no question of shutting it down – I told the bishop he'd have to use his influence to sort it out," said Mildred.

"How did you manage to get him involved?"

"Oh, I just reminded him that the West End Widows were his chief fund-raisers for all his charity events, and we had a vested interest in seeing this little venture succeed."

"Mildred – you're a wonder," said Barney. "If I weren't already married, I'd propose to you right now."

"Sorry. I only marry rich old men," said Mildred. "The older the better. When you and the bishop and Bhante Dipa get back, you can come round for afternoon tea at Beach Avenue and tell me all about it."

At Horseshoe Bay, the bishop was already waiting at the head of the queue, sitting astride his immaculately gleaming emerald green Harley with its sleek bullet-nosed sidecar. When they reached Salt Spring, they followed the directions the purser on the ferry had given them to get to the retreat centre.

Bhante Dipa was alone and didn't seem surprised to see either of them. He listened to the bishop's proposal and readily agreed to accompany them back on the morning ferry. The bishop was intrigued with the whole retreat centre and the monk laughingly invited him to come and spend some time meditating with him.

"That would really give my congregation something to talk about," said the bishop. "Perhaps when I'm retired you'll invite me again, Bhante."

The three men retired early as the ferry left at seven in the morning. The bishop insisted in sleeping in one of the meditation cabins with only a mattress and a blanket. He was already awake when the monk brought him a cup of tea at six o'clock.

With Barney in the sidecar and Bhante Dipa on the rear saddle seat, the three of them rumbled along the deeply wooded roads to Long Harbour. Two or three people came over to admire the classic bike as it sat in pride of place at the front of the ferry. When they all piled on to leave at Horseshoe Bay, a column of waiting car passengers cheered as the trio rolled down the ramp.

It was the same along the route into North Vancouver whenever they stopped for a traffic light. Heads turned and smiled at the bishop in his period black leathers and dog collar and the monk in his flapping orange robes with Barney waving to the kids. All three of them sported little black soup bowl helmets that the bishop had produced from the sidecar's luggage compartment.

They bowled over Lion's Gate bridge, round Stanley Park and along Beach Avenue to Mildred's penthouse apartment building where lunch was waiting, prepared by a group of the West End widows. It was agreed that a meeting with all the St Stephens people would be called for that evening and that Bhante Dipa would address them and then stay over on the 'Sea Mist,' as Trish was now installed on Clive's boat. Barney and Bhante Dipa went for a long walk on the seawall after lunch.

"If I pour enough oil to smooth things out tonight," said Bhante Dipa, "I think I can line up a regular roster of members of the Vancouver Buddhist community to run the night shelter – provided your motorcycle friends will continue to handle the security arrangements."

"I'll ask Marlene what she thinks," said Barney. "I understand you did latrine detail all night?"

"I recommend it for meeting people – I made many new friends while I was on duty," grinned Bhante Dipa.

"Maybe I should volunteer for next week – if both you and Gandhi found it so inspirational," said Barney.

"Yes, I had many occasions to think of Gandhi in the course of the evening – not a job for anyone with a weak stomach," he laughed. "Clive offered to spell me off around midnight but I told him to get some sleep for the morning rush and clear-up. He didn't argue with me."

"He and Trish made quite a team," said Barney. "I hope it lasts."

"Clive has been looking for the right partner for as long as I've known him," said Bhante Dipa. "I'm afraid his expectations are impossibly high for any mere mortal woman."

"Clive and I are polar opposites- maybe that's why we get along so well," said Barney. "He has spent the last quarter century looking for a partner and I've spent the same time looking for a way to be alone. I wonder if either of us will be any happier."

"It will depend how skillfully you both spend your remaining time," said Bhante Dipa. "Ultimately we are all of us alone whether together or apart."

"Lying in the hospital these last few days kind of broke my pattern of continuous activity," said Barney. "I'm finding it hard to pick up the threads again."

"Perhaps you should just lie fallow for a while – take a step back and observe what's going on before you plunge straight in again."

They had reached one of the docks for the little tub ferries to Granville Island and Barney said goodbye to the monk and handed him the keys for the 'Sea Mist'.

He walked on up to Burrard bridge and caught a trolley bus at Davie to take him downtown. He had not been to the actual venue for the art show and was astonished at how enormous the space was. In a former incarnation, the building had been the head office of one of the major banks that had migrated up Howe Street to a new glass and steel tower. The Art Deco front entrance with its huge double oak doors sat across the corner of the building and back from the main street intersection. The high windows were masked over with rolls of newsprint paper and decorated by the art students announcing the forthcoming event.

He pushed against the heavy door and entered through a wall of sound. He saw but could not hear Eugene supervising an installation that Barney recognized from his visit to Eugene's old student premises. It was the looming ship prow with the cornucopia of stuff pouring from it into the sea. A pair of arms encircled his chest from behind and he turned to see Bobbi mouthing words like a goldfish and smiling delightedly. The two of them went up to Eugene and tapped him on the shoulder. Bobbi made gestures at him and he crossed to a console and pulled down the slider on the volume control.

Barney's ears continued to vibrate and Eugene's voice sounded as if he were underwater.

"What's happened to Ralf?" asked Barney. "He's not at the apartment."

"Bobbi took him over to her mother's house when you were in hospital," Eugene said. "He's fine – I still take him out with the others in the early morning and Marlon plays with him after school. – What do you think, so far?" He waved his arm vaguely around the huge empty bank interior with its high ceilings and towering columns designed to impress its depositors. A partially constructed ramp at shoulder height projected into the main open space.

"What's this?" asked Barney.

"The catwalk – for the fashion show – and the auction," said Bobbi.

"We're going to have two enormous follow spots to crisscross the catwalk," said Eugene, pointing to some scaffolding in two corners of the foyer.

"Is the music really going to be that loud?" asked Barney. "My ears are still ringing."

"Only at the very beginning for the 'son et lumiere'," said Eugene. "That was Roz's suggestion – she said they do them everywhere in France in the summer."

"It's a little disorienting," said Barney, blowing his nose to clear his ears.

"That's the idea," said Bobbi. "We want to surprise people when they first come in – catch them off guard, then hit them with the art work – I think it's a great idea."

"I see," said Barney nodding dubiously. "Is there anything I can help with?"

"Not really," said Eugene. "Maybe later when we have more of the installations done – we're making a huge centrepiece of Roz's work – I thought sort of a collage of her collages – I hope it pans out – I've spent weeks choosing the right pieces from her collection."

"I recognize your ship's prow piece," said Barney. "This space really sets it off."

"Bobbi chose that spot – she said as it was too big to be shown on the catwalk I should have it flown in from the ceiling."

"Is there somewhere I can sit down and just watch?" said Barney. "All this stuff is a bit overpowering all at once." Bobbi showed him a big leather armchair against a wall and brought him a coffee from Blenz across the corner. He stayed for an hour watching as the students and lighting and sound crews continued rigging the space for the show. Eventually the volume of sound drove him out and he signaled goodbye to Bobbi and Eugene and escaped out to the cool of the early evening.

The days were noticeably shorter now and the temperature dropped more quickly when the sun lowered. He walked down past Canada Place, admiring the sun setting on the huge roof canopy sails and turning them a glittering gold. Long shadows stretched out into Coal Harbour as he walked back along the harbour wall. He found himself thinking of China and what it would be like living in a non-Western culture.

Although Roz's return had taken him by surprise, he saw now that he had been ready for a change – for the next stage of his voyage. He loved being in Vancouver and knew he would end up back here one day. But something compelled him on – to what? He knew the where but not the why – he would just have to rely on instinct – and Ulysses - "'Old age hath yet his honour and his toil'," he recited to the wheeling seagulls. "'Death closes all: but something ere the end, - Some work of noble note may yet be done'...."

# CHAPTER 14

Barney divided his time between the 'Sea Mist' and the apartment with only the odd side trip to the art show venue. He pottered about finishing the cabinetwork details in the galley of the boat, which he and Clive had abandoned when Trish moved aboard. In the afternoons, he took Ralf for long walks out past the Maritime Museum and along Kits beach. If the tide was out, they would carry on to Jericho Beach and Spanish Banks. Once he even went as far as Wreck Beach where the occasional hardened nudist lay in the shelter of the huge float logs, between the Asian fishermen casting their filigree nets from the shoreline. Ralf was too tired to walk back so Barney tucked the little dog inside his windbreaker and caught a Number Four bus back downtown.

Clive had the 'green dragon' overhauled and serviced, but Barney was still reluctant to take the 'Sea Mist' out on his own. The two of them had been out a few times beyond English Bay and up Howe Sound, but Clive was unwilling to leave Trish for more than a day or so and she was too busy with all her new clients to join them.

On days when he felt at a loose end, he went out to help at the Food Bank warehouse and have a makeshift lunch with Maggie from dented cans of tuna or salmon. He realized she was no longer using her crutch.

"Yes, I decided I can manage without it – it had just become a habit," said Maggie.

"What about your court appearance? – I thought that crutch was Exhibit A –"

"I know. But I've been thinking about what Bhante Dipa said – about me causing more suffering and all – I've pretty much decided not to go to court after all."

"Have you told Zeke yet?"

"We talked it over a couple of times when he came to visit Marlon – he says he doesn't want to go either. He said we should work something out ourselves – we're adults and we ought to start acting like ones."

"I see. Marlon will be pleased he's going to see his dad."

"He can't decide who he misses more," said Maggie. "– Ralf or his dad."

"I'm hoping to persuade Roz to let him share Ralf – that leaves you to deal with Zeke," said Barney. "Anytime you want me to baby-sit –"

"We'll see," said Maggie. "–I'm not convinced Zeke is the reformed character he makes out to be."

On the day before the Art Show event, Barney drove the little yellow compact out to Vancouver International to pick up

Roz. He brought Ralf with him and left him sleeping on the back seat. It took awhile to collect all her stuff from the oversize baggage department and he bundled it all into the trunk with the overspill of canvases packed into the back seat. Ralf perched on her lap in the front seat and bounced up and down trying to lick her face.

"Dogged devotion," grinned Barney. "– Judging from your luggage you had a fruitful trip, Roz."

"One of my better ones – and I made a new friend, too – Cassie."

"Yes, she told me you'd met up in Paris."

"She doesn't look like you – but she seems to have your wanderlust. She's off to Africa, she says. Turned down a plum job at the UN, too."

"I'm hoping to go out there to visit her – maybe I can get to know her a little better away from home."

"I think she'd like that – she seems pretty close to her mother but she mentioned you quite a bit. I enjoyed meeting her – she was the one who persuaded me to come back. – I hope I've made the right decision."

"Well, if Eugene and Bobbi have their way, you'll be quite a local celebrity. –Do you want to go by the venue now or go home first?"

"Home, please, Barney. – Maybe later, I'll go downtown."

At the apartment, Barney helped her unload everything and piled it in the front hall. He had systematically cleaned the place through with Bobbi, trying to remember how things were when he first arrived. All the surplus items he couldn't account for, he put in the basement storage.

"It's immaculate, Barney – are you sure you've been living here?"

"It's been a godsend, Roz. Ralf and I have lived it up the whole time – thanks. I'll leave you to unwind and unpack. I can walk down and get an aquabus over to the 'Sea Mist'. You must come and see her soon."

He left and walked back along the seawall to the tub ferry and his new floating home. Trish and Clive invited him to share a meal on the 'Betsy' but he begged off and spent the evening writing in his journal on the 'Sea Mist'. He imagined Captain Vancouver sitting in the cabin of his ship, making meticulous entries of his discoveries along the BC coast.

The day of the art show was clear and bright and after being assured by Bobbi there was nothing left to do except choose his party outfit, Barney took a bus to Value Village to find something suitably fancy. He found a two-tone pair of black and white shoes and a pair of pinstripe trousers. In amongst the suits he discovered a multi-coloured sleeveless waistcoat, but his best find was the pale lemon high-collared Nehru jacket. Pleased with his luck, he dropped them off at the boat and took the aquabus across False Creek.

He spent the afternoon walking on the seawall and wandering through the forest paths in Stanley Park. He met a bag lady who came from Seattle and said she had been living in the park for two years. Barney offered to buy her lunch at the fast food outlet at Prospect Point and drank coffee while she demolished half a pizza and a wedge of carrot cake.

He was intrigued with her story. She told him she had simply left her suburban home in Seattle one day and walked out the door. She went to the bank, cleared out her joint account and headed for the border. In Vancouver, she had quickly maxed out her credit card and lived in a series of cheap hotels until finally ending on the streets. It was summer and lots of people were living in Stanley Park so she joined them and had been there ever since. When Barney asked her what had made her leave her husband after so many years, she shrugged her shoulders.

"He was an asshole."

On his way back around Lost Lagoon he sat watching a raccoon swimming back and forth between a small island and the shore, its bushy tail floating on top of the water. He fell into conversation with an earnest young man about black holes and parallel universes. Struck with the similarities to Buddhist cosmology, Barney wondered yet again where this ancient knowledge had arisen.

He supposed that the current theorizing about the origins of the universe were our modern myths and legends and just as incredible as any of the ancient ones. Maybe Ecclesiastes was right after all and there wasn't anything new under the sun. He returned to the 'Sea Mist' and dressed for the Art Show evening.

As he approached the old bank building Barney saw two powerful beams of light swinging back and forth across the sky and over the crowd in front of the main entrance. No one was being allowed in until eight o'clock and they were being entertained by a collection of jugglers, fire-eaters, magicians and street performers. The crowd was kept back off the street by a cordon of glittering classic Harley motorcycles, driven in a slow musical ride up and down in a stately double figure of eight. He recognized Marlene's smiling face above the head of Duke.

A pair of matching electric blue 'Electroglides' with both riders in spotless cream leathers could only be Larry and Dale but he couldn't make out their faces. He watched the spectacle with the crowd for a quarter of an hour before the motorcyclists, on a pre-arranged signal, formed a double row of blatting, snorting machines lining the entrance to the building and the great oak doors swung open to a blinding blaze of white light and a wall of electronic sound.

The crowd surged forward into the building and Barney was swept along with them. A stunning mix of lasers, holographs and strobes filled the room like a summer electrical storm, matched by a symphonic soundtrack that ranged from the ethereal Parsifal to the ragged discords of John Cage.

The huge space was plunged from searing white light to total blackness; from deafening throbbing bass beats to eerie silence. The strobes darted about the room lighting first one piece of work and then another. The huge limelights swung to and fro, criss-crossing the great central display of Rozalin's collages. In the interstices of light and dark, Barney made out the mesmerized faces of the watching crowd.

Then as suddenly as it began, it was over and discreet side lighting and a low insistent rhythm began. From bars set up strategically in different corners of the old main concourse, male students in black, bearing trays of champagne flutes at shoulder height swooped in and out of the crowd, pausing for the merest brief moments, so that only the nimblest in the audience could snatch a glass.

It became a choreographed game of gliding trays and outstretched hands until the glasses vanished to be replaced by more students - girls this time, moving to the beat of the music, dressed as cigarette girls with selections of tiny hors d'oeuvres, threading through the maze of onlookers. Slowly the volume of voices rose to drown out the music and the deejay at his console played with the levels; now swelling, now diving under the buzz of conversation.

Barney drifted about the room, admiring once again Eugene's ship's prow collage, which swayed above the heads of the on-lookers. He saw Eugene and Roz, looking pleased and bemused in the centre of a knot of the Vancouver glitterati, to one side of her central collage. Bhante Dipa was sipping orange juice and surrounded by Marlene and the dentists, resplendent in their cream leathers and the bishop with a sophisticated-looking lady who Barney assumed must be his wife, Madeleine. The bishop had foregone his leathers and was dressed in raven black.

Bobbi and Mildred, linked arm in arm were promenading through the crowd, smiling and greeting everyone they passed. Barney followed in their wake for a few minutes until Bobbi became aware of him. She had gelled her hair into spikes and her eyelashes sparkled with glitter. In a very short black dress, she looked even more waif-like than ever. Mildred looked majestic in a deep aubergine purple long gown and a pearl choker. They exchanged air-kisses with Barney, careful not to spoil their makeup.

"Is there anybody here you two don't know?" he asked. "You looked as if you'd personally invited every last one."

"Oh, Mildred knows way more than me – all the important ones are her guests."

"All the colourful ones are Bobbi's – mine are the boring ones," said Mildred.

"Do you like the show, Barney?" asked Bobbi. "– Eugene was worried we'd hijacked your idea."

"It's stunning. It would have been much more humdrum if I'd organized it – the only colourful characters I know are on the streets and the only important ones are you and Mildred. – When do we get to the main event, Bobbi?"

"The auction? Oh, there's lots more softening up to be done before we hit them in their wallets. More drinks, more action, more schmoozing – come on, Mildred, we're only half way round."

"If you see Maggie, tell her I'm looking for her," said Barney. He started working his way against the flow of guests towards the main entrance. Trish and Clive had joined the group around Marlene and Bhante Dipa. He plucked Clive's sleeve and asked him if he had seen Maggie.

"Trish said she spotted her earlier over by the catwalk," he pointed over to one corner of the raised ramp. "– Did you really come up with this show idea, Barney? It doesn't sound like you somehow."

"This is mostly Eugene and Bobbi's work – I'd never have dreamt up anything like this. Enjoy the show, - it's only just nicely getting started according to Bobbi. I'm going to look for Maggie. – How's Trish?" he said. "–She seems to be having a good time."

"She's pacing herself – one drink an hour. – I told her I'd keep score," grinned Clive.

Barney headed for the side of the ramp and recognized Maggie talking with a tall, vaguely familiar young man in a white suit. She turned to greet him, holding a sheaf of notes in her hand and a drink in the other. She handed them to the young man and gave Barney a hug.

"What a night, Barney. Isn't it fantastic?"

"Knockout," agreed Barney. "–You should have brought Marlon – he'd have loved it so far."

"He was here. Duke gave him a ride home on his Harley after the opening 'son et lumière' show. – Barney, this is Zeke."

"Hello Zeke. You look just like Marlon or is it the other way around?"

"Good to meet you at last, Barney. Maggie ranks you right up there along with Brando and Bhante Dipa."

"Seeing all these classic bikes must be quite a turn-on for you, Zeke."

"One of Duke's buddies let me ride with him when we took Marlon home. – I don't know who was more excited, Marlon or me," smiled Zeke. "I haven't been on a Harley for years."

"They left me chewing my fingernails over this speech. I'm supposed to make the charity pitch for the Food Bank before the auction," said Maggie.

"Leave the notes behind," advised Barney. "– Just say what comes into your head – you'll be fine – you're preaching to the converted."

He noticed Duke coming towards them with another biker in black leathers. It was only when they were nearly together that he realized the other biker was a motorcycle cop.

"This is Barney, officer," said Duke.

"Mr. Barney Roper? I have a message for you from the British Police in London. A Detective Sergeant Hertz has been trying to reach you. He wants you to call him. Your son has been arrested on a kidnapping charge."

# CHAPTER 15

On the plane to Heathrow, Barney tried to piece together what had happened from the little the detective had told him over the phone. He said he would tell him in more detail when he arrived and offered to meet Barney's flight. He had placed a hurried call to Alice but only got her answer-phone so left a message saying he would call her when he arrived. There had been no time to speak to anyone at the party and he had only told Clive that he would be in touch soon. How had he become so estranged from his own son, he wondered, that something like this could have happened without him having any idea why?

At Heathrow, the detective was waiting with a crudely hand lettered sign reading 'Roper'. They drove into London in his unmarked police car.

"Your son is in big trouble, Mr. Roper. I'm hoping you can persuade him to talk to me before he appears in court on this kidnapping charge. So far, what he's told me just doesn't add up."

"How did you find me?" asked Barney.

"Hunter told me you were in Vancouver and volunteering at a food bank – so I got the Vancouver PD to track you down – turns out it wasn't all that difficult. The hard part is going to be yours – getting him to convince me he wasn't planning to kidnap that baby. Talk to him, Mr. Roper – prove me wrong."

In the Wimbledon Police station, Clarence escorted Barney to Hunter's cell. The older man smiled sympathetically at Barney.

"He's a nice lad, Mr. Roper. I've talked to him a bit and I don't believe he intended that baby any harm – he was just confused."

"Thanks, constable. I hope you're right."

Clarence unlocked the interview room door and Barney faced his son for the first time in two years. He took a step forward and embraced him, tears smarting his eyes.

"Hello, Dad," said Hunter. "Thanks for coming."

"Hunter – how did things get so far without you telling me?"

Hunter shrugged. "I guess we sort of stopped talking – and then it seemed kind of hard to start again. I'm glad you're here, Dad. I need you to help me get straightened out. –Did you get my letter? I wasn't sure where to address it."

"No; the first I knew was when the police got in touch with me in Vancouver. I came straight here. Hertz filled me in on what happened on the way in from the airport," said Barney, pulling up one of the hard chairs to the table opposite

Hunter. "What I don't understand is why – can you maybe explain that for me, son?"

"I got desperate, Dad, thinking I was never going to see my son. When Mona refused to even acknowledge I was the father, I panicked. I decided to visit him when everyone was asleep. That's all I wanted to do – just be able to look at him. – I'd never seen him since he was born. The first time I sneaked into the house, I spent a whole hour just sitting, staring at him sleeping – he was so peaceful, it lifted a huge weight off my chest. – I didn't plan to go back – that's all I wanted – but after a few days I just had to go and see him again."

"How long have you been visiting him like that- in the middle of the night, I mean?"

"Two months, maybe – several times, anyway. Until I got caught – he woke up while I was there and I couldn't stop him crying. Mona's husband beat me up – they thought I was trying to kidnap him but the idea never even entered my mind."

"But were you just going to go on like that indefinitely, or what?"

"I didn't have any plan - it was enough just to see him. – I suppose I hoped maybe one day Mona would change her mind and let me visit him normally."

"Jesus, Hunter, you've been going through all that on your own – I wish I'd been here to help you – I'm sure we could have worked something out."

"You're here now, Dad. It feels good to see you again."

"Me too, son. I'm only sorry I let things slip so badly between us. – Alice warned me but I didn't listen – I thought you needed the space to live your own life but I guess she was right – it probably seemed like indifference to you –"

"I was doing a lot of crazy things, too, Dad. Wandering all over Southeast Asia, trying to make sense of my life – ever since Netta went to America, I've been kinda lost – we were so close for so long – I was pretty angry with you when you told me to back off and let her live her own life."

"You did the right thing, Hunter. She had to sort out her own stuff with her real father by herself."

"And now she's with Philip."

"He seems like a good guy, Hunter. – Have you met him?"

"No, but he found me a solicitor – she's an old college mate of his."

"What's her name? – I'd better talk to her and see what she thinks we should do."

"Nadia. Nadia Kumar. I've got her number here."

"I'll call her right away. Hertz said I could visit you any day. – I'll be back tomorrow, son. Is there anything I can bring you?"

"Alice. I need to talk to her and know she understands – I know she's upset – will you ask her to come, Dad?"

"Sure thing. I have to speak to her, too."

Barney phoned the solicitor and arranged to see her after her court duties were over later in the day. In the meantime, he went to the local library and looked up private investigators in the yellow pages. He copied down the names of half a dozen and got some change to begin calling them. Something that Hertz had mentioned had given him an idea. The detective sergeant had said that Mona insisted Hunter was not the father, but she told Hunter her husband was sterile.

So who was the real father? Barney wondered. He thought it might be something that a private detective could find out. He voiced his suggestion to a man called Walter Steen, who had an office not far from Wimbledon station.

"Let me get this straight," said Steen. "You think there's another man in the picture – and that he could be the father. How does that help your son's case, Mr. Roper?"

"I'm not sure, yet," said Barney. "I'm grasping at straws – but if my son isn't the father, then maybe she's hiding something from her husband – another affair, for example."

"And if so, maybe we can persuade her to drop the charges," said Steen. "Okay, Mr. Roper, just so's I'm clear what I'm supposed to be doing. I'll start digging around – see what I can find out – it's on my patch so I have a few contacts who might help. –I'll call you as soon as I have anything."

Barney left the office and headed into the city to meet Nadia Kumar outside the Law Courts. He had some time to spare, so he phoned Alice again. She answered on the first ring.

"Hello, Alice, -it's me, Barney."

"Barney! I was expecting Netta. Where are you – do you know what's happened?"

"Yes, I know, Alice. I'm in London – I've already seen Hunter this morning."

"Oh God – how is he? – I want to see him."

"He's okay, Alice. He wants to see you, too. You could go tomorrow morning, if you like. Maybe we could meet up after and compare notes – see what we can do."

"Netta says she and Philip have found him a good solicitor."

"Yes, I'm waiting to speak to her now – she's in court at the moment. I'll tell you what she thinks when we meet up tomorrow."

"Phone me tonight, Barney. I'll be in all evening. – How did you hear – did Netta phone you?"

"No, the police got in touch with me in Vancouver and I flew back last night – I'm feeling a bit jet-lagged so I'll probably go to bed early after I see the solicitor."

"Don't forget to phone me first. Where are you staying, Barney?"

"I'm in a B&B in Wimbledon, near the Common."

"Okay, I'll get the train down from Oxford first thing. – Barney?"

"Yeah?"

"Netta says she believes him – do you?"

"About the kidnapping? Yeah, I believe him – it's the judge we have to convince."

"Call me later, Barney."

He hung up and wandered around the shops near the Law Courts until it was time to meet the solicitor. He stood outside on the street until a tall Anglo-Indian woman still wearing her little white lawyer's collar appeared. He approached her.

"Miss Kumar? I'm Hunter's father – Barney Roper."

She offered her large hand to shake. "Thanks for coming, Mr. Roper. I need to talk to you about arranging bail for your son."

They found an outdoor café and ordered some tea.

"Miss Kumar, how serious do you think Hunter's case is? Will they really push a charge of kidnapping against him?"

"The police have to convince the prosecutor that he really intended to kidnap the child – otherwise it's a simple case of unlawful entry – which is what I'm pushing for. I've spoken to Detective-Sergeant Hertz and he is far from convinced that Hunter intended to kidnap the baby but the parents are demanding he press charges."

"Is there anything we can do to help?"

"You can arrange to post bail – I'm appealing against the original refusal. It would mean putting up your house for security, Mr. Roper."

"Okay, I'll talk to my wife tonight. – Do you think Hunter had any intention of kidnapping the baby, Miss Kumar?"

"I had a long interview with Hunter the day he was arrested. He sounded confused and upset but I'm sure he had no plans to kidnap the child – in fact he didn't seem to have any plans at all, other than to just go on seeing his child – if it is his child."

"Is that how you're going to argue the case?"

"To me, it all rests on his intentions. He told me he had been entering the house unlawfully for nearly two months and simply sitting and watching his sleeping child and then leaving again. He had ample opportunity to kidnap the child before he was discovered if that had been his intention. In fact, there were lots of better occasions when the mother was alone with the child and the husband was away on business."

"It sounds convincing to me, Miss Kumar – is there a weakness I'm not seeing?"

"Hunter is deeply depressed, Mr. Roper. Understandably so, being deprived of any opportunity of ever seeing his son. The prosecution will argue that this makes him unstable and that he might try to take the child at any time – people get very emotional about child kidnap cases – the jury could easily be swayed against Hunter by a persuasive barrister."

"So we need to make sure it never gets that far?"

"That's what I'm working on now - I see the parents as the main obstacle. I think they over-reacted in pressing this charge but now they may feel they have to continue. I know Hertz is dragging his heels, hoping they will change their minds, but so far he has a lot of damning circumstantial evidence that all points against Hunter. He's really operating on a gut feeling that Hunter is telling the truth and that he never had any intention of taking the child. – Meantime I'm working on the bail appeal, Mr. Roper, so I need to know whether you can come up with the security soon. Otherwise there's no point in going ahead with it."

"Okay, Miss Kumar, I'll phone you tomorrow definitely – and thanks for taking Hunter's case. I feel a lot better now that I've met you."

"Good, I'll be in my office all morning."

Barney went back to his B&B room in Wimbledon and put on some jeans and sneakers. He'd only had time to throw in a change of clothes when he left Vancouver and would have to go out and buy something tomorrow, he decided. The Common was near his B&B and he went for a walk on one of the paths across it. Hunter had mentioned the address and described the big house to him and he suddenly decided to have a look for it.

Not sure what he had in mind, he wandered around the perimeter of the Common until he recognized the street name. He walked along the front of the houses but nothing obvious took his attention so he re-entered the Common and walked along the backs of the gardens and stopped suddenly at one with a summerhouse. He saw the garage with the window immediately above it and assumed it must have been the one Hunter had used to gain access if indeed this was the house.

He kept walking in order not to arouse suspicion, turned and came back past the garden. This time he made a note of a large London plane tree close to the side of the house and went back out onto the street. He found the house easily by looking for the tree and walked slowly by; continuing on to the corner and then crossing and walking slowly back on the opposite side of the street. He made a note of the house number and the black Jaguar in the driveway. There were no signs of activity and he walked on back to his room, stopping on the way to buy a phone card and a take-away kebab and coffee.

He phoned Alice and told her what the solicitor had said about raising bail. They agreed to meet for lunch after Alice had visited Hunter. He felt suddenly very tired and went to bed early, only to wake at three in the morning, unable to go back to sleep. He tried to read but couldn't concentrate, so he dressed and quietly let himself out of the house. He walked back toward the Common and found the street again easily.

For one wild moment, he considered trying to get into the house the way Hunter had told him he used. Instead, he went around to the front of the house. The black Jaguar was missing from the driveway, but an old dull red mini was parked on the street. A light was on in one of the upstairs bedrooms. Barney walked past the house and repeated his earlier route, crossing at the corner and coming back the other side of the street. He stopped and stood watching the house for a few minutes and then continued walking. In front of him, a car door opened and a tall man unfolded from the interior. He approached Barney.

"Mr. Roper? What the hell are you doing here?" Barney recognized the investigator he had hired yesterday.

"Steen! You gave me a fright - I couldn't sleep so I went for a walk – my son told me the address of the place and I was curious –"

"You weren't thinking of breaking in too, I hope? – Does this run in the family, Mr. Roper – breaking and entering in the middle of the night?"

Barney managed a weak smile. "No, although it did cross my mind – I can see how easy it would be once you were on the garage roof."

"So you *have* been casing the place. –Look, Mr. Roper, you hired me to do this so why don't you go back to bed and leave it to me – you could make matters much worse for your son by interfering like this."

"Have you found out anything yet, Steen?"

"I've been talking to a few of my friends at the station. It appears Mrs. Lupatti has had more than one affair with her so-called 'gardeners'. They had the place under observation after she got the restraining order against your son. In fact, she's got a visitor this evening." He nodded towards the little red mini parked in front of the house. "That car turned up less than an hour after her husband left this evening and it's been here ever since. I doubt if they're discussing herbaceous borders at this time of night."

"Do you think he might be the baby's father?"

"Who knows? I'll have his car traced and find out who he is tomorrow. Do you have a phone number I can reach you at where you're staying, Mr. Roper?"

Barney gave him the number of the B&B. "Thanks, Steen – Walter, isn't it? My name's Barney. Phone me as soon as you have anything, will you? I'll pass it on to Hunter's solicitor."

"Hold off for a day or so, Barney. Let me get a little more detail together first. Go on back to bed, now – and stay away from here, okay?"

"Right," said Barney. "Thanks, Walter." He headed off down the street and the investigator folded his long frame back into his car to resume his watch.

# CHAPTER 16

Heck turned off the A40 before the sign for Datchet and drove his battered old Land Rover down a country lane towards a small wooded copse. He pulled into a lay-by at the edge of the woods and switched off the engine. Alice sat staring straight ahead until he reached over to touch her hand.

"Sorry, Heck, I was miles away. – Where are we?"

"Datchet's Wood – some ancient woodland I used to visit – haven't been here for years. Shall we go for a walk? Your train isn't due for ages."

They left the Land Rover and climbed over a stile to follow a path into the woods. Walking single-file, they continued for half an hour until they came to a clearing. Heck spread an old plaid car blanket on the bracken and they sat down on the ground. He lay back but Alice sat clutching her arms round her knees.

"Alice, I know this isn't the right time to talk about it, but I'm not sure when I'll get the chance again for awhile. You know I've been looking for work in London – well, I've just been offered a post at Queen Anne's College in the East End. Assistant Department Head. - I think I'm going to take it."

"If it's what you want, Heck. I still think you're mad, giving up everything here in Oxford."

"It's part of what I want, Alice. I need a change – I'm too settled and smug here – you said so yourself."

"I was only pricking one of your pompous remarks. I didn't mean you should throw the whole lot over, for god's sake."

"Aren't you going to ask me what the other part is, Alice?"

"I expect you're planning to hole up somewhere in the East End with one of your adoring students."

"You're absolutely right," said Heck, reaching up to pull her down beside him. "You'll never guess which one."

"Some brazen hussy who indulges you in all your dubious fantasies?" she said, snuggling into his side.

"Right again," said Heck, kissing the top of her head. "– In fact, if this wasn't a totally inappropriate moment, I'd indulge in one right now."

"Go on, then."

"Are you calling my bluff, Alice?"

"You said we had plenty of time before the train is due."

"You *are* brazen," said Heck, "–You won't change your mind once I have my trousers off?"

"I'm not taking my clothes off – just my knickers," announced Alice, hoisting her skirt and pulling them down over one foot.

"Whose fantasy are we indulging here?" said Heck, as she pulled him on top of her. Alice only smiled and lay back on the bracken. They moved companionably together for a while. She felt him quicken inside her.

"Aren't you going to cover my mouth, Alice?"

"No."

"What if I start roaring?" said Heck.

"Roar away," said Alice, wrapping her legs round him the way she had seen it done in films. After several minutes, they finished and lay back panting, catching their breath.

Heck kissed her face "–I think I've died and gone to heaven."

"I don't think you're allowed to do this in heaven," said Alice.

"Some heaven," he said. "–Alice, when all this is over with – you know, Hunter and everything – will you call me and we can start looking for a place in London? There are some lovely Georgian terraces in the East End."

"Would you make an honest woman of me, Heck, or would I just be your bit on the side?"

"Whatever you want, Alice, - whatever you want."

"I quite fancy being a kept woman," she said. "–At least until I've finished my thesis."

"It's a deal," said Heck, glancing at his watch. "– My god, look at the time – we've got fifteen minutes to make your train –" He hopped around yanking his trousers up, while Alice stepped back into her knickers and brushed off her skirt. A sudden yelp from Heck made her jump.

"What – what is it?"

"My zip – I'm caught in my zip," said Heck, peering down at his flies. "–Oh Christ, I'm bleeding –"

"Let me see," said Alice. "– Take your hand away so I can see –" She bent down and saw that a fold of his foreskin had caught in the metal zipper. Blood was dripping onto his trousers. She felt in the pocket of her coat and found a tissue, which she used to wrap around his penis.

"How bad is it?" asked Heck, leaning over her shoulder.

"There's a little flap of skin zipped right into the zipper," reported Alice.

"Oh god, what shall we do? I can't drive like this."

"I could try to unzip it," offered Alice. "– I did it once before when Hunter was a little boy – he did the same thing. It will hurt, though."

"Go on, then – but be careful, for god's sake."

Alice gripped him firmly with one hand and gave a quick yank on the zip with the other. Heck let out a roar and leapt back out of her grasp.

"Jesus! What did you do?" he gasped.

Alice approached him again and knelt down to inspect her handiwork. "–It's out," she announced triumphantly, "– Give me your handkerchief, - it's all bloody here." He handed it to her and she dabbed gently at his limp penis as it lay in her hand. "-It's a bit mangled, I'm afraid. I think there's a little piece missing – it's still in the zip."

Heck winced and bent over to look at himself. "Christ! That is so painful – goddammit!"

"Poor Heck – I'll wrap it in your handkerchief – like a bandage, see?" She wound it round his penis to stem the bleeding. "– Is that too tight?"

"No, no, it's okay – thanks."

"There," said Alice, "- all better." She kissed the protruding tip and carefully tucked it back inside his trousers and stood up. "-You okay, Heck?"

He nodded and gingerly zipped up his fly. "– I hope you didn't do that to Hunter," he grinned shakily.

"No," smiled Alice, "- but I don't remember him making quite as much fuss." She kissed his chin. "–I'm afraid you're going to be out of action for awhile. – Do you think you should go to the doctor?"

"I don't think I could handle the embarrassment – did Hunter go?"

"No, he refused point blank. I just bathed it each night until it healed."

"Ahh, sounds wonderful," said Heck. "– Will you do that for me, too, Alice?"

"Sorry, I'll be in London, remember?"

"I'm afraid I've made you miss your train, Alice. I could drive you down – it's the least I can do, considering…."

"No, you'd better go home and recover – there's another train in half an hour – just drop me at the station."

# CHAPTER 17

When she emerged from Wimbledon Police Station, Alice found a café and sat at a table outside. As she fumbled through her handbag, she saw that her hands were trembling. She only just managed to grab a hankie as the first wave of sobs washed over her. She stuffed the hankie in her mouth and pressed hard with her fist, trying to stifle them, but they kept coming, wave after wave.

The young waitress who had come out to take her order stood at her side and patted her shoulder. The sobbing slowly subsided and Alice dabbed at her eyes and tried to reassure the girl.

"– Sorry – I'm sorry. – I didn't mean to...to...."

"Oh, that's okay – we're used to it," the waitress replied, still stroking Alice's shoulder.

"Pardon?"

"We're the first cafe near the police station," explained the girl. "I've had grown men sitting right where you are, crying their eyes out over a bacon sandwich. - It happens all the time," she smiled at Alice. "– You ready to order now?"

Alice nodded. "– Yes, I think so – a black coffee, please."

"Anything else?"

"I don't think I'll risk the bacon sandwich," Alice smiled weakly.

"So is it your husband, then?" The girl nodded towards the station.

"No. No, it's my – son," said Alice, hesitating, then deciding against further explanation.

"You wanna talk about it?" said the girl. "– I'll get your coffee. I'm not busy."

"Thank you," said Alice, "– I don't think I'm up to it right now – but thanks."

"Just the coffee, then," nodded the girl and moved off to the counter. She returned in a moment and set the cup down in front of Alice.

"I'm sorry about your son," she said. She put the bill on the table under the coffee cup. Alice thanked her with a smile and sipped at the black coffee.

The girl gave her directions to the hotel where Barney had suggested they meet for lunch. It was quite nearby so she finished her coffee and left a large tip. She had brought only a light coat and the weather looked threatening as she dawdled her way along the street, idly window-shopping.

At a menswear shop there was a sale on boxer shorts and she toyed with the idea of buying some for Barney but decided against it. For over twenty-five years, Alice had been buying his clothes and it seemed odd to think of him living independently of her. She looked for a bookshop but there were none in the area and in the end, she bought him nothing. At the hotel, she waited for him in the foyer. When he arrived a few minutes later, they embraced awkwardly.

"You're looking well, Alice."

"So are you. You've lost weight, Barney."

"I wish," said Barney, patting his paunch "– but it's nice of you to say it anyway. Are you ready for lunch, yet or…?"

"I'm not hungry at all, but you go ahead," she said.

"Shall we go for a walk on the Common, then?"

"Okay. Hunter has been telling me all about - everything," said Alice.

They left the hotel and started walking. The sky had become overcast and it was definitely cooler. Alice buttoned up her coat and Barney tucked his hands in his jacket pockets.

"So, how did you find Hunter – did he sound alright to you – considering?" he asked.

"I suppose so – considering. He just seemed so vulnerable and all I wanted to do was take him home with me – and I knew I couldn't. It was horrible, actually." She started to sniffle and fumbled for a tissue in her pocket. "– I tried to warn him about this woman when he came to Oxford to see me – I had the feeling she was going to use him and he'd get hurt. But I never imagined it would come to this – poor Hunter, what he must have been going through – and all he wanted was to see his baby son –"

"Well, it turns out it may not even be his son," said Barney.

"You mean you believe Mona's story about Hunter not being the father?"

312

"I had a phone call this morning from a private investigator I hired when I arrived," said Barney. "He's been watching her house and he tracked down another young man Mona has been having an affair with, long before Hunter came on the scene."

"Did she say he's the father?"

"The investigator hasn't spoken to her, yet. He wanted to know whether he should approach her or not. He seemed to think the only real way to find out would be a DNA test."

"Do you think she'll agree?"

"She might. – If she doesn't want her husband to know about her affair with this other young man, she might be persuaded. I'm hoping we can even get her to drop the kidnapping charge."

"Doesn't she live right around here? Hunter told me her garden backed onto the Common," said Alice.

"That's right; I walked by it the other night."

"I want to see it too, Barney. Show me which one it is."

"What for? Alice, you're not thinking of speaking to her, are you?"

"Maybe. Why not? Perhaps I can persuade her to change her mind."

"But she might not be home –" stalled Barney.

"Just show me which one it is, Barney. I want to see it anyway," said Alice.

They followed the little path, which led out onto Mona's street, and Barney pointed to the big plane tree beside the house.

"That's it – but there's no car in the drive – she's probably out."

"You wait here; I'm going to try it anyway."

"Alice – I'm not sure this is a good idea – what are you going to say? – we haven't even talked about it yet."

"I don't know – I'll think of something when I get in there. – Keep walking up and down, Barney. Don't hang around out in front and make her nervous."

Alice crossed the street, climbed the wide steps to the front door, and pressed the buzzer. Barney waited until the door opened then started walking on down the street. Out of the corner of his eye, he could see a dark-haired woman speaking to Alice. She was holding a baby.

Barney walked up and down both sides of the street for what seemed like an hour before the front door opened and Alice re-appeared. The rain that had been threatening all morning spattered the pavement lightly. She crossed back over the street and caught up with him as he finished a lap.

"What happened?" asked Barney. "– What did she say?"

"She was pretty shaken when I told her we knew about how long she had been seeing this other young man. She said her husband only very reluctantly agreed to her involvement with Hunter and made her promise to break it off as soon as she was pregnant. She was only using Hunter as a cover and had really been seeing this other man for ages."

"And is he the real father?"

"She's convinced he is and she wants to keep on seeing him."

"And she told you all this? - Why?"

Alice shrugged, "- I'm not sure – she was bored and her husband was away constantly – she met this guy and they started having an affair – she doesn't want to give him up but she doesn't want her husband to know about it either – I think she's been playing a dangerous game and she needed to talk to someone."

"What about the kidnapping charge – did you ask her about that?"

Alice nodded, "It was just a way to get rid of Hunter – to stop him pestering her – she thought it would really frighten him off for good. Her husband isn't so sure – he doesn't want the publicity, she says."

"Good god – has she put us through all this for some kind of stunt?" said Barney.

"I told her if she agreed to the DNA test to prove Hunter wasn't the father, he wouldn't have any reason to bother her and she could simply ask the police to drop the kidnapping charge."

"What did she say?"

"She said provided her husband didn't find out anything – about the DNA test or her affair, she wouldn't press the kidnapping charge."

"She actually said that – she'd drop the charge?"

Alice nodded and smiled. The two of them stood hugging each other in the middle of the street. The rain was increasing in volume.

"Jesus, Alice – that's wonderful! You're amazing." He hugged her again and lifted her off the ground, swinging her round in a circle,

"Come on, let's phone Miss Kumar and tell her the good news –"

The two of them started walking rapidly down the street, faster and faster, grinning at each other and finally breaking into a run as the rain poured down in torrents.

# CHAPTER 18

The celebration had been going on at the old mansion flat in Highgate for nearly an hour when George finally announced that dinner was ready. Everyone filed in from the garden and Martha seated them all round her large dining table which had been extended to its impressive full-length.

She had not had so much 'family' together for years; for she now included Cassie's boyfriend, Zinadine and her Czech friend, Lottie from Paris, who had arrived unannounced at the last minute. Martha seated her beside Hunter and already Lottie was regaling him with stories of the swathe Cassie had cut through the male Sorbonne undergraduates.

Cassie was torn between monitoring Lottie's exuberant anecdotes, which were clearly fascinating Hunter and Barney; and Alice, who was quizzing Zinadine on his intentions for her daughter in the Sudan. George did the rounds replenishing everyone's drink and raised his glass.

"I think a few toasts are in order," he announced. "First, to our grandson – welcome home, Hunter." –They all cheered and drank and Hunter nodded and smiled at everyone, particularly Lottie. "And next, - to the person who made it all possible; Miss Kumar. Nadia. Thank you, Nadia, for what you've done for us. We are in your debt – To Nadia," and he clinked glasses with Hunter, who sat beside him.

They all cheered loudly while the solicitor sat smiling happily and waving a large expressive hand at Hunter, who blew her a kiss.

"And I know Martha wants to offer the next toast," said George, nodding to his wife at the far end of the table. She rose and raised her glass, turning to Netta beside her.

"To our first great-grandchild, courtesy of Netta and Philip - Congratulations!" She bent over and hugged her granddaughter, who sat beaming and contented, with her hands folded over her stomach. Hunter was the first to rise from his chair and embrace Netta. He shook Philip's hand.

"Look after her, Philip – precious cargo."

Everyone insisted on following suit and a queue formed to hug and kiss the couple, including Lottie. When the congratulations subsided, George tapped his glass again.

"And we are still not done. –Alice – your turn." Alice rose and raised her glass.

"To Cassie and Zinadine – and Africa! May they all be good to each other." She turned and clinked glasses with them as they sat either side of her and another round of cheering and congratulating followed.

"Now can we eat?" said Barney.

After the meal, Martha announced that she had enough tickets for everyone to go to the last concert of the season at Kenwood House. They could all walk across the Heath – there was plenty of time. Barney and Alice excused themselves, saying they would join them later. They walked down the hill to the local pub and sat outside in the cool evening air.

"You didn't quite have your full gap year," said Alice.

"Ten months," said Barney. "Close enough. I got the feel of it. –"How about you?"

"Me too. Thanks."

"For what?"

"Forcing my hand. – I hated you for doing it at the time –"

"And now?"

"I've sort of got the bit between my teeth and I don't want to let go – yet."

"Me either. - Are you still angry with me, Alice?"

"Yes and no. You didn't leave me much choice, did you? Take it or leave it."

"I'm sorry I made such a hash of it. At the time, I felt I'd painted myself into a corner and I guess I panicked and just bolted for the exit. In retrospect, I see I wasn't thinking too clearly."

"It was a painful period – for both of us, I guess," said Alice.

"And now – is it still?"

"Only when I laugh, as they say."

"The kids are pretty tight-lipped about you, Alice. I don't really know much of what you've been doing – do you want to tell me anything?"

"They don't give much away about you either, Barney. I guess we've put them in an awkward spot – straining their loyalties; expecting them to take sides…."

"Jesus, Alice, why is everything so hard?"

"Because it's life, Barney and life is messy."

"Mine sure as hell is – being back in Canada hasn't changed any of that. What's it like in Oxford, Alice? – Peaceful? I think of you sometimes, wandering about 'the dreaming spires.'"

"Hectic is more like. Exhausting."

"Not satisfying, then?"

"Oh yes, very. – Just tiring. – I'm sixty now, remember?"

"Burning the candle at both ends, are you?"

"Something like that, I suppose. I seem to have got in a bit over my head."

"Meaning?" prompted Barney.

"Meaning I've met someone – and it's all moving faster than I expected.  - I just wanted to go along at a nice leisurely pace - but he wants to –"

"- Cut to the chase?"

"Sort of – it's too complicated to explain – and anyway I'm not sure I want to – it's too embarrassing talking to you like this – Ask me again in a year's time. Tell me what you've been up to –what's it like being a Third Age Explorer?"

"Like you say – exhausting but exhilarating. Riding madly off in all directions. In over my head most of the time too –"

"'Not waving, but drowning?'"

"Yeah," laughed Barney. "Feels like that on occasion."

"So tell me about it, then."

"I'm not sure I know where to start. – What do you want to hear?"

"You know me, Barney. Leave out all the big boys' adventure stuff and give me the up-close and personal bits."

"It's too sordid, Alice. – Like you say, too embarrassing."

"Now I really want to hear about it – you can't leave me hanging like that, Barney."

"Sorry, I'm not sure I could handle your censure, – Anyway, it's over – it's history. Maybe in another year's time we can have a 'true confessions' session."

"I guess I'll just have to wait, then."

"So, what do you think we should do now?" he asked.

Alice gazed at the other couples nearby. "I suppose we could get divorced?"

"Is that what you want?"

"I don't know yet. I'm not sure - You?"

"Not me – I'm not ready for that," said Barney.

"What, then?"

"How about another gap year and then decide?"

"What for – more exploring?"

"What else?"

"Same time, same place then?" said Alice.

"Same time, same place," he smiled.

They sat for a while, finishing their drinks, then walked slowly back over the Heath. The faint sounds of the orchestra floated out towards them from Kenwood House and Alice slipped her arm through Barney's as they headed into the warm autumn night.

\*\*\*\*\*\*\*\*\*\*\*\*\*\*\*

*The Blue-Eyed Boy* is the next novel in which Barney continues his 3rd Age explorations and travels to the Far East in his search for answers to the conundrum – how shall a man live?

Published by 3rd Age World Publications, Vancouver & London.
www.3rdageworld.com

Printed in the United Kingdom
by Lightning Source UK Ltd.
121238UK00001B/346-429

9 780978 207403